THE MODERN SINNER

ೞೞೞೞೞ

THE MODERN SINNER

by

CAROLINA INVERNIZIO

୯୨୯୨୯୨୯୨୯୨

Translated with an Introduction by

Andrew Edwards

ITALICA PRESS

NEW YORK & BRISTOL

2023

Italian Original
Peccatrice moderna

Translation & Introduction Copyright © 2023
Andrew Edwards

Italica Press Italian Crime Writers Series

ITALICA PRESS, INC.
99 Wall Street, Suite 650
New York, New York 10005

Library of Congress Cataloging-in-Publication Data
Names: Invernizio, Carolina, 1851-1916, author. | Edwards, Andrew
(Translator), translator.
Title: The modern sinner / by Carolina Invernizio ; translated by Andrew Edwards.
Other titles: Peccatrice moderna. English
Description: New York : Italica Press, 2023. | Series: Italian crime writers | Includes bibliographical references. | Summary: "The Modern Sinner by Carolina Invernizio incorporates all the elements of the classic noir or the Italian "giallo." The author was a pioneer in mystery, psychological, detective, and crime fiction, and this novel, written near the end of her life, spotlights formidable female characters, both good and evil, who operated within the strictures of early-20th-century Turin society and family life"-- Provided by publisher.
Identifiers: LCCN 2023003710 (print) | LCCN 2023003711 (ebook) | ISBN 9781599104324 (hardcover) | ISBN 9781599104331 (trade paperback) | ISBN 9781599104348 (kindle edition) | ISBN 9781599104607 (pdf)
Subjects: LCGFT: Noir fiction. | Novels.
Classification: LCC PQ4821.N9 P4313 2023 (print) | LCC PQ4821.N9 (ebook) | DDC 853/.912--dc23/eng/20230201
LC record available at https://lccn.loc.gov/2023003710
LC ebook record available at https://lccn.loc.gov/2023003711

Cover Image: Portrait photo of Pola Negri (1894-1987), Polish actress. Photographer unidentified.
(https://monovisions.com/vintage-portraits-of-pola-negri-silent-movie-star/)

For a Complete List of Titles in Italian Literature
Visit our Web Site at:
www.ItalicaPress.com

ABOUT THE TRANSLATOR

Andrew Edwards is the co-author of *Sicily: A Literary Guide for Travellers*; and *Andalucía: A Literary Guide for Travellers*; *His Master's Reflection*, a biography of Lord Byron's doctor, John Polidori; *Ghosts of the Belle Époque: The History of the Grand Hotel et des Palmes, Palermo*; and *Down to the Sunless Sea: A Troubled Samuel Taylor Coleridge in the Mediterranean.*

He is also the translator of *Agony* by Federico De Roberto — also in the Italica Press's Italian Crime Writers Series — and the books *Borges in Sicily*, *The Sicilian Defence*, and various academic treatises. He spends his time between the UK and the north coast of Sicily.

CAROLINA INVERNIZIO
AN INTRODUCTION

Carolina Invernizio has passed under the radar of most contemporary readers, whether in Italy or the rest of the world, which makes it very easy to underestimate the degree to which she held the attention of the public during her lifetime. In fact, she would be a strong candidate for the title of the most famous Italian writer to have completely disappeared from the public consciousness. Yet her authorial footprints have indelibly signalled the direction for a significant strand of popular Italian fiction.

Yolanda Romano, the author of *Del amor y de la muerte en los relatos de Carolina Invernizio* (ArCiBel Editores, 2017) has written extensively on the subject. It is clear from Romano's introduction how much of a sensation Invernizio made in the rather staid editorial world of fin de siècle Italy: "Without a shadow of doubt, Carolina Invernizio was the most important publishing phenomenon at the end of the nineteenth and beginning of the twentieth centuries. She was the initiator of a genre of popular novel dealing with romantic themes but tinged with shades of Gothic darkness, where the chilling plots, whose essential ingredients were love and death, were carried out by women of all classes and conditions."[1]

Invernizio was born in Voghera in the province of Pavia, although there is some question surrounding the actual date. Like many stars of stage and screen, she was somewhat reticent about declaring her actual year of birth. The local town hall has an archival record that suggests she was, in fact, seven years older than the 1858 she declared. Much of her adult life was spent in or near the two cities of Florence and Turin. In the former, she established a lucrative relationship (for both parties) with the publisher Salani, but also worked with papers such as *L'Opinione Nazionale* and *La Gazzetta de Torino* from both cities.

---

1.   Yolanda Romano, *Del amor y de la muerte en los relatos de Carolina Invernizio* (Seville: ArCiBel, 2017), p. 7.

Commentators have noted that Invernizio was influenced by the French *feuilleton* or serialized story exemplified by the likes of Alexandre Dumas père, Eugène Sue, Frèdèric Souliè, and Victor Hugo. Stories in this format, known as *romanzi d'appendice* in Italian, burgeoned after Italian unification, chiefly due to rising literacy rates in a hitherto largely illiterate population. It is important to remember at this point that Italy was, and still is, a mosaic of languages, which for political expediency are usually called dialects. Standard Italian, or the "right kind of Tuscan" as Lord Byron called it, was to be the linguistic glue that would bring this new country together. As schools produced students literate in the national language, a new readership turned to serialized stories as a popular form of entertainment.

Invernizio knew her readership well and included elements that would appeal to it. Daniela Bombara, in her article on Invernizio and her contemporary Matilde Serao, notes how the inclusion of adventurous and fantastical elements in her stories supposedly fed on the Italians' penchant for superstition, a tendency frowned upon by the communist thinker Antonio Gramsci. Bombara, however, goes on to say that these elements are often key to understanding the characters' actions and belie the charge that Invernizio was simply using such elements as a consumerist draw to attract more readers.[2]

Herein lies the chief dichotomy when discussing her work: she was loved by her readership, but almost universally derided by Italy's coterie of mainly male critics. That said, even Gramsci conceded that she was "the honest hen of Italian literature" while, at the same time, decrying the fact that she did not aim higher in her literary ambitions. The epithet "hen" can be read as derogatory, and it is difficult to deny the assumption that it was in part aimed at her prodigious output. Invernizio wrote well over a hundred stories, and there are some that genuinely broke new ground. If you are looking for the first Italian woman to pen a detective story, you need look no further than the woman from Voghera.

2.   Daniela Bombara, "Real or Alleged Ghosts and Monstrous Dead Children in the Italian Fiction of Carolina Invernizio and Matilde Serao," *Women's Writing*, 28.4 (2021): 512–28, DOI: 10.1080/09699082.2021.1985289

Both Serao and Invernizio dealt with themes of criminality and investigation, but it was Carolina who turned to the subject a few years before her Neapolitan counterpart. The critic, Emilio Zanzi, recognised her posthumously in 1932 as "the woman who anticipated by half a century *gialla* and *supergialla* fiction." *Letteratura gialla* is the Italian term used to describe mystery, psychological, detective, or crime fiction, and it is key to understanding her work to know that she was a forerunner in these fields. The titles of her stories certainly make no attempt to hide the preoccupations of the text: *Il bacio di una morta* (*The Dead Woman's Kiss*, 1886), *Il delitto della contessa* (*The Countess' Crime*, 1887), *La sepolta viva* (*The Woman Who Was Buried Alive*, 1896).

In 1894, she wrote *I ladri dell'onore* (*The Honorable Thieves*), which features a police investigation. By 1909, she had named her female protagonist in the title as the chief investigator of the crime: *Nina, la poliziotta dilettante* (*Nina, the Amateur Sleuth*). Nina is originally accused of killing Count Sveglia but, once freed, swears to find the real killer. The working-class heroine, through a plan involving disguise and gender-switching, undercovers the truth behind the count's death. Invernizio's women are heightened versions of reality that some have dubbed "super women," whether driven towards decent or evil ends. Vittorio Spinazzola, in his introduction to *I sette capelli d'oro della fata Gusmara* (The Seven Golden Hairs of Gusamara the Fairy) points out that "the female frees all her positive and negative potential. Angelic martyr, evil monster, hardworking innocent or mistress of the dissolute, the woman always dominates her partner, reducing him to a faded subservient role."[3]

Spinazzola correctly identifies the strength of Invernizio's female characters, particularly in relation to the men, something which is very evident from the story that follows this introduction, *La peccatrice moderna* (*The Modern Sinner*, 1915). To say that Alceste Bianco

3.   Vittorio Spinazzola, introductory note to *I sette capelli d'oro della fata Gusmara*, by Carolina Invernizio at https://www.liberliber.it/online/autori/autori-i/carolina-invernizio/i-sette-capelli-doro-della-fata-gusmara/, p.11 adapted from the 1975 edition (Milan: Moizzi), p. 65.

deserved his fate is a step too far, but his weak-willed behaviour is unlikely to engender sympathy in the reader. When faced with the high-handed opinions of critics who disparaged her entertainments for the female bourgeoisie and lower classes, she hit back at this male bastion of letters with the riposte that her readers and friends were precisely their wives and sisters, thus implying that they enjoyed seeing the male characters humiliated. The tide of male criticism continued after she had died, with critic and writer Luigi Bàccolo going so far as to call her "Sade's little niece," despite the kind words he had written for her obituary.

Her portrayal of worldly-wise seductresses, strong working-class women, and females who carve niches for themselves in a male dominated society would suggest Invernizio as a feminist in the contemporary manner. She was, however, an upholder of the status quo. Her characters always wish to avoid a scandal and to maintain appearances. Decisions are taken in *The Modern Sinner* for specifically that reason, so that society continues to see a character in a favorable light, notwithstanding the hurt caused beneath a thin surface veneer. Despite rumors to the contrary, Invernizio's books were never placed on the Vatican's prohibited list. Yolanda Romano makes the point that this may well have been due to her religious beliefs and "non revolutionary feminism."[4] Anna Maria, Alceste Bianco's fiancée, is torn between revenge and love, but it is not even questioned that she will give up chasing her dream of a singing career to marry. In doing so, she will conform to societal and ecclesiastical norms.

The Modern Sinner was published the year before Invernizio died and contains many of the themes that she had developed throughout her career. The seductress, the exotically named Sultana, is every bit the *femme fatale*, luring men from a righteous path towards dissolution and betrayal. The male characters either capitulate before her bewitching manner, are too mentally frail to escape, or are too unaware to notice the turn of events. The crime that takes place near the beginning of

4. Romano, *Del amor,* 27.

the text haunts the protagonists throughout the story, binding the characters to each other and their fate. In opposition to the aristocratic Sultana, we have the country girl from a humble background, Anna Maria. The juxtaposition of these two protagonists is the technique used by Invernizio to set up the book's moralizing tone, an approach common to much of her work and perhaps another factor in her avoiding the attentions of the Vatican.

To borrow a phrase from Joseph Kesselring, "arsenic and old lace" are much in evidence. To reinforce this image, the crime writer Elena Forni had this to say in 2011's *Atti del convegno Govone* about Invernizio and female writers of the Victorian age: "perverse souls under mountains of feathers, lace and needlepoint, but profoundly innovative and aware."[5] The key words in Forni's description are *innovative* and *aware*. In contrast to male protagonists of the era, Forni elaborates her argument to suggest that Invernizio's female killers think through their deeds in a premeditated manner, confined as they are, along with all her female characters, to act within the limitations of their social context and sexual identity in a fast-changing patriarchal society. Invernizio knew, as Forni and Romano indicate, that her primary objective was to entertain her target audience, but in doing so she gently attempted to fray the edges of her ordered, neatly stitched world. Incredible cruelty, overt passion, and catastrophic deeds lurk beneath the Pirandellian masks of daily routine.

By the end of her life, Invernizio was not only established as a publishing phenomenon in Italy, but also in countries like Brazil, Spain, and much of Spanish-speaking America. Sadly, just one of her books has been translated into English. The publishing house, Manucci, run by an Italian ex-patriot in Barcelona, churned out a great deal of her work. The expression *churned out* is appropriate in this instance because the works, as Yolanda Romano laments, were

5.   Ornella Ponchione, and Antonella Saracco, *Carolina Invernizio, Il gusto del proibito? Atti del convegno Govone* (Turin: Daniela Piazza Editore, 2011), p. 84.

hastily prepared, cheaply translated, and printed in a mediocre manner. Nevertheless, there were some instances of her texts being rendered into Spanish by notable figures including Ramón Del Valle Inclán. Whether time and care were invested in her stories or not, they certainly achieved success. In many respects, their *romanzo d'appendice* nature resembles the soap operas found on modern-day South America television. They are nicknamed *culebrones* in Spanish due to their serpent-like capacity to twist and turn while never-ending.

Invernizio's tales, although punctuated by suitable cliff-hangers, do, of course, reach a conclusion. The nature of the endings in some of her stories have maintained their capacity to surprise the reader. She brings together multiple threads without neglecting the moral dilemmas faced by the protagonists and the strict norms accepted by society as a whole. The punishment meted out to the culpable, though, may not always reflect the neat conclusions expected of a judicial outcome.

Andrew Edwards

The Modern Sinner

ଔଔଔଔଔଔ

Once the lawyer Bruno Sigrano had put his elegant case in the rack of the first-class carriage of the direct train from Turin to Genoa, he climbed down onto the platform again. The train was due to leave at three o'clock, so he passed the remaining ten minutes with his wife and children: Ottorino, a five-year-old little boy, and Mina, a charming infant of three, who was holding onto her governess's hand.

The lawyer enjoyed great renown and, at the age of forty, remained a good-looking man of considerable stature with a tanned face and black sparkling eyes that lent him a soft, affectionate, and kindly appearance. He had married Sultana Flaminio eight years before, meeting her at a country ball, after which he soon fell for her charms.

Countess Sultana was then twenty-two and cut a magnificent figure: slim, elegant, with a regal head of golden hair, deep blue eyes, a luminous complexion, and a sensual mouth that would part in a smile to show the intense whiteness of her teeth.

Despite her beauty, however, she had lacked suitors, since she possessed no other dowry than the nobility of her family. Nor was she a young woman capable of adapting to a modest marriage, although she lived in genteel poverty with her parents in a villa above an alpine village. The property was largely dilapidated, a remnant of the past that had only retained some of its former splendor from the stunning plants and a few hectares of land, which represented the entirety of the household's remaining assets.

Sultana was aware that Bruno, in addition to being a parentless only-child, also had a considerable fortune and a law firm in Turin making him in the region of thirty thousand lire a year. Therefore, when he asked her to marry him, she thought she had exceeded her wildest expectations and accepted with enthusiasm, foreseeing a marriage that would make her dreams of prosperity a reality.

To possess such a beautiful creature, who seemed happy to be his, increased the lawyer's feelings still further, and it was easy to let Sultana hold sway over him and the house. Extremely intelligent, she knew how to flatter her husband with the subtlest of attentions and tender caresses delivered with the abandon of a child. He had, consequently, good reason to believe he was loved, if not with an ardor equal to his, at least with the same degree of fidelity.

Sultana acted so deftly that she managed to stop Bruno from setting up his office at home. Three years after their marriage, on the birth of their first child, the couple settled into a small palazzo that they owned on the outskirts of the city. It was the happiest day of Signora Sigrano's life.

Until that point, she had only kept two servants, sisters from her village, who were dedicated to her with a devotion bordering on fanaticism. Caterina, the elder, was the cook, but also helped with other household chores, and Teresa, the younger, acted as a waitress and dresser.

In their new home, as well as the nanny for the baby, there was the caretaker and porter, Batista, a decent man, loyal to Signor Sigrano, having looked after his office for several years. He was the custodian of the porter's lodge and took care of the garden. His wife, Sofia, a hardworking woman, performed the most important services in the house. After Sultana's two children had been weaned, Teresa became their governess. Sigrano then wanted to do something nice for his attentive wife, so he bought a lavish car and employed a chauffeur who also acted as a waiter. He was the son of an old retainer working for the Flaminio family.

Never once had a cloud hung over the Sigranos. Sultana enjoyed complete freedom, living according to her whims. With regard to her dignity and honor, she was considered one of the most inflexible and serious of women, whether due to her overarching pride or the love she had for her husband. The lawyer spent all day at his office and, on returning home, always found his wife, welcoming him with a radiant smile, and the children, who distracted him with their lively chatter. He wished for no greater kindness, comfort, or attention. Accordingly, he was never haunted by jealousy, and life passed delightfully, in a manner that he hoped would continue.

Sultana and the children always used to accompany him to the station when he had to leave on business, a tonic he greatly appreciated.

"So, will you be away for three days?" asked Sultana, as he lifted Mina from her arms, covering the girl's face with kisses while Ottorino grabbed his legs.

"Yes, dear, but I'll try to get things done sooner."

"Have you forgotten anything, my love?"

"I forgot to tell you something. When I went back home to pick up my case, I took five one-thousand lire notes out of my wallet so I didn't take too much money with me. I temporarily put them in the dressing-table drawer, intending to pick them up after shaving and put them in the safe. But I forgot."

"I'll do it. Don't worry. Call me on the telephone when you arrive."

"Of course."

"And let me know when you're back."

"Yes, yes, my treasure!"

He had given the child back to the governess and was looking affectionately at his wife while holding her hand gently. Suddenly, a thought flashed into his mind.

"I'm sorry, not realizing that I had to leave this morning, I gave Alceste permission to visit his village for the patron saint's feast day celebrations. I know he wanted to go."

His wife's attractive face clouded over. Her blue eyes were but a dull reflection.

"That's fine!" she forcefully interrupted. "I can gladly do without Alceste, especially when you're not here. He abuses the familiarity we've granted him just because he's the son of poor Giacomo. He was a decent man who was around when I was born and remained faithful to my family through thick and thin. Alceste's not like his father. Our indulgence has almost made him insolent."

"I must admit that I've never noticed it, but if he is disrespectful to you, just tell me, and I'll fire him immediately."

Sultana had no time to answer, hearing the announcer: "The train is about to depart! The train is about to depart! Travelers are kindly requested to board, as the train is leaving."

Between two passionate kisses, Sigrano hugged his wife tightly.

"See you soon!"

"I love you so much! Think of me," Sultana whispered in turn.

"Thoughts of you and the children never leave me for a moment!"

He kissed the little ones, shook hands with the governess, then quickly climbed the carriage steps, the door shutting immediately behind him. He leaned on the open window to see his dear wife's face once more as she was smiling at him. Ottorino and Mina blew him kisses, and he felt the all-embracing warmth of Sultana's gaze. The train moved off. The signora kept waving her lace handkerchief until Bruno had faded from view.

Once the train had disappeared, Signora Sigrano turned to her governess.

"It's still early, take the children to Valentino. I'm going to the seamstress. Tell Caterina that dinner should be ready by seven."

"Yes, signora."

While Teresa quietly walked away with Ottorino and Mina, Sultana took a few steps to the telephone kiosk, entered, and asked the operator to put her through to 7-14. The telephone soon started to ring.

"Hello? Who am I talking to?" Sultana asked. "Ah, it's you! Excellent. Everything went as you wanted. I'll definitely be there in fifteen minutes. See you."

She replaced the receiver and walked out with her head held high, leaving a delicious waft of violet perfume behind her. Passing a tram in the street, she made a gesture with her gloved hand to stop it and climbed aboard. Without looking at anyone, she took a ticket and sat down. Seemingly absorbed in contemplating the street beyond, though seeing nothing, her thoughts drifted away. It was the end of October, and the trees were beginning to turn yellow, but the temperature was still mild, the sky blue.

Sultana got off at the corner of Corso Vinzaglio and passed under the arcades. She walked the distance to Via San Quintino without hurrying, occasionally stopping to look in a shop window.

In San Quintino, she turned right, walked a short stretch further, then entered the entrance hall of a modest building. Without paying any attention to the concierge, she went up to the first floor, and being careful to remain unobserved, pushed a door ajar to one of the apartments on the landing. She went in and closed it again.

Immediately, two arms enfolded her, an ardent mouth kissed hers.

"My angel,…" a hoarse voice whispered, choked with emotion.

Sultana freed herself quickly.

"Don't be such a child, Mario! At least let me in. Calm yourself."

They were in a small dark hallway.

"You're right! Forgive me," replied the young man.

Signora Sigrano was the first to enter the graceful living room in the stylish apartment belonging to Count Mario Herbert, a second lieutenant in the cavalry. Mario had just turned twenty-one and was a handsome young man, tall, blond, with dark eyes, a slim moustache — he was the architype of a carefree, boisterous, but gifted officer, capable of making himself a hero if the occasion arose.

As a lawyer, Sigrano was a consultant to the Herbert family, but also a friend. They had placed a civil lawsuit in his hands that had dragged on for many years. The Herberts had filed a complaint against another noble family who had unjustly stripped some of their assets. Sigrano won the case, and they were able to take possession of their rightful holdings.

Consequently, when Count Mario Herbert was posted to Turin, his father warmly recommended him to the lawyer, asking Sigrano to administer his large monthly allowance so that the young man could nobly hold his place in society and fulfil the commitments he could not satisfy with his salary alone.

Mario was, therefore, required to attend the lawyer's office, where he met Sultana Sigrano, born Countess Flaminio. Her beauty struck him immediately, but he would never have thought of seducing her if it had not been for the fact that Sultana, attracted by his looks and name, invited him, with an attentiveness Bruno saw as maternal, to one of her receptions. For the young officer, Sultana represented the unknown, the frightening yet enticing. For the lawyer's wife, the conquest of Mario was a sensual pleasure.

Mario, in spite of himself, felt a shadow of remorse in deceiving the lawyer, who had always received him with kindness and given him paternal advice. He, therefore, stopped frequenting the house, and Bruno never saw him again at his wife's receptions. On one occasion, while handing the monthly allowance check to the young officer, he commented on the matter. The count flushed with embarrassment.

"I have missed them," he said, "but, I'm always very busy. Please apologize to the countess."

The lawyer mentioned it to his wife, who remained calm, letting a faint smile play on her lips.

"As far as I'm concerned," she replied, "I'm not bothered by his absence. I'm sorry, though, that he lied to you about the real reason preventing him from visiting his friends."

"And you know what that is?" Bruno asked sympathetically.

"Everyone knows except you, as you're so wrapped up in office work. Mario is reputed to have become involved with a married woman from high society who occupies all his free time. I can't believe there are women like that who deceive their husbands and corrupt the youth!" Sultana added with singular audacity.

"Unfortunately, they do exist. I feel sorry for Mario, I would've liked to have seen him married to an attractive, decent girl, perhaps someone who had lost their parents and had a decent inheritance."

Sultana shrugged.

"Don't bother mentioning it to him. It would be a waste of time," she said. "He's too young, has no judgement, and prefers married women to girls. Let him indulge his caprices. Not everyone is as wise as you were at his age, nor is he father or marriage material like you."

"I never envied the reckless and still don't."

"And you're right! I wouldn't love you as much if you were like that."

The conversation ended there. The following day, Sultana laughed about it with her lover. The lady with the angelic profile and austere ways, to whom the world bowed and gave respect, was a fake, corrupt. She returned her husband's love, kindness, and generosity with the basest ingratitude, with the most odious of betrayals.

Her relationship with Mario had been going on for two months, and nobody had ever suspected their assignations. The officer's refreshing youthfulness pleased Signora Sigrano, and Sultana's beauty almost drove him mad. Neither of them thought the relationship should end.

2

When Sultana, still elated, left her lover's apartment, it was almost seven o'clock. She got into a passing public carriage and was driven home. The governess had already returned with the children, and in the dressing room, Sultana found Caterina waiting to help her change her clothes.

"Will the signora be going out again this evening?" asked the maid.

"No," she answered. "You know very well that when my husband is away, I prefer to stay at home. Give me my purple robe."

Caterina followed instructions.

"Has Alceste gone?" she added.

"No, madam."

Sultana flinched slightly, and a flash of anger crossed her eyes.

"Why not? He should have left at 4:00 o'clock!"

"Yes, madam, but when he came back to the house with some little gifts he wanted to take to his relatives and heard from the porter that the master had gone to Genoa, he said he'd wait for him to return in case the signora needed anything."

Sultana frowned.

"I don't know what to do about him," she interrupted. "If I need a car, I'll get one in the square. Bring Alceste here, and I'll tell him. Also, I'm warning you not to let either your sister or the children come in here while I speak to him. As I'll be rebuking him, I don't want to humiliate him in front of anyone."

"Don't worry, signora. Nobody will disturb you."

Left alone, Sultana's attractive face took on an energetic yet stubborn expression. She wondered at his temerity in clashing with her and whether he was challenging her because she didn't want anything to do with him anymore. She knew that she had to get rid of him at any cost because he was becoming too dangerous and intrusive.

Rather mechanically, she looked at herself in the mirror for some considerable time. Her low-cut dressing gown with its wide sleeves above the elbow perfectly outlined the contours of her shapely figure, adding much charm to her dazzling blonde beauty. She smiled with pride, but it soon faded from her lips when she heard the chauffeur's footsteps in the corridor.

Alceste knocked before entering.

"Come in!" said Sultana, opening the door herself and retreating a little to let him through.

Alceste stepped forward as it closed, and when she turned, they found themselves face to face. He was a striking young man, mild-mannered and good-looking, but in reality, proud and stubborn. He was also strongly built, with thick curly hair and luminous darting eyes.

"Why haven't you left?" asked Sultana in a brusque rather imperious voice.

Alceste stared at her eagerly.

"That's a peculiar question," he replied. "Before, when the master left, you begged me to stay."

Sultana bit her lip.

"Well, today, instead, I'm ordering you to go!" she added in a pungent tone.

"Get out of the way for someone else? I wouldn't bet on it! I'm not going to be your laughingstock, and I'm not the type of lover who is picked up and put down at will. I've no intention of going, and tonight I'll come to your rooms as before, otherwise...."

Sultana's lips started to twitch as her nostrils flared restlessly.

"Threats?" she said in a hollow voice.

Alceste crossed his arms and continued to look at her.

"I'm not making threats," he replied. "I'm warning you. I didn't come looking for you. Remember that. When I was called to your house to serve as a chauffeur and waiter, I knew, through confidences passed to me by villagers and the family, that you were a morally bankrupt individual, that you took pleasure in teaching your evil ways to children of the same age and that you beat them if they dared to rebel, even accusing them of being the instigators if anyone spoke about your misbehavior. Nevertheless, I treated you with the respect due to the lady of the house, and I began to think that the rumors were nothing but slander, given that you were so thoughtful and tender with your husband."

Alceste remained silent for a moment as Sultana had said nothing. She was bent double on the sofa and had buried her pretty face in one of the silk cushions. The young man sat next to her, and trying to contain the turmoil he felt, continued to speak.

"Never, I swear, did it pass my mind that one day you'd lower yourself enough to be interested in me. I admired your beauty, but I wasn't troubled by desire. I loved the girl I'd left back at home and who I innocently imagined would one day be my wife. I was happy with my life. Do you remember the day that you and I were left alone in the building because your husband had gone to Milan, the children had left with Teresa, and you had sent Caterina on various errands that I suspect were pointless?"

Seemingly lifeless, Sultana did not answer or make a move. Alceste carried on.

"I was trying to dust some knick-knacks in the living room when you called out to me. You were in this very room, half-naked, provocative. I didn't dare look at you when you said to me in a strange voice: 'Alceste, don't you think I'm more beautiful than your Anna Maria?' I felt the blood rush to my head, and shaking, I stammered: 'Yes, signora, you're much more beautiful!' You then burst out laughing and threw your arms around me."

Incensed, Sultana rose from the sofa forcefully and spoke with a voice somewhat tinged with remorse.

"Yes," she exclaimed, "I was guilty, I don't deny it, and I wish I could forget! I acted stupidly because I loved my husband and I still love him. It was a moment of weakness that I've often lamented. But you can't understand how we women have feelings full of impulses that can't be smothered, which lead us to do bad things against our will!"

"I only know," interrupted Alceste, "that ever since that moment, I've suffered a great deal. My inner voice told me that I was shameful because I'd betrayed a nice girl who loved me, a good employer who had full confidence in me, yet when I intended to follow a dutiful path, I heard your voice, and I couldn't think of anything else except losing myself in your embrace. Now you say that you love your husband, that you feel remorse! Lies! You've got no heart, not even with your children. And if you're trying to distance yourself from me, it's because you've got someone else, someone with higher status, rather than a poor deluded fool like me."

Alceste spoke with a broken voice, painful to hear. Nonetheless, Sultana interrupted him abruptly.

"Enough!" she said in an overbearing manner. "I won't allow you to delve into my business, and since you don't want to leave on your own terms, when my husband returns, I'll have you dismissed. I can't tolerate insolence and people who disrespect me."

As soon as she had said these words, she regretted it. Alceste snapped, his gaze clouded, his attitude unwavering.

"Are you threatening to have me chased away?" he shouted. "Be careful, instead, that I don't get you thrown into the street as a dissolute woman who dishonors her very name and the house that welcomes her. Remember that I wear a chain with a locket, close to my chest, that could compromise you. You gave it to me. It has your portrait, a passionate dedication, and a curl of your golden hair!"

"Give me that right now!" demanded the countess.

"I'm not that stupid! It's precious to me, just like the letter you had the recklessness to ask me to deliver to Count Mario Herbert."

Agitated, shaking, Sultana grabbed Alceste by the arm.

"The letter to the count?" she repeated. "How could you have kept it? Tell me! The count received it, he answered me!"

An ironic smile parted the chauffeur's lips.

"As he went into the drawing room to answer you, I picked it up off the rug where he'd dropped it, thinking he'd put it in his inside pocket. I retrieved it since I was curious to know what commission your husband had given him, which was what you'd told me. But as soon as I read the first line, 'Mario, my darling', I realized you'd taken me for a fool, making me play a vile part in all of this. So in retaliation, I kept the letter, knowing that at some point it might prove useful. If the young count had realized the letter was missing and suspected me, I would have explained the facts, and I doubt he would have continued to share your favors with a servant. But he didn't mention it, so I went home and gave you his reply unopened, while your letter was still in my wallet where it remains today."

Sultana shuddered as she listened, her lips pressed tight with repressed anger. Suddenly, her face was transformed, her smile returned, and with feline grace, she approached the young man, throwing her arms around his neck. Her blue eyes locked with Alceste's as if trying to hypnotize him. Her lips brushed his.

"Jealous!" she said in a charming tone of voice. "What do you care about Count Mario? I understand. Your jealousy of him makes you come after me, me,... who gave you such pleasure — the kind of pleasure any other man would give his life for!"

Alceste became agitated, desire prompted beads of sweat to run down his forehead.

"But I,..." he stammered.

"Shut up, let me speak! When I got involved with you, I told you immediately that I didn't want us to be linked forever, that we would each remain in control of our own will, our own actions, that I wouldn't have cared if you loved someone else more than me, and that it had to be the same for you."

"I haven't forgotten!" Alceste interrupted. "In fact, knowing about your infidelities, I stayed in the shadows, ready to defend you in case of danger and contenting myself with the little time you allowed me without asking for anything more. I've realized for a few weeks now that you want to get rid of me entirely. I saw the happy glow in your eyes when I asked your husband if I could go to my village for the patron saint's feast day. I knew that you were fed up with me and during my absence would decide my fate by getting Signor Sigrano to fire me. I was confused. I didn't know what to do, nor could I find the strength to leave when I found out that the master was going to Genoa for a few days. I wanted to take the opportunity to find out what you have in mind for me, so I stayed behind!"

"I don't deny that I've occasionally been cruel to you," said Sultana, "but I never thought of abandoning you. I wanted to put you to the test to be sure that, at any given moment, I could count on you, on your affection. And, instead, you insult and threaten me!"

Alceste's handsome face changed with the emotion.

"Forgive me," he murmured, "but I love you so much. I need you so much, that when you treat me with indifference, it's agonizing. Believe me, Sultana, nobody will ever love you more than I do!"

"Well, prove it," she whispered while kissing him, "by giving me back the count's letter and the locket. I want them!"

Alceste freed himself from her grasp. The spell had been broken.

"I told you," he repeated, "they are my guarantee and defense. If you want them back, you'll have to kill me, a prospect that doesn't frighten me in the least. However, I swear they won't find their way into anyone else's hands as long as you continue to grant me your favors."

Sultana hid the anger boiling inside, and appearing to remain calm, she smiled.

"I didn't think you were so stubborn!" she exclaimed. "I admire you for that, and it's something we have in common. Ok, since they are safe in your hands, just keep them. I'll be yours again tonight."

Alceste went pale.

"Truly? Can I come to you? Won't you be expecting someone else?" he said, delighted, but choked with emotion at the prospect.

"No!" Sultana answered, turning her magnetic gaze to him. "Wait! You've made me forget the respect I owe to my husband's house."

"Oh, please! I really do love you!"

"Now, listen to me. You know that none of the servants suspect our relationship…."

"And nobody will ever suspect it!" Alceste interrupted.

"You're wrong! Today, you were most imprudent and did something that could compromise me. You remained here without the master, as if I really needed you!"

"Forgive me! I was going mad."

"Forget it, especially as you can make up for it."

"In what way? Say it, tell me!"

"You're going to tell Caterina and the others that you'll be leaving on the eight o'clock train because I don't want you to give up the time off you were granted by my husband. Then leave and take your case with you. At eleven o'clock, return through the service door using the key you must have."

"Yes, signora."

"I'll wait for you in this same room, so come through the corridor and I'll leave the door ajar. If by any chance the porter or his wife see you returning, say that you missed the train."

Sultana spoke with such simplicity and naturalness that it would have been impossible for even the most accomplished of men to guess that she was creating a trap.

"Have you got all that?"

"Yes, yes."

"Now go away, and tell Caterina to prepare dinner, I'll come immediately."

Alceste left the room, elated.

Sultana, when left alone, gestured angrily to herself. Her eyes expressed the terrible thoughts going through her head. She realized that the wretched man did not fear her. Although he believed he had the upper hand because of her weakness for his looks, she knew that she had to regain her serenity and break the chains binding her, even if it meant preventing him from seeing another dawn.

3

All the public clocks in Turin were displaying eleven at night when an unsteady Alceste cautiously opened the service entrance door to the Sigrano building from the courtyard side.

The silence was total.

The young man's heart was racing, his head full of feverish thoughts. He always reacted in this way, every time he came to Sultana, the siren. He was bewitched by her perfume, her smiles and kisses…yet in truth, he had no love for her. Deep down, he longed for a woman like his Anna Maria, full of sweet simplicity, not a wanton woman greedy for an illicit affair like Sultana.

Nevertheless, although his spirit wandered far from Turin, Alceste did not know how to split from the sorceress who had mesmerized him.

As Signora Sigrano had indicated, he had taken leave of the other servants, telling them that he was going because the mistress had told him she could dispense with his services while her husband was away. In fact, during the few minutes he spent chatting with the porter, he complained about her, saying that she was proud and arrogant. He added that, were it not for the master, he would gone back home permanently.

"My wife and I think the same way!" Batista replied. "We also stay because of the lawyer, the nicest gentleman I know. Perhaps he's too good as he lets the lady dominate him."

Alceste agreed. Under the pretext of not wishing to miss the train, he hurried off only to slow his pace when he was just far enough away from the palazzo. Carrying his case, he stopped in at a modest restaurant owned by a certain Matteo Ferpio, a friend from his village.

"It's great to see you!" Matteo exclaimed as soon as he saw him. "Are you going on holiday?" he added with a smile, noticing the case.

"Signor Sigrano gave me permission to go to the saint's feast day celebrations and, after I accepted, I thought I'd see if you wanted to come with me."

"This evening?"

"Why not?"

"But don't you know there'll be no coach to meet us tonight, and we'll have to walk about ten kilometers. You're mad! Stay for dinner with me instead and spend the night if you don't want to go back to the palazzo. I'll leave with you on the five o'clock train, and by eight, we'll easily have reached home."

Alceste knew full well that he would not be leaving.

"You're right! I was a fool not to check the timetables. I really don't want to walk for hours along those treacherous roads. Very well, I accept your offer of dinner, but afterwards I'll take the opportunity to go and see a friend who thinks I'll be traveling, just to check on her loyalty," he replied nonetheless.

"Ah, you rascal! If only Anna Maria knew!"

"I hope you're not going to give me away. It's nothing but a small dalliance, a brief pause before I hopefully marry my dear fiancée. I'll leave my case in your care, and I'll be back around two or three in the morning."

"As you wish!"

Alceste was very cheerful during dinner. He spoke with enthusiasm of his master's kindness, of Countess Sultana's beauty, and her loving relationship with her husband and children.

"Really?" interrupted Matteo's wife at that point. "I'm amazed that little Countess Flaminio has been an exemplary wife and mother! I've heard so many stories about when she was younger."

"Nothing but lies!" exclaimed Alceste impetuously. "All the girls envied her beauty, and the young men of the village, failing to gain her affection, belittled her instead. It's true, you can't get close to her without the desire to possess her, but…."

"Rogue! I bet you too," interrupted Matteo, "would have gladly betrayed the master for her."

Alceste's face flushed, but he smiled.

"You're joking! Certain tasty morsels aren't meant for the likes of me."

He changed the subject.

It was ten o'clock when Alceste left the restaurant. The weather was fine, and the young man had an hour before going to his rendezvous.

Some hundred paces from the Sigrano house, he sat down on a bench in the avenue and his thoughts began to drift. In the anxiety of waiting, he felt an inexplicable turmoil, which forced him to get up and move on. He glanced at his watch constantly.

At five minutes to eleven, he walked resolutely towards the building and, as we know, silently opened the service door and entered. The building was in darkness and silence reined. He went up the service stairs to the first floor and opened a door that led to the owners' rooms. Their main bedroom was separated by a lounge area from the room where the children and governess slept.

From the Sigranos' bedroom, there was an entrance to the dressing room and from there a door to a luxurious bathroom, which, in turn, led to the corridor. Through this door, left ajar by Sultana, Alceste entered. He immediately saw her appear before him, wrapped in a light green bathrobe accentuating her curves. A shaded electric lamp cast a dim light.

"You're on time!" Sultana said in a singular voice. "Before we go into the dressing room and start to enjoy ourselves, I want to make a deal. Sit down."

She pointed to a stool near the pink marble bathtub while she sat in an armchair. Alceste obeyed without any hesitation.

"I'm ready to listen," he replied in thrall to the woman who, without being able to explain why, both attracted and terrified him.

"You say you love me, right?"

"Perhaps you don't believe me."

"Oh, I believe you, but there may come a day when you don't and then, through excusable vanity, you might boast of the favors I showed you or produce the locket I gave you...."

"Don't worry," Alceste interrupted, "I'll jealously guard the locket. Moreover, I'll carry my love for you to the grave."

"Words! Words! I want deeds instead. In short, if you still want to continue this, give me back the locket and the letter to Count Herbert."

Sultana spoke with a certain animation, betraying the agitation she felt underneath, but Alceste was not won over.

"I've told you, and I'll say again. Those objects are safe, and I will never use them to harm you."

Sultana lent towards him, enveloping him in the intoxicating scent of her perfume. He could see her shapely breasts under the light fabric of her bathrobe.

"Give them to me," she repeated. "I want them!"

"No, no, I can't," Alceste said again. "If you truly loved me, you'd trust me and would let me keep them."

"I want them!" repeated Sultana boldly.

Her attitude struck Alceste, and he began to understand that Sultana had only created this outrageous charade of love and abandonment in the hope of getting the objects in question so she could rid herself of him.

It was just one more proof that Signora Sigrano despised him after poisoning his soul by making him betray Anna Maria.

He, therefore, had to be spirited and insolent in his defense.

"No, I won't give them to you!" he exclaimed with his head held high. "Your kisses aren't enough to pay for them, nor to destroy the relationship between us…or between you and the count!"

"You're despicable! You insult me."

"I'm not insulting you, just defending myself."

Sultana, in a fury, rushed towards him, trying to rip open his waistcoat and shirt so she could tear the locket from his chest.

They tussled in silence, but Alceste was stronger. Without hurting her, he managed to hold her back by the wrist.

"No, you won't get it! The count isn't worth my sacrifice and I'm not going to leave you free to laugh at me like you laugh at your husband. Nor do I want you to judge me in the same way you judge your other lovers. As long as I hold on to these objects, I'll have the upper hand and you'll keep on giving yourself to me, willingly or otherwise."

"Don't bet on it!" she shouted vehemently. "You disgust me now."

Alceste turned pale but undaunted, managed to maintain his indignant demeanor. On the contrary, he had the strength to smile, to joke, even though he was tormented with anguish.

"Ah!" he said. "How you've changed. It hasn't been a month since you held me in your arms, yearning for my touch, my kisses, calling me your treasure, your only love!"

Sultana clenched her teeth and stared intently. "Stop it!"

Alceste laughed again.

"We haven't even started yet!" he retorted. "Come on, let's go into your room. It's about time!"

Sultana was beside herself. She knew that all hope of getting the items back was gone. A mute anger crept over her and seared her thoughts. She looked him in the face once more.

"Are you going to persist in your refusal?" she said.

"Yes."

A wild glint flashed across her eyes.

"Very well. Wait here a moment."

Alceste had no idea what was going through her mind but remained motionless.

Sultana walked into her dressing room for a few seconds then returned. She was still livid, but resolute.

"For the last time, will you give me the items in question?" she said, holding her right hand down between the folds of her robe.

Alceste took a step towards her and faced her.

"No!" he answered immediately.

Without hesitation, Sultana's arm rose and extended, a shot echoed through the room. Alceste, struck in the forehead with a bullet, barely had time to utter a few words.

"Murderer! Oh, poor Anna Maria.…"

He staggered back and fell forward to the ground. In an instant, Signora Sigrano had put down the revolver and rushed to the body. She had no intention of helping, simply wanting to make sure he would never move again and to rummage through his clothes. As she turned him over, Alceste flinched before dying.

Sultana, realizing he was dead, let a malevolent smile play on her lips.

"Well, you can't stop me now!" she murmured. "I'm taking them back, and I'll be rid of you."

She had removed his wallet from his pocket but had only found two five-lire banknotes and a letter from Anna Maria inviting him to the village for the festivities. Nothing else! She couldn't find the letter to Count Herbert or her locket, which Alceste had said he kept jealously guarded close to his chest. It had all been pointless! She had freed herself from the man who was becoming a dangerous nuisance, but still the compromising items remained the same and, if discovered, could cause her dishonor and ruin.

Where had the wretch hidden them? Then she remembered the case that Alceste had taken with him to feign a trip to the station, but which he had not brought to their meeting. To whom had he entrusted the case? Had he hidden the items inside?

Despite the scene before her, Sultana's brutal attitude had not altered. She cursed her luck. Suddenly, she came to her senses. How could she get out of the frightening situation her rash actions had created? What could she do with the corpse?

Sultana was not a woman prone to losing heart, and she soon had an idea that gave her some reassurance. She ensured the corpse was face down, then opened the dressing table drawer where her husband had told her to find the five-thousand lire notes, which, in fact, she had forgotten to move. She then knocked over a chair.

She went into her bedroom, took off her dressing gown, crumpled the bed covers as if she had already gone to bed, and barefoot, wearing only her nightgown, went into the dressing room and opened a window. She fired another shot from the revolver since no one had noticed the first.

"Help! Thief!" she shouted.

In a few minutes the caretaker, his wife Caterina, and Teresa rushed to Signora Sigrano's apartment. She ran to meet them looking disheveled, crying with the revolver in her hand.

"God, what a fright!" she stammered.

As if fainting, she fell into Caterina's arms, dropping the revolver on the floor, which Batista then picked up.

"What's happened?" they all anxiously asked.

Sultana spoke hoarsely in a faltering agitated voice.

"I'd been asleep for perhaps half an hour after reading the newspaper," she said, "when I was woken up by the dull thud of an object falling to the ground. I jumped out of bed, picked up the revolver that I always keep by my bedside in my husband's absence, went into the dressing room, and turned on the lights. I didn't see anyone, but then, from the half-closed door of the well-lit bathroom I saw a dark shape move.

"I remembered that my husband had said before he left that he had put some five-thousand lire notes in the dressing table drawer and, as he'd forgotten them, had asked me to put them in the safe. Woozy from interrupted sleep, I suddenly thought of burglars…and while I was thinking about shouting for help, the door opened, and I saw a man in front of me. Scared, I fired a shot, the man fell, and I went to the window, opened it, and cried out for help."

"Is he dead?" asked Batista.

"I don't know," answered Sultana. "I was only thinking of defending myself and, when I saw him fall, of making sure I was safe."

"We'd better check!" they all agreed.

Sultana's two children were still innocently asleep as neither the sound of the shots nor the cries of their mother had awakened them. Teresa, to be sure they would not stir, went to close the door of their room, and then followed the others.

Both the dressing room and bathroom had the doors wide open. In the second of the two rooms, lay the body of a man in a pool of blood. Although they all believed him to be a thief, they felt a strong sense of emotion.

Batista finally gathered enough courage to turn over the corpse and see the face. Sultana's desperate cry pierced the exclamations of surprise from all present. Despite the blood splattered across his face and the bullet wound that had torn his forehead and fatally entered his brain, everyone recognized the Sigranos' chauffeur.

"It's Alceste," they said in unison.

"Yes, it's really him!" Batista said, "And there's nothing we can do for him. He's dead alright!"

"That can't be true! We must be seeing things," stuttered Sultana, brushing a hand across his forehead. "He promised me that he would be leaving!"

"In fact," remarked Batista, "he went to the porter's lodge at eight with a case in his hand and told me that he was going to his village."

"Perhaps he missed the train," observed the cook, "and came back via the services stairs."

"But he wouldn't have come back this way," said the governess in turn, "knowing full well that he was entering the mistress' apartment."

"Ah, the wretch!" the countess exclaimed in a stinging tone. "Now I realize what led him to sneak in here secretly! No, Alceste didn't want to steal the master's money, he wanted to steal my honor!"

As if inspired by the sound of her own voice, she continued in an increasingly unsettled manner:

"For quite a while, I've been aware of the inappropriate feelings he had for me."

"We've all noticed!" Caterina interrupted. "I once had to scold him precisely because he was talking about you without due respect."

"He also mentioned it to me," Batista said gently, "but I made him see that the signora wasn't for the likes of him."

Despite the tragedy of the moment, a fleeting smile touched the lips of Teresa, Caterina, and Sofia, the caretaker's wife.

"Precisely for that reason, regretting that I'd treated him with familiarity in recent months and because I believed him to be a decent lad, I kept him in his place, never letting him into my apartment without being called. I was almost unkind to him...I'd even been thinking about getting him fired. Yesterday, when my husband regretted giving Alceste some time off, assuming that I'd need him during his absence, I was actually relieved he was going. And when I came back to the house and found out that he'd said he wasn't going, I was irritated and told Caterina to send him to me immediately. I wanted him gone at any cost," added Sultana breathlessly.

"It's true," Caterina confirmed emphatically.

In an increasingly hysterical voice, Sultana continued her story.

"I'm not going to repeat the conversation I had with Alceste, who even dared to talk to me about his feelings. I reprimanded him harshly and threatened to tell my husband everything if he didn't leave. He wept and pleaded with me, but I was unrelenting. He then said to me, 'Well, I will leave, but remember, signora, even if I'm no longer around, I'll have you where I want you'. The wretch certainly didn't think that he'd sealed his fate at that moment, but his recklessness and criminal intent have ended up in his death. Although he died at my hand, my conscience is clear, because I didn't kill a thief after money, but someone who wanted to take away my honor, something more precious than any jewel. Batista, call the police headquarters, and tell my husband at the Hotel d'Italia in Genoa. I'm going to withdraw to my room as I'm devastated by all this. I don't want to see the body anymore. I just can't!"

In truth, although incensed, Sultana looked washed out and was trembling as if from a fever, to such an extent that the other three women present felt the death of Alceste more keenly. Caterina and Sofia comforted her with a few kind words, urging her to rest and remove herself from the macabre spectacle. Teresa gently took her arm and led her away.

As soon as her door was closed, Sultana slumped into an armchair.

"What misery! He's ruined me!" she said hesitantly.

Teresa knelt in front of her.

"Don't despair, don't cry! We're all willing to testify that you're not responsible for Alceste's death. He entered your apartment as a real thief," she said, her voice cracking with emotion.

"I didn't intend to use the revolver, only to shout. All of you would have rushed in and discovered his outrageous intentions. I acted foolishly, but I was so scared!" she sobbed, wringing her hands.

Teresa felt her beloved mistress' anguish to the very core.

"Try to stay calm. Calm yourself!" she repeated. "At the end of the day, what can they do to you? Your husband will know how to defend you when he finds out what's happened."

"Ah, you don't know everything my dear Teresa!" Sultana said, lifting the hair that had fallen across her neck and shoulders. The governess was transfixed by the dark reflection of her eyes.

"My God, what else is there?" asked Teresa.

"Yesterday, when Alceste came to me, he returned my reproach with threats, saying that if I didn't consent to be his lover, he would tell my husband that not only had I been his mistress but also Count Mario Herbert's, and he would show the evidence," Sultana answered in a low voice, interrupted by tears.

Teresa looked dazed.

"The evidence?" she said. "What evidence?"

"As you've always been faithful to me, I'll tell you everything. A few months ago, I bought a very plain locket to wear around my neck where I intended to keep a picture of my husband and children. One day, I discovered that the locket had disappeared. I thought I'd lost it during the hustle and bustle in preparing to leave for the public baths. Nor did I notice the disappearance of a photograph taken of me that had an affectionate dedication. I intended it for Bruno. Now the locket and photograph, along with a lock of my hair almost certainly taken from the comb I keep in my dressing table drawer, are in Alceste's possession. He wanted to believe that I'd given them to him myself."

"I dread to think," interrupted Teresa, "that if the master or anyone else found the locket among the dead man's things, they might believe that the wretch had a hold over you!"

"And that's what I'm afraid of, do you understand? So, before the magistrates arrive, look for his case yourself. Rummage through his trunk without anyone noticing."

"I will, signora!" exclaimed Teresa. "But what if he was wearing the items?"

"No, I can't believe he would. I can't believe it!"

"You also spoke about a Count Herbert...."

"Yes, a letter that appears to be written by me to Lieutenant Herbert, but it's a fake."

"That's awful!" said Teresa. "But have no doubt, even if I can't find the objects, you won't be accused. We'll all defend you."

"I know you will. I know how good you are to me. My honor is now in your hands. I'm not the least bit afraid of scandal as long as my husband and children are convinced of my innocence. To remain worthy of them, I've turned into a killer!"

"Don't say that! Alceste deserved his fate."

"But I'll always blame myself for his death. I didn't intend to kill him." She began to sob. "Go, don't delay," she added, extending a hand to Teresa.

The governess kissed her hand warmly and scurried away.

Sultana straightened up and clenched her fists tightly. She cursed Alceste, who, although dead, still had the potential to ruin her. She vowed to stop it at all costs and to see to it that people would remember him with disgust, believing only her.

4

An hour later an officer from the bureau of public security, accompanied by a doctor and two other agents, arrived at the Sigrano home. Teresa had been allowed plenty of time to search on Sultana's behalf but had failed to find Alceste's case, nor was she able to find any of the compromising items when looking in the dead man's room.

Sultana, having somewhat recovered from her low mood, received the officer and his entourage wearing a simple dark blue dressing gown which exacerbated the intense pallor of her face. She informed them of the incident and, followed by the servants, led them into the room with Alceste's corpse.

She spoke in a broken voice and her attractive features were contorted with distress. She repeated the story she had told to the servants, showing the officer where her husband had left the bank notes. In the belief that it had been a thief, she described how she had failed to notice the features of the individual who had appeared before her in the bathroom. And how, terrified, she had fired without any intention to kill. She explained that, only when the servants had rushed to the sound of the gunshot and her screams, had she and the others recognized the chauffeur who everybody thought had left.

"Why do you think he returned unexpectedly, and how would you explain his presence in this room?" asked the officer. "Do you think he knew about the money left by your husband?"

"No, absolutely not!"

Sultana looked at the servants as if trying to avoid adding anything else, already deeply regretting the confidences she had revealed, since it would have been easier to pass Alceste off as a thief. However, there was the question of the objects. What about the missing objects?

"Alceste had a more devious motive than theft when he secretly came back to the palazzo in the absence of the master," Batista immediately added with his admirable sincerity.

"Which is?"

Sultana started to confess the nature of the chauffeur's infatuation, but with great tact and dignity and without ranting against the dead man, thereby establishing how he had met with his tragic fate. During this testimony, confirmed by the servants with frequent nods, the officer took several notes. He sent an agent to the magistrates to explain what had happened. They were obliged to come to the scene since the officer had no responsibility for investigating the circumstances of the mystery. He witnessed the doctor's brief examination of Alceste's corpse, then asked the countess to hand over her revolver. Sultana followed him as he subsequently made his way to Alceste's room to undertake a search.

For a servant's room it was bordering on elegant. It had an inlaid wooden bed, a mirrored wardrobe, a chest of drawers, a small desk in front of the window, a sofa, two chairs, and floral print wallpaper. There were some books and illustrated newspapers on the desk, a box of writing stationery, a paper folder, and a glass ink well. No letters were found inside the folder. The desk drawer contained two packs of cigarettes, a picture of a young man in a bersagliere's uniform bearing the dedication 'To my friend Alceste, in fond memory,' some postcards, but nothing else. Neither the wardrobe nor chest of drawers held anything capable of shedding light on the events of that night.

Batista mentioned the case that Alceste had taken with him when he pretended to leave the building. Searches were made throughout the house, but to no avail.

"Has your husband been warned of events?" the officer turned and asked Sultana.

"Yes," she replied, full of anguish. "Poor Bruno! When he left, he couldn't have imagined what would await him when he returned. As usual, he was so happy when I accompanied him to the station with the children, who, God willing, will continue to sleep through this in blissful ignorance. My husband telephoned around eight o'clock to say his journey had been fine. He must certainly have had a rude awakening when, on my request, Batista called him to say he should leave immediately as the household had been greatly saddened by a terrible misfortune that had befallen Alceste. He replied that he would leave on the direct train at two-thirty and be here by seven-forty in the morning. Now, if you will allow me, sir, I would like to withdraw as I can't handle this anymore."

Indeed, the pallor of her face and her anxious eyes completely confirmed her discomfort, so much so that the officer was moved to allow her to get some rest. However, he informed her that, along with the other agent, he would not be leaving the property until the end of the initial investigation.

"As you wish, sir!" the countess murmured softly.

In reality, although strong in spirit and resolute, Sultana was beginning to feel fragile. As soon as she reached her room, she collapsed on the bed and, still dressed, drifted off to sleep. She was plagued, though, by frightening dreams in which the threatening figure of Alceste repeatedly appeared before her saying that she would fail to get her hands on the missing proof, that he had foreseen her actions and taken precautions to defend his memory and exact revenge. She had heard him say he would always be a presence disrupting her future affairs.

Sultana squirmed on the bed, mumbling incoherently, but remained asleep. She was unable to say how many hours she had slept, when a kiss on the mouth made her open her eyes and cry out. Her husband, who had already been there for an hour, stood before her. Sultana threw her arms around his neck.

"Bruno, you know that I killed him?" she said amid tears.

"Don't say such things!" he replied, holding her tightly. "You did nothing but defend yourself. You were alone, and you didn't just fire on a thief but a man who'd betrayed our trust. He deserved his fate. I know about it all as they've told me everything."

Sultana moved even closer to him.

"Can anyone hear us?" she whispered.

"No."

"I lied. I clearly recognized the thief, and it's for you, dear Bruno, that I killed him, so I could still be worthy of your love!" she added almost inaudibly.

Her tears stopped, and her eyes expressed an excess of pride and dignity.

Bruno Sigrano was deeply moved.

"Why didn't you speak out earlier?" he stammered. Sultana kissed him passionately.

"Because I didn't want to upset you. I didn't think he would go as far as sneaking into our apartment and trying to rape me during the night while you weren't there. If I had hesitated for a moment, if I'd let him get into the dressing room, all would have been lost. Thank God I heard the noise he made when he entered the bathroom, and it was then I remembered the money you had left behind. I first assumed it was a thief as I thought Alceste had left. Pale, out of breath and full of lust, he took a step towards me with every intention of grabbing me. I realized that my honor was at stake, and I fired. I didn't think I'd killed him, though. Dear Bruno, I've suffered so much for you!"

"And you will have to for a while longer, my angel!" Sigrano added with anguish in his voice. "But everyone is ready to testify that you were just defending yourself. Nonetheless, the law makes no exceptions. You will be arrested, and a judicial process will be started for involuntary homicide...."

Bruno was dejected as he spoke, tears rolled down his cheeks. Sultana tried to console him: "What does it matter?" she said, proudly raising her head. "As long as my honor remains intact, and I'm still worthy of you, I'm yours alone?! I would also hate the children to know about or see any of this...."

"Rest assured," the lawyer quickly replied, "they're already far from here. The magistrate himself advised me to do that before they started to understand the situation. I've entrusted them to Teresa with orders to take them to their grandparents, where they'll wait for us. I asked her to tell them that you'd gone to join me in Genoa."

"It's better that way!" Sultana exclaimed.

"Cavalier Alessio, the magistrate in charge of completing the investigation and instituting judicial proceedings, asked me to wake you up and be of some comfort to you. He's waiting for you in the living room so he can ask you some initial questions."

"I'll get up, get changed, and come right away. Send Caterina to me."

Her strength and self-assurance had returned. The alarming expression had disappeared from her face, which now revealed nothing more than the trauma of events. Her husband, reassured, left her to get dressed. With the aid of Caterina, it took no more than fifteen minutes.

In anticipation of being transferred to jail, she wore a simple, dark-colored dress, which made her look even younger. She quickly gave a series of instructions to Caterina, who was as devoted to her as Teresa.

Cavalier Alessio, young for a magistrate, knew Bruno Sigrano by reputation and, although he had never had personal dealings with him, held him in high esteem. He had only glimpsed Sultana a few times, but nevertheless had eagerly agreed to take on the investigation. Immediately, from what he had heard from the officer and members of the household, he guessed that he was facing a very personal and enigmatic case. He was, though, careful not to express his initial impressions.

As he was still in the room with Alceste's corpse when the distressed lawyer arrived out of breath, he took him to the living room and spoke to him in an effort to calm the situation. Along with the officer, they agreed to arrange matters so that the scandal would not break straight away.

When Sultana appeared, Cavalier Alessio was rather taken aback but regained his composure quickly.

"Forgive me, signora," he said with a slight bow, "if I woke you, but I need to ask you some questions before I arrange for the body to be moved."

"I understand, sir, and I'm ready to give you some answers," Sultana said with great simplicity, avoiding any emphasis or exaggeration. "Maybe you find it strange that I've been able to sleep after the events of last night, but the emotion of it all has taken its toll, both physically and mentally. So much so that all I need is to rest."

"That will certainly have helped you," replied the magistrate, "as your mind will now be clearer and you'll be better able to enlighten us regarding the sad events."

She sat facing Alessio, while the officer and Bruno were to the side.

"Alas, sir," added Sultana, "I can only repeat to you what I've already told the officer here. I went to bed early, as I usually do when my husband is away, and I put the revolver on the bedside table within easy reach."

"So, you were afraid of being attacked?"

"No, but our home is a bit isolated, and the porter's lodge is far from the house, which, at the time, only had three women and two children in it. It didn't, given the circumstances, seem an excessive precaution. Ever since I was a child, I've known how to handle a gun. My father taught me to use one in case I needed a means of defense, especially as we lived in the countryside where ambushes are frequent. Returning to matters in hand, I'm not sure how long I'd been sleeping when I was suddenly awakened by the creaking of a door. Only the bathroom door that leads to the service corridor makes that squeak when it opens. My mind turned to the five-thousand lire bank notes my husband had asked me to put away. In the confusion of waking abruptly, I thought thieves had broken in. Without thinking, and with courage driven by fear, I jumped out of bed and grabbed the revolver.

As I walked into the dressing room, which was lit by a single bulb, I saw the figure of a man standing before me. Frightened beyond belief, I shot at him, then returned to my room and cried out for help. The porter, his wife, and the other women came rushing to me when, overcome with emotion, I collapsed."

"And you didn't recognize your servant as the intruder?"

"No, and I wouldn't have even guessed since I thought he'd gone. All the servants, including the porter, saw him leave at around eight o'clock last night."

"It seems he had some criminal intent, secretly returning to your apartment like this at night!" said the magistrate. "What did you think when you recognized the chauffeur?"

"Nothing!" Sultana answered without lowering her head before Cavalier Alessio's gaze. "I felt great pain at having killed another human being, even though I'm convinced I have a right to defend myself from a thief or attacker. But it wasn't my intention to kill him."

Her voice sounded sincere.

"I believe you, signora, and, for now, I'll stop the questions as I have to finish off some other investigative matters," said the magistrate. "I'm sorry to say that I have to order your arrest. Anyone who kills, even if it's involuntary homicide, has to submit to the due process of law. However, I can assure you that you will be treated with respect and that your imprisonment won't last long."

"I respect the law," Sultana answered, exaggerating her usual air of insouciant pride, "and I am entirely at the disposal of the forces of justice. Although my conscience is clear, I will endure my penance. It's you, my dear Bruno, who I feel sorry for."

Without worrying about the presence of the judicial officials, she rose to fling her arms around her husband. As they embraced, they both began to shed tears.

5

When the news spread throughout Turin that Alceste Bianco, the chauffeur, had been killed by Signora Sigrano, there was much surprise. The particulars divulged in the newspapers aroused a great deal of comment.

Although Sultana had been able to keep her good name intact, it seemed to many rather unlikely that she had killed the young man by mistaking him for a thief. Instead, it was assumed that the servant, in love with his mistress and rejected by her, had secretly returned to the building to try and take the countess by surprise. She, in fear of a brutal assault, had then taken precautions and, at the first appearance of the young man, had shot and killed him.

But why had she not warned her husband, instead of committing a crime? The lawyer, Bruno Sigrano, would have been able to deal with the young man without drawing undue attention to events.

For days, the city news concentrated on nothing else but the shooting committed by a woman who enjoyed the esteem of many. Silence was to follow, enabling justice to take its course. In the meantime, the majority thought that the countess would be released free of charge at the end of the investigation and that she had acted in self-defense.

The news of the crime, committed in such mysterious circumstances and leading to the arrest of Signora Sigrano, was a real shock to two people, namely Mario Herbert and Matteo Ferpio. The cavalry lieutenant learned of the incident while he was having a meal in a restaurant with some friends. Given that he had alluded to the beautiful and virtuous Signora Sigrano out of vanity after one drunken dinner full of champagne, during which others detailed their conquests of supposedly unapproachable ladies of rank, it was no surprise to his friends that he went pale at the news. And to think that he had made an appointment with Sultana that very evening!

"You fooled us," a friend told him, "by letting us think Signora Sigrano had some weakness for you."

"When did I ever say that?" replied Mario, increasingly irritated.

"Come on!" the others answered as one. "Don't you remember that night at Molinari's? You let us think such wonderful things, but nobody really believed you."

"Well, there you are then! I had to be drunk in order to insult the good name of a lady I respect."

"Signora Sigrano is an awful woman who welcomes lovers like thieves, with a revolver," one of the other's added laughing.

"I hope you're not suggesting that a servant was her lover?" snapped Mario in a more serious tone.

"Who knows!" said a handsome officer twirling his mustache. "Ladies are so capricious they often prefer a chauffeur to a gentleman. Then they change their minds and try to get rid of the rogue, even by violent means...."

"Oh, really!"

A smile was on everyone's lips, even briefly on Mario's. His cheeks soon flushed, though, at having found such malice amusing.

"I don't want to hear anymore!" he said, rising from his seat to lace his saber. "I'm going in search of some news."

"Try to console her husband. It's your duty," they exclaimed in unison.

Mario thought it best not to reply and left the restaurant. He was reeling from the news, thinking as he walked along. Was it likely that Sultana had shot the chauffeur thinking he was a thief? Was he wrong to exclude the possibility that Alceste was her lover?

Mario was well aware of what Sultana was capable of doing. He knew her to be cynical, corrupt, lascivious, daring — to be a fake. How many times he had wanted to silence her when, with supreme impudence, she had laughed about her deceived husband who only wanted her happiness. Mario often paled at Sultana's temerity in wanting him to write passionate letters addressed to her home under the reassurance that her husband never interfered with her mail. He knew that she was intoxicated by the danger, which added a certain frisson to her passion.

"If someone started to harass me or tried to get between us, I would resort to any means to keep us together," she had said to him one day.

Damn! He hoped that Signora Sigrano, under questioning, would not let anything slip about their relationship and that a search of the house failed to find any trace of the two or three notes he had reluctantly sent her. She had fallen from her pedestal. He cursed the day he had crossed paths with such a dangerous woman, someone who could involve him in a scandal which would prove painful for his family.

How many times had his father and mother reminded him to "Treat Bruno Sigrano with the affection, gratitude, and devotion of a son, because you owe the well-being and wealth of your family to him. It's thanks to him you will be able to honor the glorious name of your ancestors." And he had shown his gratitude by taking his wife! But had it really all been his fault?

Matteo Ferpio, one of Alceste's closest friends and compatriots, who ran the restaurant he had visited that night, had waited without undue concern for Alceste to return so they could leave at daybreak and enjoy the saint's feast day. The innkeeper's wife, Marietta, who was staying in Turin to mind the business, had said to Matteo as she had gone off to bed that she thought Alceste, since he had come to Turin, had turned into a rascal.

"He always talks about women, and on the eve of going to see his fiancée, he spends the night having fun with someone else."

Matteo laughed.

"It's better to sow your wild oats before the wedding than after!" he exclaimed.

"Big talk! When men start to take pleasure in elicit affairs, they end up bored with those who truly love them."

"Don't believe any of that. Alceste is warm and lively by nature, and he's got a heart of gold. He adores Anna Maria, who'd be a tasty morsel for any king. She's a beautiful and virtuous girl, and when he's married her, he won't think of other women anymore. He'll be a decent, faithful husband like me, although I was more of a rascal than him when I was free and single."

Marietta smiled and decided not to reply.

When daybreak came, Matteo was ready. Marietta had prepared some good coffee for Alceste, but he did not appear. The innkeeper decided not to leave on his own. By noon, Alceste had still not been seen by anyone. Matteo was beginning to feel restless, and his wife had also lost her air of calm. It was at midday that some guests at the boarding house came to the little restaurant, and it was from them that the couple learned how Alceste had been killed by Sultana thinking he was a thief.

"Accidentally? Is that possible?" Matteo stammered.

Straight away, he decided to go to the Sigrano home to get some on-the-spot information. When he went upstairs to get changed, his wife followed him.

"Don't be too impulsive," she told him, "and don't get in the way of the law."

"But don't you see, Alceste was having dinner with us just last night." Matteo added. "Several people saw him. Besides, I must hand over his case, because if people find out that he left it with me, they might think it contains something valuable and that I intend to keep it."

"You're right," observed Marietta, who was known for her honesty, "but maybe we should look and see what it contains, not so we can take advantage, but in case we find some papers that poor Alceste didn't want to fall into the wrong hands."

"That's not a bad idea! Let's take a look, especially as we've got the little key."

Although the case was closed, the key was tied to one of the leather handles. Opening the case, the couple found some handkerchiefs, two pairs of socks, three starched collars, a tie, a brush, a comb, a box of chocolates, a candy bar, a tin containing a silver chain with an effigy of the Madonna della Consolata, and some small items of custom jewelry perhaps intended as gifts. In a separate bag, there was a carefully sealed package which bore the singular wording: 'To Anna Maria. To be opened only in the event of my death, or to be returned to me intact on the day of our wedding.'

"You see!" exclaimed Marietta. "I guessed there was a secret in there. We won't tell anyone, but let's take the package out and deliver it to her ourselves. We'll be carrying out Alceste's wishes."

Matteo agreed and his wife swiftly locked the package away in a place chosen by her husband, where he kept his valuables and where nobody would think to look. Marietta then went downstairs to avoid arousing suspicion, and Matteo took the case to the nearby Sigrano home.

Outside the palazzo, he found a huge crowd had gathered. There was much comment on events, and some were trying to enter and get a look at the body, which had not yet been removed. The countess had already been transferred to the prison a few hours before the rumors had started to spread.

At the entrance to the building, some municipal guards and public security officers were preventing anyone from entering. However, when Matteo made his way through the crowd and informed a guard that he was from the same village as Alceste and had a case of his, given to him the night before by the deceased, he was allowed to enter. Knowing he wanted to hand it to the authorities, the guard accompanied him to the room where the investigating magistrate and the chief officer were continuing their inquiries.

While the guard informed Cavalier Alessio who he was and what he wanted, Matteo caught sight of the body of his friend and could not hold back the tears.

"Poor, Alceste! To think that only last night you were full of the joys of life. So happy!" he exclaimed with emotion in his voice.

The magistrate approached him.

"Did you see him last night?" he asked. "Did you talk to him?"

"Yes, sir," Matteo replied raising his eyes, damp with tears. "He had dinner with me in my restaurant, and we had arranged to leave together this morning for the saint's feast day celebrations in the village where I have relatives and where Alceste's fiancée was waiting for him. But after dinner Alceste left saying that he was going to visit a female friend who thought he was already traveling home. He wanted to make sure of her faithfulness."

"Did he really tell you that?"

"Yes, sir, and my wife can testify to it. We scolded him for his infidelity to his fiancée, who loves him a great deal. Alceste replied, laughing: 'It's nothing but a small dalliance, a brief pause before I hopefully marry my dear fiancée. I'll leave my case in your care, and I'll be back around two or three in the morning.' But we waited in vain. It was only a few minutes ago that I found out he had been killed in error by the signora. Neither I nor my wife can understand how he returned here. I thought it my duty to come and find out, also to hand over the case he left behind."

"You've acted like a good citizen. Do you know what's in it?"

Matteo managed not to blush or blink before the inquiring gaze of the judge.

"No, sir!" he replied. "I didn't think I had the right to open it."

The magistrate took it from his hands and, in turn, passed it to the officer.

"We will examine it presently," he said. Turning back to Matteo, he added, "Didn't he tell you the name of the friend he was going to see last night?"

"No, sir, but perhaps she was in this building."

"Do you have any suspicions about any of the servants?" asked the magistrate. "Did he mention anything about it to you?"

"Never. When Alceste chatted to me and my wife, he was enthusiastic about the qualities and beauty of the signora. That's all. He even remembered her last night. And to think that he's been killed by her! It feels like a nightmare. My poor friend! What will become of his fiancée when she learns of his tragic death?"

"The lawyer, Signor Sigrano, took it upon himself to inform her when he told the countess's parents and Alceste's only relative, whom I'm sure you know."

"Yes, sir, I know everyone there, and everyone knows me, but I wouldn't have the courage to go and announce this dreadful misfortune because Alceste was well-liked by everyone, and I'm sure the whole place will be saddened by his horrible demise. Perhaps they'll have some bad things to say about Signora Sigrano as she's not well thought of in those parts."

"Why?" asked Cavalier Alessio.

"I'm not sure how to explain it! They say she's haughty, has a violent nature and a difficult character."

"Well, they appear to be wrong!" the magistrate interrupted rather severely. "I understand that the signora is a very affable lady, a good wife and mother."

"Alceste also said so, and I wouldn't want to assert anything different, but I'm simply referring to country gossip. Nonetheless, despite all her decency, she had the nerve to kill the servant who was most devoted to her."

"The fault lies with the unfortunate man there. He secretly came back to the palazzo without telling anyone and, taking the side door, entered the mistress' rooms. The signora, who thought he was away, was awakened by the noise he made. Frightened, she jumped out of bed and, assuming it was a thief, grabbed her revolver. Seeing a man move towards her, she fired at random and struck him without realizing it. It's not the time now, however, to explain in more detail. You may go, but just remember that you must remain at our disposal as we'll have to question you again."

"I'll always be happy to tell you what I know. But before I go, I'd like to ask what will happen to poor Alceste's body."

"An autopsy will be performed, then they'll bury him," replied the magistrate. "Signor Sigrano has already ordered a funeral and reserved a place in the cemetery."

Matteo asked no further questions. Giving his personal details, he looked once again at his friend's corpse and retired from the room with more tears in his eyes.

His wife was waiting anxiously for news. The restaurant was deserted, and Matteo was able to sit down and tell her everything. Marietta listened to him in silence without interruption.

"I can't get it out of my head that it was Signora Sigrano who Alceste went to see last night," she said.

"Certainly not with her consent, though, otherwise she wouldn't have killed him," Matteo observed.

"Who knows!" added Marietta. "Alceste wouldn't have been capable of violence, nor would he have entered her rooms at night while the lawyer was away, unless she'd allowed him to. Believe me, the countess was so shameless when she was younger, and she can't have changed. She would've used Alceste as long as it pleased her. When she got bored, she killed him. She must have arranged everything to look like he'd left and then lured him into the ambush she'd set up. The whole thief story is a lie to hide the murder."

"But that would be terrible!" murmured Matteo.

"And then," added Marietta, "the package Alceste left for Anna Maria, to open only in the case of his death, makes me think that our friend had an inkling that something could happen to him. I bet that package can explain the mystery of his tragic end. We ought to respect his wishes, though and deliver it unopened to the sole person who, if necessary, should be responsible for acting on it."

"You're right, but in the meantime, I could, even without mentioning the package, bring your suspicions to the attention of the magistrate."

"What's the point? We could be brought up on charges for slandering such a noble lady. Be careful about saying anything. Let's see how things go and wait for Anna Maria."

"Perhaps it would be better if I went to the village myself so I could deliver the package and talk to her."

"No. It's not the right time to move about. If the girl doesn't come, I'll go to her, but for now it's better to avoid even the shadow of suspicion as those with an interest in saving the countess will be watching Alceste's friends for fear they will try and discover the true cause of his death. We'll wait. Sometimes you can never have enough prudence and patience."

Matteo surrendered to his wife's reasoning, knowing it to be right, but swore that, if the countess was really guilty, she would eventually pay for her crime.

6

Until the age of fifteen, Anna Maria Tosingo, poor Alceste's fiancée, had been one of the happiest girls in her small Alpine village. Her father was the local schoolmaster and her mother a skilled embroiderer and exemplary housewife. They owned a modest house on the outskirts of the settlement, surrounded by a small, enclosed garden.

Anna had been raised there with much loving care, inheriting her clear mind, rapid perception, intelligence, and education from her father. Whereas her mother gave her a healthy energy, deep religious belief, and a sense of virtue.

Anna Maria and Alceste, who was three years older, had known each other since early childhood, as he was her father's favorite pupil. He often accompanied him to the local festivals and even gave him some extra lessons, also allowing him to play in their garden with his daughter. On a few occasions, she had gone with Alceste to the Flaminio villa where his father, Giacomo, lived and worked as a servant, although he received scant reward.

Giacomo's wife and son lived with her brother, Tommaso, a wealthy bachelor farmer, who adored his sister and nephew. Anna Maria and Alceste had not really known Countess Sultana, who had married the lawyer, Sigrano, when they were both still children, Anna Maria being fourteen and Alceste seventeen. At the time, they took little interest in the village gossip concerning the malevolent behavior of the conceited countess.

Two years after Sultana's marriage, when cholera was raging in the village, Anna Maria lost both her parents within a few days, and Alceste lost his mother. It was a massive blow for Anna Maria. What was she to do all alone in the world? Back then, she was kept isolated from everyone for fear of contagion. Neither acquaintances nor friends came near the house, leaving one local woman to bring food and quickly depart. Anna Maria even prayed to God that she might also be taken.

The night after her parents were buried, kneeling before an image of the Madonna, she was praying, when, full of tears, she heard someone call out her name from the garden. It was Alceste, who had come to mourn with her, both for the loss of his own mother and his beloved teacher. They were forever united by their common grief.

From that moment, Alceste knew he wanted to marry his childhood companion, but they were both too young, and he knew that his father and uncle would not allow it. However, they swore to remain faithful to each other and considered themselves engaged before God.

Anna Maria's aged godmother, who was said to be monied, came to live with her, and Alceste remained with his uncle, Tommaso. As he had no desire to work the land, having a talent for automobile mechanics, his father, under advice from Count Flaminio, sent him to the city to learn the trade and gain his driver's license.

The separation was painful for Anna Maria, but Alceste often went home to see her and wrote long passionate letters, which were a consolation that made her dream of a happy future. These dreams continued until she learnt that Alceste was to be employed by Bruno Sigrano as a chauffeur. The news provoked tears because she had a premonition of misfortunes to come.

By now, Anna Maria, who was mixing more with people in the village, knew of the rumors circulating about Countess Sultana.

"Make sure she doesn't steal your fiancé!" one particular friend had even told her.

Anna Maria replied honestly: "I'm not worried. Alceste loves me and the countess is married now with children."

"Which doesn't prevent her from flirting with everyone," added her friend. "Last year, when she came up to the countryside, she ruined Clielia's marriage to Bastiano's son. And you know what a bad end he then came to!"

"I know he drowned by accident."

"Well, they said that, but it was deliberate."

Anna Maria continued to brood on the situation but began to calm her fears when Alceste came home and assured her that the rumors were nothing but slander, painting Sultana as a model wife and mother devoted to her husband and children, in addition to being esteemed by society.

"Did you tell her about me?" she asked naively. "Does she know I'm your fiancée?"

"Of course, and she told me that I couldn't have chosen better. She praised you a lot."

Anna Maria smiled, fully persuaded.

In the meantime, Giacomo, Alceste's father died, leaving him some savings and a parcel of land with a sunny aspect. When he went home for the funeral, Uncle Tommaso suggested he leave his job and come back to be with him.

"You don't need to be a servant to anyone," he told him. "You should live well with your own people. What I have will one day be yours, so you can marry Anna Maria, live here with her, and be a consolation in my remaining years. Give me the joy of kissing a grandchild."

Alceste replied that he liked his job as a chauffeur too much and that Signor Sigrano did not treat him as a servant but as a friend. He said that he would not be suited to living as a farmer in such a small place and that Anna Maria was still young and could wait another year or two before getting married.

Anna Maria heard of this through Tommaso and was saddened by Alceste's news. She was gripped by concern and decided to talk to him about it. She let it slip that perhaps his decision was due to another woman, and for the first time, he replied with irritation, which led to an argument.

Immediately regretting it, he asked her forgiveness, inventing lies to assuage her, whilst swearing that she was his only love. To please her, he would bend to his uncle's wishes, but not straight away, as he did not want to leave his employers suddenly since they had been so good to him. He promised profusely that he would come back for the saint's feast day and that they would then arrange everything for their future happiness.

Anna Maria let herself be persuaded, as she loved him dearly, but could not shake her sad feelings, which only increased in the intervening months before the celebration, during which time Alceste wrote to her less often. Although his letters were more affectionate than before, she felt that the words did not come from his heart but were a mere echo of his conversations with her, repeated so she did not forget them.

Anna Maria confided in her aged godmother and Tommaso, who loved her.

"If Alceste is late in marrying you, maybe I'll take a wife," he said, laughing affectionately.

"Really?" she answered brightly. "Who will you marry?"

"Your godmother. We think along the same lines and get along well enough. That way I'd still have you near me as well."

"And Camilla, who has served you for so many years?"

"She wouldn't be jealous of Orsola or of you since she wishes you all the best. It was actually she who suggested the marriage."

"Would you like me to speak to my godmother?"

"Let's wait until the saint's feast day. If nothing happens with Alceste, I'll come forward. At least I'll be sure not to lose you and die a lonely old man. In the meantime, you would do well to remind Alceste that the celebration is approaching and we're expecting him."

In fact, Anna Maria had written to him, reiterating her invitation, and it was that letter that Sultana had found in his wallet. On the morning of the festival, Anna Maria went to morning mass, then tidied the whole house in readiness for Alceste's arrival. She also made donuts, which she knew he really liked. She was in a cheerful mood, at peace with herself. Nothing had made her foresee any misfortune.

She was dressed simply, in a plain manner, wearing a pinafore dress. Graceful and seductive, her figure had developed in the months previous, and she was now in the full flush of youth. She was tall with dark brown hair, shiny and wavy, parted with hair bands from her forehead. Her dark eyes were deep and expressive, occasionally veiled by sadness, but always loyal. She had delicate features, a perfect complexion, and sparkling white teeth. Owing to the kindness of her soul, she exuded an indefinable charm.

If Anna Maria had wanted, she could have had her pick, but she paid no attention to anyone else because her heart belonged to Alceste. Nobody could replace him.

On returning from mass that morning, in the alley leading to her house, she came across Antonio Didier, a soldier in the Bersaglieri corps and Alceste's closest friend. A handsome young man, frank and jovial, he had obtained a short-leave pass to attend the festivities. He was happy to see Anna Maria.

"It's great to bump into you!" he exclaimed, holding out his hand. "If you hadn't smiled, I wouldn't have recognized you. You're taller and more beautiful than ever!"

Anna Maria blushed but refused to lower her eyes. She squeezed the young man's hand.

"And you've become a flatterer, but you're forgiven as I'm happy to see you. Alceste will be really pleased!" she replied.

"Is he here?" Antonio asked.

"No, but he should be here today."

"Are his employers coming too?"

"I don't think so."

"Then it will be a bit difficult for them to give him permission."

Anna Maria grimaced.

"Why? Do you know something?"

"I don't know anything. I just meant that it'll be difficult for Countess Sultana to find a replacement for him."

"The countess can do without a car for two or three days," she added. "And she'll have to look for another chauffeur if Alceste keeps his promise to marry me before the beginning of winter and he accepts his Uncle Tommaso's suggestion. He won't then leave the area anymore."

"He'd be a lucky man. If he comes, I'll have a word with him as well to see if we can't sort things out."

"Thank you! You're a good friend to him."

"And to you too, Anna Maria. See you again."

Around ten o'clock, back at home, she heard the noise of a car going up through the main road to the center. She ran to the window, and although she was unable to see the vehicle or distinguish the passengers, she convinced herself that it was the Sigranos' car. Until that moment, nobody else had passed along that road.

"Maybe," she thought, "the countess wants to spend the holiday with her parents and has come with her husband and children. He must be behind the wheel and won't be long in showing up."

With delight, she went to warn her godmother. She could not sit still, pacing up and down from the house to the garden. She ran up the path to look around the village, returning to check the kitchen. By dinner time, Alceste had failed to appear. Anna Maria had gone silent, and her smile had disappeared.

"The boss will have stopped him from coming, or he'll have dropped in to see his uncle," observed her godmother.

"He would've come to warn me," she answered. "Taking the shortcuts, Alceste could've been here in five minutes, and Tommaso wouldn't have kept him before he'd come to see me."

"You must have been wrong. That car was being driven by someone else."

"Surely that's not right."

Dinner was ready, but Anna Maria had little appetite. Without success, Orsola did her best to distract her goddaughter.

"If Alceste couldn't come," she said, "he would've written to me. I can't explain his behavior."

"Well, after we've finished dinner, we'll go and see Tommaso, who may know something. Perhaps he wrote to him."

"Yes, you're right!" exclaimed Anna Maria, "But let's go now." She was impatient and full of nerves.

The streets were deserted at that time of day since everyone was eating. Passing the houses, the two women heard laughter and happy voices, which only served to increase Anna Maria's anxiety. As they entered Tommaso's courtyard, they heard voices in the dining room.

"He's got some guests," observed Orsola. "Who knows, maybe Alceste is there too!"

Just at that moment, Camilla, who was looking through the kitchen door, saw the two women. Instead of coming out to meet them, she quickly turned back inside. This made Anna Maria think that her godmother may be right.

With a turmoil of thoughts, she entered the house and reached the dining room door.

"Can we come in?" she asked.

"Yes, come in," replied a chorus of men's voices.

To her surprise, she saw Antonio, the bersagliere, approach her. His face, which had been so happy, was now pale and gloomy. Anna Maria felt sick with anguish, which made her tremble with bewilderment.

"Hasn't Alceste arrived?" she asked.

"No, he can't come…he won't come!" Antonio answered in a peculiar voice.

Anna Maria, who was still walking towards them, then realized that the table was not set. She saw Tommaso sprawled in an armchair, weeping, surrounded by some men from the neighborhood. Before, their voices could be heard outside, but now they remained silent. Anna Maria, burning with anxiety and sensing something serious, rushed towards the old man.

"Uncle, Uncle Tommaso, what is it?" she asked, her voice convulsed. "Tell me. Tell me now! Don't make me suffer. Don't hide the truth from me. You know I'm strong."

At the sight of the girl and hearing her words, the poor old man sobbed, extending his arms wide.

"Oh, Anna Maria," he gasped, "they've killed him, you know, they've killed him!"

"Who?" she cried, her eyes wide. She fell to her knees before the old man, grabbing his trembling hand.

"Him, our Alceste." Tommaso exclaimed, bursting into tears once more. "We'll never see him again, never again."

"No, no, that can't be right!" Anna Maria screamed out. Tears came to everyone's eyes as she continued:

"Killed, my Alceste? But when? How? Who?"

"It was an accident," Antonio said amid the others' silence, "or so Teresa Mombello said when she came to bring the sad news to the Flaminios and to leave the Sigrano children with their grandparents. She then came to tell Tommaso. The aristocrats didn't deign to set foot here."

Anna Maria ran a hand over her feverish forehead.

"I don't quite understand all this," she stuttered, disoriented.

"According to Teresa," added Antonio, "Alceste said goodbye to everyone last night, saying he was leaving. Indeed, just before, he'd shown the other servants some gifts he was going to bring to you and friends in the village. At eleven o'clock, everyone in the Sigrano household had gone to bed and were sleeping soundly when the servants were awakened by a gun shot and the desperate cries of the lady of the house calling for help."

Antonio paused for a moment. Anna Maria, leaning on the old man's knee, heartbroken, looked at the younger man without speaking. All the others kept their silence. Antonio continued.

"They all ran to Signora Sigrano's rooms. She was alone, because her husband had left for Genoa, and she said that, after being awakened by a noise from the bathroom, she'd remembered that her husband had left some five-thousand-lire bills in a drawer. Fearful that a thief had entered the house, she jumped out of bed, grabbed the revolver she kept on the bedside table when the lawyer wasn't there and went into the next room where a light was switched on. Seeing a man in front of her, she fired a shot. He fell to the floor, and she cried out for help?"

"Did she think Alceste was a thief?" Anna Maria said mechanically.

"According to Teresa, yes. When they all realized that it was Alceste who'd been killed, everyone was dismayed. The lady collapsed from the shock. It was assumed that Alceste had missed the train and, having dined out, had returned rather tipsy, mistaking the door and going to the countess' rooms in error. This blunder cost him his life. However, I don't believe this version of events."

"Nor do I!" Anna Maria said with a shudder.

"Do you have any evidence to prove it's false?" old Tommaso added.

"Unfortunately, no!" they answered in unison.

"In any case," continued Tommaso, "whatever the cause of his death, the worst thing of all is that we'll never see him again. Oh, if only he'd stayed here with me and been the husband of this dear girl who would have made him happy, instead of being someone's servant. Poor boy! Poor Anna Maria!" His words moved those gathered in the room. Although Anna Maria's young features bore the signs of grief, she still had an inner strength.

"Uncle Tommaso," she said, "why don't we go to Turin and try to find out the truth? Are you really going to let poor Alceste be buried down there?"

"You're right!" Tommaso agreed, rising from his seat. "We'll leave today and have that poor boy brought back here so he can have an honorable burial with his loved ones."

"First," observed Antonio, "you should go to see the Flaminios."

Tommaso shook his head.

"It's useless. They won't receive anybody. Teresa told me. The poor old couple, they're also very upset because of their daughter, and they have to keep it all hidden from their grandchildren."

It was agreed that Anna Maria and Tommaso would leave without notifying anyone. Those present promised not to mention the plan.

7

In the elegant society frequented by Signora Sigrano and in the legal profession, everyone was persuaded of Sultana's innocence given no evidence had been discovered confirming an intimate relationship between her and the victim. Her unprompted confession, made with firmness and without confusion, also convinced them. Even her arrest was condemned, with people saying that she had fired to defend herself from a thief after money or her honor and that she bore no blame.

Sultana had never denied anything during her questioning, and in their depositions, all the servants had asserted that Signora Sigrano was a model wife and mother. They also said that Alceste was a decent, helpful young man who, nevertheless, had the fault of falling in love too easily and being a bit foolish. Although he was engaged to a nice young woman from the countryside, he had boasted of other loves and harbored mad hopes for the signora.

However, he had always spoken of her with the utmost respect, even though he found her so beautiful, she could tempt a saint. And, they added, if he had the intention of trying something that night, he must have been the worse for drink, because he knew very well that such an attempt would not succeed, and he would be chased away and punished. Indeed, his punishment had been a terrible twist of fate, leading Bruno Sigrano to disregard money as the cause of the unintentional crime.

It was mentioned that a witness who had made an insinuation about Signora Sigrano but was unable to substantiate his words, had been ignored. It was the statements of Uncle Tommaso and Anna Maria that finally ended up affirming Sultana's innocence.

When they arrived from the country, they went to Matteo Ferpio, where they decided to lodge. Matteo and his wife told them what had happened that evening when Alceste had gone to the restaurant. They gave Anna Maria the package they had found in the case. The young woman turned pale when she read the strange wording on the outside and asked permission to retire to her room to see what it contained. They respected her wishes and her grief. Anna Maria was absent for almost two hours and when she reappeared, although her eyes still had signs of tears, her expression had a certain calm.

"Signora Sigrano is truly innocent of any wrongdoing in these unhappy events," she said slowly. "Alceste confirms it in a letter that he left for me and asked me to destroy as soon as I'd read it, which I've done. The poor unfortunate confessed his love for the signora and revealed that he would try to approach her by surprise, declaring his feelings, before killing himself. Yes, he would have killed himself because of the signora if fate hadn't intervened. Alceste asked my forgiveness and wants me to forgive the countess who is not to blame for his folly. He begged me not to hate his memory, although deep down he knew he was guilty, because he swore that he only truly loved me and that his soul would remain close to me. He left me this portrait of him as a memento: here it is."

The girl took a small, framed photograph of Alceste from her dress pocket. On the reverse side was written: "To you alone — be happy and be blessed!"

"And do you forgive him?" asked Matteo's wife.

"Yes," answered Anna Maria, "I want Alceste to rest in peace, and I've also promised that you too, Uncle Tommaso, must forgive him."

"Oh, yes, the poor boy!" stammered the old man showing the simplicity of a kind and honest heart unburdened with hate. There were tears in his eyes as he kissed the portrait.

Matteo and his wife were unconvinced by Anna Maria's explanations, perhaps regretting they had not taken the opportunity to examine the package when they had the chance. Nonetheless, , unable to do otherwise, they voiced the same opinion as their visitors.

When Anna Maria and old Tommaso found themselves before the magistrate, they did not accuse the countess, instead defending her by saying that the poor lady must also be desperate on account of the unfortunate events. They declared themselves convinced that she had no intention of shooting to kill.

Anna Maria and Tommaso then reached an agreement with the lawyer, Sigrano, for the transport of Alceste's body to their home. He refused to let them bear the costs as he felt it his duty to the unhappy young man, whom he sincerely pitied. Even if he had intended to do something utterly stupid, he must have been drunk.

The day before the planned transportation of the body, Signora Sigrano was released from custody with "no case to answer." The outcome, however unforeseen, failed to raise comment. By now the dead man had almost been forgotten, and the keenest sympathy was reserved for Bruno Sigrano. He continued to admire and esteem his beautiful wife, who must have suffered because of the incident, given that the memory would stay with her.

Sultana was dazed by the impossible speed with which she could return to her family and without any malicious allusion to the crime committed. Nobody, during the investigation, had mentioned the locket or the letter — a clear sign that they no longer existed. She believed that Alceste, fearing that his fiancée would find them when he travelled to the village, had disposed of them and that he had claimed to still have the evidence so he could try his luck again.

When her husband took her back home, holding her tight, he tried to comfort her with tender words, but she was overcome with raw tearful emotion when she met Anna Maria and Tommaso who had been waiting. Bruno had already warned her of their presence and, despite anxiety almost preventing her from taking a breath, she bowed her proud, blond locks before the girl.

"Anna Maria, Tommaso, will you forgive me?" she stuttered between sobs.

Since his throat had tightened, the old man could only nod his head.

Anna Maria replied, her voice soft: "I forgive you, signora, as a I understand you're suffering. As for poor Alceste, he met his own misfortune head on, he welcomed it, and we can only pray to God to show him mercy.".

"You're a good person, Anna Maria. Thank you, thank you!"

Sultana threw her arms around Anna Maria's neck and burst into tears, which, on this occasion, were sincere. When the young woman broke away from the embrace, she was more ashen faced than a dead woman, but the smile of a martyr played around her lips.

The following day, after receiving authorization for the burial and with all the formalities completed, Alceste's body was driven to his village. It was enclosed in a triple-lined coffin and placed in a small truck cloaked in black and decorated with wreaths. The driver was accompanied by a priest, and the vehicle was followed by another car carrying the Sigranos, Anna Maria, and Tommaso.

The forewarned parish priest performed the service in the church and at the graveside. No one went to the fields that day. It was rumored that there would be a hostile reception for Countess Sultana, but when she appeared, pale, distraught, and tearful, held gently by Anna Maria, and when they saw Uncle Tommaso tottering on the count's arm, they behaved respectfully without a single shout of protest.

After the priest gave absolution to the body, he said some touching words about the young man whom fate had mistaken for a thief and struck down. When he enumerated Alceste's qualities, his affection for his employers, the countess's desperation at her error, and his fiancée's grief, nobody, owing to the emotion, was left unmoved and unable to forgive. The simple, decent folk of the village did not know how to hate.

With Sultana acquitted and Alceste buried to the accompaniment of prayers, flowers, and many tears, the countess's meeting with her parents and children was a moving occasion. Ottorino and Mina had already been warned that they would no longer see Alceste, understanding he had died in unfortunate circumstances. The two children had come to love the chauffeur, who often played with them like a child, and they sincerely mourned the loss of their faithful servant. Nor were they surprised that their parents grieved for him and had accompanied his body to the cemetery.

Sigrano and the countess had to leave for Turin on the same day. The little ones, however, would remain with their grandparents for another fifteen days, and Teresa would stay with them.

Before leaving, Sultana had a chat with Anna Maria. She wanted to persuade her to come to Turin.

"You'll stay with me," she told her. "I'll treat you like a sister."

"Thank you, signora," she replied, "but I can't accept. I'll stay here for now, with Uncle Tommaso, as the shock has dealt him a great blow, both mentally and physically. I can't leave him in such a state. One day, though, we'll meet again, as I don't intend to end my days here.…"

"Make me a promise," interrupted Sultana, "that if you come to Turin, you'll look for no other place than mine. My husband would like it too."

"Thank you for the kindness, perhaps I'll accept. But for now, I can't make any promises not knowing whether I'll be able to keep them."

"Let's hope you do."

"Yes, so do I, signora!"

Sultana kissed her on the cheeks, and Anna Maria, kissing her hand, left in a hurry with her hand to her eyes.

When Signora Sigrano found herself alone with her husband in the car as they travelled back to Turin, she leaned her head on his chest. In an uncertain voice, through tears, she said: "Forgive me, Bruno. Forgive me!"

"What do I have to forgive you for, my poor dear thing!?" the lawyer said affectionately. "What you've suffered over the past few days and today are enough to atone for anything you did."

"But I can't help but think how much I've made you suffer! I would put up with any kind of martyrdom to spare you!"

"But I'm only thinking of you, my love, and I wish you could forget."

"I'll try."

Sultana remained quiet for a few minutes with her head resting on her husband's chest. She then lifted her head and look at him, her eyes still misted with tears.

"Bruno!"

"Yes, dear!"

"All our friends will avoid us now."

"On the contrary, your misfortune has consolidated our old friendships even more, and we've acquired some new ones." Bruno said with a lightness of tone. "If you could have seen how many business cards and telegrams of comfort and then, subsequently, of congratulation I received when you were quickly acquitted. Believe me, everyone will love you more than before and will make an effort to show it in order to comfort you."

Sultana looked at him.

"Have you seen Count Mario Herbert?" she asked with some difficulty.

"Yes, for a moment, but the young man could barely say two words to me. He seemed confused, scared…. At any other time, it would have made me laugh. He told me that he was going home on leave and would stay there for some time. I don't know if he's left as his family have neither written nor sent a telegram — a sign they don't know anything."

"It's better that way!" Sultana whispered, collecting herself. "I want everyone around me to ignore things and keep quiet. What about Anna Maria?"

"Poor girl, a true angel with a lovely, kind heart. Alceste didn't know how to appreciate her enough, otherwise certain stupidities wouldn't have crossed his mind!"

"You're right!"

The car made its way through a sad stretch of autumnal countryside, yet Sultana saw nothing. Sphinx-like, her eyes were cloudy and set firm. Only she knew the images passing through her mind. Suddenly, as if overcome by a radical change, she felt a surge of tenderness and gratitude towards her husband, a man who was nothing but kind and generous to her. She hugged and kissed him with intensity.

"Keep on loving me, Bruno. If you want me to forget all this, keep loving me. I adore you!"

8

A year had passed since the events of those days. The personal drama that cost Alceste his life and convulsed the Sigrano family had largely been forgotten. Sultana had settled back into her comfortable life, more cherished by her husband than ever, and regarded with benevolence and esteem by all.

All that remained of what had happened was, for others, an aura of melancholy, which made her beauty all the more fascinating. Her conscience, that of the culprit, was mute. She felt that she had acted as she ought to have done, and by eliminating Alceste, believed that she had simply removed an obstacle standing in her way.

If Alceste had proved to be reasonable and had agreed to go away, to give her the items she wanted, and to marry Anna Maria, not only would he still be alive, but Sultana would have always been grateful to him for his discretion. She would have come to his aid in any circumstance and would not have forgotten.

In the first few months, Signora Sigrano was troubled by the items that had not been found, given that they had constituted the main reason for the turn of events. However, she persuaded herself that Alceste's threats had no basis in truth and that he had actually destroyed the evidence, perhaps in fear that one day they would fall into the hands of his fiancée. His threats, therefore, were hollow, and had no other purpose but that of continuing to enjoy her favors. He had still thought he could bend her to his will even though she had taken against him.

Anna Maria certainly had no suspicions as she had written to her several times giving news of Uncle Tommaso, who neither she nor her godmother could leave because his health had taken a turn for the worst. The doctor had said that he would not recover from the grief of Alceste's death and would not be long in following him.

Anna Maria's letters, written with great feeling and simplicity, had amazed Sultana, who showed them to her husband.

"I didn't realize that country girl was so educated," she said.

"I did," replied Bruno, "since your old parish priest once told me when I asked him about Alceste's girlfriend. He said that 'she's a delightful girl' and went on to tell me that she'd been educated in the manner of a gentleman's daughter. Her own father taught her, and her mother imparted the best of virtues.

"Well, the parish priest was right!" Sultana exclaimed. "And it seems a shame that she's stuck in rural isolation."

"What are you suggesting? I think she'll be happier that way!"

They did not discuss the matter again. Signora Sigrano refused to employ any more chauffeurs, which her husband agreed to. Instead, they reached an arrangement with a local garage from whom they hired a monthly taxi service. With the minimum of inconvenience, they had all the advantages.

Count Mario Herbert, who had spent more than two months on leave, paid a courtesy visit to the lawyer and the signora on his return. He found himself embarrassed in front of Sultana when alone with her in a reception room.

"Are you afraid of me now?" she could not help but say.

"No," the young man replied, his face flushed, "but after what's happened, signora, you must also understand that we can't be imprudent. We can only see each other in the company of others."

"Is that what you really think?" Signora Sigrano asked. Without raising her voice, she settled back in her armchair. "Well, I think differently, but I can't explain to you here. I'll come to your place tomorrow at four."

She stared at him so intensely that he could not find a reply. Mario remained quiet and shortly afterwards took his leave.

Left alone, Sultana lost the color in her cheeks. She bit her lip. Her thoughts turned to his wish to leave her, but she knew she still loved him and that her murder of Alceste had all been for him. A bitter anger took hold of her, yet she was unsure whether resentment or love was gaining the upper hand. Fighting to regain her composure, she recognized that she had been foolish to get so upset. She knew she had Mario in her power and that he would find it difficult to leave. She received other visits that day, but owing to her gentle, polite words and melancholy smile, no one realized the war raging in her soul.

The following day, Sultana boldly went to the appointment she had set up. Mario was waiting for her but made no attempt to embrace her. He timidly held out his hand, and Sultana took it, noticing that it was shaking. She straightened up, her beautiful form accentuated by a black cotton dress. She smiled to show the whiteness of her teeth.

"You are decidedly afraid of me," she said.

"Perhaps, yes!" he replied. "Your recklessness disturbs me, and I wouldn't like our relationship to be discovered."

"You're such a coward. You should be ashamed," she said impetuously. "I'm not reproaching you for staying away these past months without sending me any news that could've comforted me, but now you're getting tired of me and wish to end things. I won't tolerate it. You should know that if I killed him, it was because of you."

"Because of me! My fault!" Mario answered, stunned.

Before replying, Sultana took off her hat and gloves and sat down on the low sofa. She gestured for the young man to sit in a small armchair.

"Yes, for you. Let me explain." Looking him directly in the eyes, she continued, "You don't remember losing one of the letters I'd written to you in which I said that I'd have to miss our meeting because my husband wanted to take me with him on a work visit and that I'd see you here the day after."

Mario was startled, the color draining from him.

"Yes, yes, I remember perfectly well," he replied. "The letter was brought to me by your chauffeur, who was waiting for an answer. I was convinced that I'd put the letter in my jacket pocket, and I went into the adjoining room to answer it."

"Exactly, but instead, the letter fell on the carpet without your noticing, and Alceste picked it up."

"But I didn't notice it was missing until the following day, and I didn't want to bother you with it. I searched in vain everywhere but eventually forgot about it."

"Well, my chauffeur certainly thought about you. He took advantage of my husband's absence and snuck into my apartments, threatening to hand the letter over to Bruno if I didn't succumb to his demands. You can imagine what he wanted! I rejected him with disdain and tried to get the letter back by offering him money. I didn't succeed, and he violently tried to grab me, so I picked up the revolver on my bedside table and fired."

Mario felt sick.

"And did you get the letter back?" he tentatively asked.

"Yes," answered Sultana brashly, "but it cost a man's life and destroyed my peace of mind."

"I ask your forgiveness!" said the young man, kneeling before her, with tears in his eyes.

A flash of triumph passed across her face. She had won.

"I hold no more grudges," she replied, stroking his hair with a caressing hand, "but I want you to know how much I love you and how nothing can separate us, given you, too, must take a share in the responsibility for my crime."

Mario was shaken, bound by a chain he could see no way of breaking. Yet at that moment, he was just about able to hide his anxiety and irritation. Their relationship, as the count saw it, was now condemned to continue as a form of punishment.

For a year, life continued in the same vein until, one morning, Signora Sigrano received a letter from Anna Maria.

Dear Countess,

It is one month to the day since poor Uncle Tommaso's suffering ended. I did not write to you immediately because I was grief-stricken after the long nights awake at the bedside of the unhappy old man, who could no longer sleep. Until his last moments, his nephew's name was on his lips. We buried him next to Alceste, and today, on the anniversary of my fiancé's death, I covered the two graves with flowers and placed the wreath your parents sent me and the one your husband sent me in your name.

Sultana paused for a moment, her face reddened, her gaze dimmed. "Bruno remembered!" she thought. "Without him, Anna Maria would've believed I'd forgotten...and that could have caused some resentment.... Dear Bruno!" This moment of tenderness towards her husband disappeared almost as quickly as it had emerged. She continued reading.

Thank you, thank you! This lovely gesture of yours, together with that of your parents, is a balm, and I'm sure, if Alceste were here, he would curse the madness that cost him his life and would have nothing more than infinite praise for you.

Uncle Tommaso, unbeknownst to me, has left me everything in his will. He owned several parcels of land with advantageous leases, which yield an annual income of five thousand lire. In addition, he had several bearer bonds and Martino, the notary who kept them, wanted to give them to me immediately. The same notary will look after my interests and those of my godmother, Orsola, who has her own money, which she will leave to me.

Forgive me, dear countess, for all these details, which cannot be of interest to you, but I would like to explain the decision I have made, of which I am sure you will approve. In the coming month, I will come and settle in Turin with my godmother because, as my means now allow, I want to study singing, which has always been my passion. I

*know musical notation and solmization, so with a good teacher, I hope
to be able to go on stage one day.*

*You, signora, will perhaps say that I am choosing a perilous career,
but I believe that you can keep your integrity whatever the situation
if you have a decent heart and good intentions, just as anyone can be
dishonest, even in the most beneficial settings, if you are dissolute and
devoid of conscience.*

On reading these lines, Sultana turned pale. The thought crossed her
mind that she had written them for her, but she dismissed it as foolish,
believing that Anna Maria had expressed herself with the sincerity of
a villager who knew nothing of the world or life. She considered her
incapable of deceit and thought it better that way. She resumed her
reading.

*My godmother is happy with my decision and has written to one of
our friends who will find us a modest lodging, but one in a dignified
residence. We will take Camilla with us, poor old Tommaso's servant,
whom he highly recommended. She has grown fond of us and is a good
cook and housekeeper, so I will have the freedom to study, and my
godmother will be able to rest. As you have always been kind to me,
signora, I will be happy to be near you. I hope you will allow me to come
and visit some time and I hope, through your contacts in high society
and among performers, that you might be able to help me achieve my
dream. I kiss your hand with devotion and kindly ask you to pay my
respects to your husband.*

Your humble servant,
Anna Maria

Sultana gave the letter to her husband so he could read it. Bruno
smiled.

"I have to say that Alceste's death has been lucky for the girl," he
exclaimed. "First of all, he was too frivolous and vulgar for her. Even
if he'd married her, he would have done it to please Uncle Tommaso,
who wanted the marriage. But he didn't love Anna Maria and would
have been a bad husband. Now, though, free from any commitment,

she can start her life again. We'll introduce her to fashionable society, where she won't make a bad impression given her education and the wealth she now possesses. Tell her that we fully approve of her decision and are looking forward to seeing her."

"Yes, I'll do that."

Sultana thought that if she showed concern for Anna Maria, the young woman would never suspect her and, on the contrary, would come to her defense if someone accused her of having been the chauffeur's lover. She also felt that she owed her something for taking away her fiancé.

She replied to Anna Maria with a very affectionate letter, approving of her decision and expressing a desire to see her again soon, also adding that she would find her to be a friend and like an older sister. It is true to say that such demonstrations of humility, which she did not feel, were somewhat repugnant to Sultana's pride, but she had to be ready.

She went to post the letter before going to meet Count Herbert without the least intuition of what the future held for her.

9

It was a Thursday, four o'clock, on a wet and cold December afternoon, and Signora Sigrano was holding one of her receptions. Despite the weather outside, it was as warm as a greenhouse in the room where Sultana was offering tea. She was dressed attractively in a blue dress that hugged her shape.

She managed to avoid neglecting anyone. While she served the drinks, helped by a young lady who brought cups, sugar, and biscuits, she chatted away confidently, a smile on her face. Nevertheless, to a close observer, there seemed to be something worrying her, something troublesome. From time to time her eyes, which looked gently on the people she served, drifted away to Mario Herbert, who seemed little interested in her, intent as he was on talking to Signora Leberto, the wife of one of Bruno Sigrano's colleagues. Signora Leberto was an alluring brunette, witty, beautiful, and very lively, who had just started to make her mark in society.

Sultana's blue eyes hardened, expressing a certain malice, but these were fleeting flashes that nobody noticed. She had finally taken a seat on a small sofa next to the Marquise Grandi, when Caterina announced: "Miss Anna Maria Tosingo-Belgrado."

At the door, an appealingly attractive young woman retreated slightly on seeing so many people. With a quick glance, Sultana had already observed Anna Maria's elegant attire and how she wore her hat with much grace. She hastened to get up and meet her, extending her hand.

"What a wonderful surprise," she said as she did so. "Come in, please! Have you just arrived?"

Without waiting for an answer, she introduced her. The ladies had ceased chatting when she appeared, and a murmur of admiration passed among the men.

"She is a compatriot of mine, who I advised to come and settle in Turin as she's now all alone in the world except for an ageing guardian who acts as her mother. Isn't it such a shame to stagnate in the countryside when a young woman is rich, beautiful, and educated?"

They all approved. Sultana made the girl sit in an armchair.

"I'm genuinely happy to see you, and doubly happy that you have arrived on the day of one of my receptions so I can start introducing you to people," she added.

"Madam countess, you're too kind!" Anna Maria answered softly but without humility. "These ladies, however, will have to take a great deal of pity on me since I'm not used to being in society."

"You're too modest, signorina!" Mira Leberto observed cheerfully. "You'll soon get used to it though. I should tell you that until two years before I married, I was locked up in a convent with very strict rules."

"You wouldn't think so!" remarked Sultana with a slightly ironic tone.

"And yet it's true," Signora Leberto replied, graceful yet flirtatious. "I spent eight years there after the death of my poor mother. Luckily, I'm adaptable…and know how to get the best from life. Even in the austere surroundings of the convent, I spent some delightful hours with my friends and the nuns, who had a great deal of affection for me. Of course, when I found myself married, out in the world, and my husband began to introduce me to society, I looked like a complete goose."

"I can hardly believe that!" Mario exclaimed with some enthusiasm. "You've too much spirit, and you're just perfect as you are."

Sultana bit her lip.

"Count Herbert is right!" the others agreed.

The young man's name startled Anna Maria, and her eyes fixed intently on the officer. She noticed that he appeared boyish and saw him blush on meeting her gaze. Did he know who she was? As she asked herself this question, two more ladies were announced, and others got up to leave.

There was a moment of confusion and an exchange of compliments. Mira Leberto shook Anna Maria's hand and spoke to her with lively frankness.

"If you come and see me, signorina, you'll make me very happy. I receive people on Saturdays. Signora Sigrano will give you my address."

"Thank you, signora. I'm much obliged to you."

Sultana made no mention of the invitation. She had seen Mario about to leave and called out to him.

"Lieutenant, don't flee," she said with a smile that accentuated her words. "It's your turn to serve these ladies tea. Come and get the cups."

"At your command, countess."

Now that calm had returned to the room after some of the guests had left, Anna Maria noticed that Signora Sigrano, approaching the table where the tea was served, was speaking in a low voice to Mario who had followed her. She realized that Sultana was agitated, nervous, her nostrils flared, and her lips pale, whereas the officer looked extremely annoyed.

When they came over to her and the other ladies to hand out the cups and biscuits, Signora Sigrano had regained her composure, her grace and spirit restored. A melancholy cloud, though, was hanging over the young man's face.

Sultana retook her seat and began the conversation again. She talked about a new novel then in vogue, adding that she did not understand the curiosity it had caused given that it was so silly and full of disgusting realism. She discussed the fashions of the day with great panache, often provoking laughter with truly amusing anecdotes.

Anna Maria listened, without losing sight of Mario. He had remained standing, leaning against a door jamb, while following the conversation. She realized that he was impatient, and she saw something approximating discomfort on his face, as if he were unhappy to be there. Twice the eyes of the two young people met, and

Mario's face flushed on both occasions, making Anna Maria deceive herself into thinking that he knew who she was.

Seeing himself observed with a certain insistence and curiosity, although her family meant nothing to him, he believed that the young woman had guessed his relationship with Sultana, especially since he had learned she was a compatriot and friend of hers. This annoyed him, as it aroused a sense of shame. The young woman was so beautiful, yet her intelligence and decency were apparent in her eyes alone.

However, just like Sultana, perhaps she was hiding her dishonesty well. He would have given so much to be able to break his bond with that woman for whom he had lost any affection, instead feeling something bordering on hate. But she had him in a vice-like grip.

The room was emptying, and most of the other ladies had departed. Mario, having plucked up the courage, took his leave.

"I'd like to stay longer, countess," he said, "but I'm on duty tonight."

"Well, you must go," answered Sultana, "but remember that on Sunday you're invited to dine with us. My young friend will be there too."

He bowed deeply in front of the two women, thanking Sultana for the invitation, then he withdrew. Two other gentlemen followed him.

"Count Mario Herbert," said Sultana, turning to Anna Maria, "is as dear to me as a son because he was warmly recommended to me by his mother. Therefore, I feel a certain duty to keep an eye on him."

"Hmm, it seems a bit onerous for him to listen to you," Anna Maria observed somewhat naively. "He seemed rather bored, impatient…."

"You're right, my dear. I noticed that too!" said one of the ladies, who was accompanied by her rather plain daughter who, nonetheless, had a handsome dowry and liked Mario a great deal. "Sultana, you would do well to keep him under your watchful eye for a while as I think the young count would like to sow his wild oats. Did you see how he was flirting with Signora Leberto?"

Sultana, although agitated, smiled and answered sweetly: "He's wasting his time since Mira is a very honest woman."

"I think so too," retorted the lady, "although her coquettish behavior suggests the opposite. She's not just satisfied with having Lieutenant Herbert flirt with her in her friend's house, but she also met him in Valentino, out in the street."

Sultana raised her eyebrows.

"Who told you that?" she said in a dull, irritated voice. "Who saw them?"

"We met them last week, didn't we, Giulia?" said the lady. "And others saw them too. But, as if she were doing the most innocent thing in the world, Signora Leberto didn't get upset. She didn't try to avoid us either."

"Exactly, as if she were doing nothing wrong," replied Sultana with a degree of effort. "Anyway, I will chastise Mario because if Mira is still a giddy goose, as she herself said, he must make the effort not to compromise her."

"How wise. That's why we all look up to you," said the older lady.

At that moment, Signor Sigrano entered. The few remaining guests took their leave since it was getting late. Bruno approached his wife who cheerfully pointed to Anna Maria.

"Look who's here!"

The lawyer's face beamed.

"What a nice surprise!" he said, shaking the young woman's hand. "In truth, if Sultana hadn't asked someone to tell me, I wouldn't have recognized you. You look like a princess.... You have my compliments."

"And you should hold them dear, Anna Maria," added Sultana, laughing, "because my husband doesn't often give out praise to ladies."

"That's not the case with you, my love," he replied, his eyes darting to his wife so eagerly that it startled the girl. Anna Maria realized that he loved her deeply.

Meanwhile, Sultana turned to her.

"Now that I can devote myself entirely to you, I ought to ask you to take off your hat and gloves. You must stay."

"Of course!" added Bruno.

"I'm sorry to say no," said Anna Maria, "but I can't. My godmother is waiting and will be worried. I came to thank you for all your kindness and to explain, contrary to my letter, that I didn't accept the accommodation I was offered. Do you, by chance, know Matteo Ferpio, signora? He's the owner of a modest but respectable restaurant not far from here, and his wife, Marietta, is distantly related to my godmother."

Sultana knew very well who he was.

"No, I don't know him, although his name isn't new to me," she replied.

"Well," continued Anna Maria, "Matteo came to spend a few days in the village and, hearing I was coming to settle in Turin to study singing, told me that some rooms above his restaurant had just been vacated by a captain and his family who had moved to Sardinia. The captain, himself, had asked Matteo to sublet the accommodation and sell the furniture. It couldn't be a better opportunity for me, so I decided to take everything and pay in cash to get a discount. I wrote to the captain, who accepted my terms. My godmother and I have settled in. The Ferpios send us up breakfast and dinner from the restaurant and help us with things around the house."

"You really couldn't have found anything better," said Signor Sigrano.

"So," added Sultana, "if your godmother lacks for nothing, you can stay and eat with us."

"Sorry dear lady, but I can't accept tonight. I'll come another time."

"Then you must come on Sunday," replied the countess. "I've invited Count Herbert, and I told him that you'd be there too."

The lawyer smiled in a good-natured manner.

"Bravo Sultana!" he exclaimed. "You are consideration personified. The poor boy would have been bored stiff just with us. The presence of a beautiful young lady will make him happy."

Anna Maria was embarrassed. "I don't flatter myself that I could possibly distract the count."

"We've heard some interesting things about him, isn't that right Anna Maria?" said Sultana. "Can you imagine, Bruno, who meets up with Mira Leberto in some of the quietest avenues in the Valentino."

The lawyer raised an eye.

"I'm sorry to hear that," he remarked. "If somebody were to tell my friend and colleague, who adores and trusts his wife, goodness knows what would happen. Leberto is a good man but, like me, he wouldn't tolerate such things, however innocent. You did well to warn me, Sultana my dear. I'll speak to Mario and tell him that a lady should not be compromised so lightly. I'll add that he'd be advised to take a wife, especially as his family also wish to see this happen."

"You won't be able to convince him!" Sultana interrupted. "But we've talked too much about him. Now, Anna Maria, really, won't you stay?"

"I can't, signora."

"So be it. Bruno, take her home. I won't allow her to leave alone at this hour."

"You're right," said the lawyer.

"But I'll have to get used to going out alone," Anna Maria exclaimed.

"Later, my dear, but for now you should do as I ask," Sultana replied. "Don't forget my invitation. On Sunday, you'll be able to meet my children. Also remember that from now on I'll address you more informally, as you're too young for stiff formalities, and I consider you a friend," she added as the young woman took her leave.

"You're too kind, madame countess!"

A few minutes later, Anna Maria left with Signor Sigrano, and Sultana went back into her apartment, at which point the masked dropped. Anger spread across her face. She felt that Mario had been challenging her by demonstrably showing he was tired of her affection. She realized she couldn't get rid of him like Alceste, but she vowed to bring him down a few pegs and make life difficult for anyone who tried to take him from her. She felt an overwhelming sense of possession driven by her twisted sense of love.

Sultana dropped into an armchair, shaken, her face pallid. Murmuring to herself, she mused on why she had killed Alceste, knowing full well that she would continue to suffer the consequences. Perhaps, she thought, he would have grown tired of her anyway after seeing Anna Maria again. She was surprised, though, that the girl was being so friendly to the woman who had killed him. It led her to believe that maybe she was less fond of him than people had supposed.

She found it strange how the daughter of a country bumpkin could have such outward and internal poise. Anyone unaware of Anna Maria's humble origin, who had not seen her in country clothes with an apron and clogs, could easily believe her to be of a noble family. And she had agreed to marry a simple chauffeur! No, no, Sultana reasoned, perhaps in her heart Anna Maria was thanking her for having cleared a man like Alceste from her path, especially since he was indifferent to her. She knew, however, that with his death, she had lost Mario's love and that he now feared her. Nevertheless, she still felt a burning passion for him although she realized nobody would be able to understand it.

Standing up, she looked at herself in the high mirror in front of her. She drew back, almost scared of the reflection. Never had she looked so drawn, her eyes so haunted. Shocked, she berated herself for getting that upset, knowing that emotion would age her and contribute to the loss of her looks, not to mention the possibility that she might reveal her feelings.

She collected her thoughts, regaining the terrible hauteur and iron will that few knew. All trace of the negativity was banished at a stroke.

When she appeared at the dining table, her cheeks had a healthy glow, and she wore an expansive smile. Her eyes had regained their vivacity, and a smile parted her lips. Her beauty had been restored along with her energy. She kissed the children, who had stayed with Teresa while she had been receiving guests. She turned to her husband, who had just come back. "Well then?…"

"Well, I took her home," he replied, "and I got to meet her godmother. She has a very distinguished manner and speaks well."

"Like her goddaughter then."

"Precisely. Signora Orsola thanked me a great deal for the interest we're showing in Anna Maria and asked me to pass that along to you as well. She deserves all our protection and, by doing so, we'll help her to forget her fiancé."

"I think that Anna Maria has long since forgotten him," Sultana replied calmly.

10

No, Anna Maria was not one those of those young women who easily forget, but no one could have known the secret she kept inside. When Matteo Ferpio handed over the sealed package that poor Alceste had left for her, she had run to her room and locked herself in so she could be alone to witness its contents.

For a while, Anna Maria, eyes wide open, stared at the words that expressed Alceste's wish that only she should open the packet in the event of his death or return it to him, unopened, on the day of their wedding. Did he, therefore, have a feeling that something would happen to him? And why, if he had lived, if he had married her, did he want to keep the secret hidden?

The package was still unopened when her tears began to stain these enigmatic words. Forcing herself to calm down, she regained her strength of mind. As the tears dried, she broke the seals with a steadier hand.

She was immediately presented with a photograph of Alceste and for a few minutes she contemplated the portrait of the man she had loved so much, who now appeared before her as if he were still alive. But his attractive eyes would no longer gaze on her, and his mouth would no longer utter words of affection. Anna Maria kissed the image then put it aside.

She now took a silver locket from the package, which had a date engraved on one side and the initials A. B. on the other along with the words "My only love" followed underneath by "forever." The two initials certainly referred to Alceste Bianco and the dedication was for him, but what did the locket contain?

Anna Maria was not long in finding the catch to open the cover, but as she pushed it to open the locket, she winced, and the color ran from her cheeks. Her eyes widened with surprise. To her astonishment, a small portrait of Sultana Sigrano was revealed, a painted photograph resembling a miniature. Yes, it was indeed her, smiling sardonically, with her blond hair and languid eyes, Madonna-like.

On the reverse side, under glass, was a golden curl held by a light blue ribbon. Anna Maria's mind was immediately troubled by thoughts that everything she had heard about the Countess Flaminio had an irrefutable and frightening reality. From the depths of her decent heart, an otherwise dormant jealousy rose to the surface. The very woman who had killed Alceste must have been his lover! But was she right or wrong? She needed to know at any cost.

She threw the locket on the table and noticed that there were two envelopes remaining inside the package. One was already open, and it was with surprise that she saw, written in a female hand, the name of the addressee "To Count Mario Herbert. S. M." Picking up the sheet, which still retained an intense perfume of violets she read:

Mario my beloved,

I have not been able to come to you today or to call you from home. And lest you worry, I am sending you a couple of lines, which my servant will bring. I have told him that I must pass on something to you on behalf of my husband. You will say, as always, that I am imprudent, but if only you knew how strong and bold I feel when it comes to you!

And while you tremble at the sight of danger, I, instead, feel fortified with increased strength…and feel able to challenge anything or anyone to keep you. I love you, Mario, as I have never loved anyone until now. My thoughts are always with you, and I feel the overwhelming need not only for your kisses but for your whole soul.

A day without seeing you, without hearing a word from you, is just torture. Mario, answer me with a simple line to say that you are thinking of me, that you love me and will make me happy.

I will not miss tomorrow at four. I am already looking forward to the delight of reassuring you with my kisses that I am all yours, that I desire nothing but you.

Always, in life and death,
your Sultana

Anna Maria was stunned. Why had a letter from Signora Sigrano to young Count Herbert found its way into Alceste's possession? Had he intercepted it instead of delivering it to the person concerned? And why? The young woman's brain was awhirl. Perhaps, in the other envelope, she would find the explanation to the enigma. On the outside, Alceste had written: To you alone, Anna Maria.

She opened it with a degree of tranquility, bordering on calm. She found some pages written by Alceste, each numbered. On the first sheet, she read:

My dear Anna Maria,

I am not writing a love letter to you, my sweet Anna Maria, but the confession of a sin that, when I am dead, you will hopefully pardon. This confession has almost been imposed on me by a horrible dream and, since I don't want to die without the hope of someone avenging me, I am writing to you with faith in your wisdom and the love you have for me, even though I am unworthy. Nobody else will understand me, but you surely will.

So, I had a dream about being killed. I didn't recognize the face of the person who shot me since the figure was wearing a mask, but I saw the hand that held the revolver, and it was her hand! Please listen to me, and have mercy on me.

You and Uncle Tommaso had a feeling that I would get lost in big city ways when I came to the Sigrano house, but I laughed at your fears back then. My love for you was so great that no other woman could replace you in my heart. I was so grateful to Uncle Tommaso for all the decent things he had done for me and my mother, so I was convinced that I would be with him, marry you, and finish my days in that way. But in the meantime, I wanted to experience the world a little and the distractions of the city.

Blessed are those who have no desires, who limit their horizons and find themselves happy, even in the most modest of dwellings, cheered by the work they do and the affections of just one soul! Indeed, it was an enormous, wicked, and irreparable mistake coming to the city and above all to the house I find myself in.

I have remained silent with you, dear Anna Maria, but now I must speak — a higher power tells me I should do so. If nothing happens and you have no cause to see these pages, you will be unaware of anything, and I, who will then have had the strength to tear myself away from this bad situation, will be able to make you happy. Yet, if the opposite happens, you must know everything.

For a long while, I did my job honestly, in the manner I was taught as a boy. I respected and liked the master of the house and, although the lady is very beautiful, I did not cast an indiscrete glance in her direction. I would have thought that I was profaning her modesty with even a single word of admiration. How naïve I was!

What I would never have had the courage to try, she did, without hesitation, scruple, or shame. And so, I became Signora Sigrano's lover!

Anna Maria stopped reading for a moment, nausea and horror overwhelming her. Was it possible that a rich, noble lady, a mother of two children, adored by her husband, could give herself to a servant? And Alceste had, therefore, lost his dignity, betrayed the employer who held him in esteem and the fiancée who adored him. Had all his delicate feelings faded away, the feelings that had once endeared Alceste to her? He had preferred a fleeting intoxication of the senses to a love blessed by God. It was not jealousy that swamped Anna Maria, but disgust and pain, as she reeled from the emotion of her discovery.

Deathly pale, she resumed Alceste's letter:

Yes, I was guilty, but you, my dear innocent girl, the only one I have loved in the true sense, will not be able to understand what it means to be in the possession of such a creature, overcome with passion. She entraps you with the coils of a devilish serpent while whispering words to send a man straight to hell.

I confess — even without forgetting you, my soul mate — that I started to live for the woman who had thrown herself into my arms and to whom I would have given my youth, my honor, and drop by drop, all the blood in my veins. Anna Maria, don't condemn me! I felt as if I were going crazy!

The young woman stopped again. She made no sign of protest but felt wounded to her core. Certainly, she could never hate Alceste, especially after his tragic demise, but the idol who she had adored, who had made her happy, lay broken in the dust.

Anna Maria no longer pictured him with the kind smile of a child and the loyal eyes that revealed the decency within. She imagined him hungry for pleasure, corrupted by a tarnished passion, convulsed, repugnant, feverishly embracing the wretched woman who had led him astray. Disgust rose in her throat, stifling any idea of pity or indulgence.

She finally turned to continue the letter, her tears having ceased. She was overwhelmed by an unflinching sense of bitterness:

My madness was suddenly cut short by a horrible discovery. The woman who had taken me as her lover was, after a few months, cheating on me with another — a younger man, noble and rich! She granted her favors to him, favors I wanted for myself alone.

I could have easily unmasked her before her husband and her new lover by showing them the locket she had given me with her portrait and a piece of her hair. However, I would have ruined her without any benefit, and perhaps she would have proven her innocence. (She is a terrible woman, full of cunning).

The poison she had dripped into my veins corroded my poor soul, and I could not bear the idea that she no longer belonged to me. I wanted her, and in order to have her again, I lowered myself to the basest of levels, taking a letter written from her to her new lover and then threatening to denounce her if she abandoned me or refused me.

You see how low a man can go for the passion of a woman like Sultana. To share her favors with another and not to feel sick or revolted!

I should not confess all this to you, my chaste Anna Maria, but if only you knew what tortures are needed to atone for my madness.

I can only calm my spirit by thinking of you. I feel an indefinable sense of peace, just like when I was a child and prayed to Our Lady, whose sacred image you must remember. But Sultana would soon reappear, insidious, triumphant, and my fever, my delirium, would return.

All my prayers, my threats, however, were not enough to get Sultana back. She was in love with someone else and tired of me so I would never be hers again. Instead, she feigned a glimmer of feeling in order to try and retrieve the compromising items she had given me, but I saw the anger, disgust, and cruelty in her eyes.

Yet, when I threatened her again, she seemed to fold and has agreed to meet me tonight, while her husband is away and everybody in the house has gone to bed, believing that I have travelled home for the saint's feast day.

I will go, but my heart tells me that Sultana is setting a trap so she can get the objects back. I can sense the danger hanging over me because Signora Sigrano hates me now and sees me as a stumbling block in her way.

Well, I am going to ensure those objects are safe by entrusting them to you. I am writing to you, not only to tell you of my fears, but to confess my guilt and ask for your forgiveness. If I die, above all, I would like you to exact my revenge and to do the same for yourself. I am giving you the means. Use them well.

I have talked about my death because she is more than capable of killing me. Maybe I should run away, forget about meeting her, escape the sorceress, and come begging to you to save me. But I am not able to. She has me in chains, and I still want her despite her having damned my soul and knowing well that I am playing with my life.

Don't think ill of me, Anna Maria. I am unworthy of you yet it is you to whom I turn at this hour with a smile on my face. God, what remorse! But I cannot tear myself away from this passion. I cannot escape. No, I really am not able to. Anna Maria, forgive me! Have mercy on me! Avenge me if I die…because if I live, I will overcome this madness and make you happy.

At the moment, my brain is on fire, my heart breaking with the pain of it all. Why did I come to the city? Why did I not listen to you and Uncle Tommaso? It is too late now. I cannot go back. My fate is sealed. I am going to die. I can feel it. But I will not rest in peace until that woman has experienced all the tortures she has inflicted on me.

You, alone, my dear, can repay the harm she has done to us both. Farewell, Anna Maria, my childhood friend through all the happy and sad times. Bless you for all the joy you have given me. Bless you for this mission I have given you that I know you will accomplish.

I kiss your forehead, your unhappy
Alceste

After she finished the letter, Anna Maria remained rooted to the spot. Those words had destroyed, in an instant, all her faith in Alceste, all the illusions about the man she had greatly loved and for whom she would have given her life. No, he had surely never loved her if for a moment's pleasure he had betrayed the trust of a man like Signor Sigrano and wept for such an unworthy wife and mother. He was even prepared to trample on his sense of duty to meet her and would defy death rather than give her up.

The memory of his fiancée was not enough to keep him from a hellish path laden with guilt and shame. Nothing had been more powerful than the dishonest kisses of his very own Messalina, thirsty for lust and blood. And for that, he had damned himself. Anna Maria refrained from crying but picked up the portrait of Alceste and stared at it full of pain and reproach. It was not jealousy that piqued her anger but regret that he had proved so weak and cowardly.

She could not bring herself to curse his memory, instead she forgave him, but could no longer think of him as she had in the past. Love had faded. However, she knew she had to accept the mission he had entrusted to her. She would not swerve from the revenge that she must take on the woman who had stolen her fiancé, silenced his sense of duty and love, and taken his life regardless of his despair. Perhaps she was smiling still at the thought of removing him from her path.

It would almost certainly be a deadly fight between her and Sultana, but a silent fight in which no one else had the right to take part and nobody should be aware of until the supreme moment of victory. Anna Maria felt an energy surge through her as she imagined the torments and deceptions she could inflict on the wretched woman who really had no right to be a wife, a mother, or even to live. She decided to trap her in such a net that she would only emerge trampled and mortally wounded with nobody to lament her fall.

Anna Maria would have to put in place all the tricks necessary to deceive Sultana so that she would suspect nothing and place the utmost trust in her. In the heart-breaking couple of hours the young woman had spent in that room, she formulated her entire plan. With her life in tatters, she was convinced that she had the right to show no mercy. To forget? To forgive Sultana? Never! He had died for love, so she would live to hate, to punish the sinner.

She folded Alceste's letter, the one to Count Herbert and along with Sultana's locket, jealously hid them all from prying eyes. She then calmly went downstairs to the room where her godmother, Tommaso, Matteo, and his wife were gathered. As we know, she told them that the package only had one letter from her fiancé, which she had destroyed on his instructions. She admitted that he had confessed his obsessive love for Signora Sigrano but said that he intended to take her by surprise and then commit suicide. She added that he had asked for her forgiveness and begged her not to hate him.

Anna Maria also suggested that fate had wanted Signora Sigrano to shoot the chauffeur, mistaking him for a thief, and so it was clear how Alceste had met his tragic end. The countess was not guilty of his death. She said that she had decided to forgive him the moment of madness that had cost him his life.

She showed them all the photograph that Alceste had left her as a memento and prayed that the others would forgive him and the woman who had killed him in error. The kindly group assembled in the room, and subsequently, the magistrate, believed her, accepting her story. Nobody guessed the thoughts that lurked beneath her pale forehead, nor the internal storm that had gathered to upset her gentle equilibrium.

11

Anna Maria had already finished dressing, knowing that she had to go to the Sigrano house for dinner as well as staying for the evening. The slim, attractive curves of her graceful figure were accentuated by a simple woolen dress of white stripes on a black background with a lowish neckline trimmed with lace. The effect was one of singular elegance.

Her stunning hair was twisted at the nape of her neck, framing her attractive face, which hid the mysteries of her soul, masked by that sweet smile and loyal aspect. She wore no jewelry, just a simple spray of violets pinned next to the lace.

Before putting on her coat and hat, Anna Maria went to her godmother's room.

"How do I look?" she asked candidly.

"You look beautiful, really lovely," she replied, sincerely admiring her, "even more than Signora Sigrano."

A tinkling little laugh parted Anna Maria's coral lips.

"And yet," the young woman answered, "the countess knows how to awaken such passion that even death by her hand is accepted with a smile."

"Because men are such idiots and, I'm sorry to say, that Alceste was the stupidest of them all!" her godmother retorted rather indignantly. "To have a fiancée like you, whom a prince could be proud of, and to be killed by another man's wife in the act of trying to have his way with her, is either crazy or degenerate. Because of this, you'd do well not to regret things so much. Of course, his brutal death affected me a great deal, but thinking about it, perhaps things are better this way. A womanizer, a vain man like Alceste, who only thought about conquests instead of devoting himself exclusively to you, would have ended up making you unhappy."

"You're right," Anna Maria said in a serious tone, "God moves in mysterious ways! Give me a kiss…and I'll see you later."

When she arrived at the Sigrano home, it was four in the afternoon, and although Sultana had suggested she arrive early, the countess was not in the house. Anna Maria was received by Teresa and Signora Sigrano's children, both of whom she had seen in the village but had never approached.

"I'm sorry the lady countess is still out, but she shouldn't be long in returning. In the meantime, stay with me and the children," said Teresa on seeing her.

Anna Maria smiled. "Of course!" she replied. "It was a bit intrusive of me to arrive so soon. But, dear Teresa, I absolutely won't allow you to be so proper with me. You know we've always addressed each other informally."

"It's true, but you're a young lady now.…"

"No more so than you. I like to treat everyone the same way."

"Oh, I know, you're very kind."

Anna Maria bent down to kiss Ottorino and Mina, who immediately attached themselves to her with the expansive nature of children faced with youth and beauty.

"Do you think we will be the best of friends?" asked Anna Maria graciously.

"Yes, yes, so much, because you're so pretty!" the boy answered.

"Me too, me too!" Mina added. "Give me another kiss."

"And me," shouted the boy.

Teresa led the young woman to the countess' dressing room so she could remove her hat and coat. The children dutifully followed.

"Do they understand our local dialect?" asked Anna Maria.

"No," Teresa replied, "I always speak to them in Italian just as the countess and her husband wish."

"I'll be going to school this year, and I'll also be learning French," Ottorino exclaimed.

"And me!" Mina said.

"No, you're not. You're too small," replied her brother.

"But I can say my prayers better than you!" Mina snapped.

Anna Maria smiled, kissed them both, then turned and reverted to dialect for Teresa's benefit.

"I'd like to ask you a favor."

"Name it."

"Can you show me the room where poor Alceste was killed? When I came with Uncle Tommaso to see Signora Sigrano, I didn't have the courage to ask her because the pain was too recent, but I'm calmer now."

Teresa opened the glass door at the end of the dressing room and, also speaking in dialect, replied: "Here it is, this is it. To tell you the truth, if I'd been the countess, I would never have had the courage to go inside, but she continues to bathe there every morning. Look! Alceste entered through the door that leads to the corridor from where you can get to the service stairs and out into the garden. From this room, he could go into the dressing room, which has an entrance to the lady's bedroom. As you know, the countess, on hearing a noise and thinking it was thieves, went to check that she wasn't mistaken instead of immediately asking for help, which she feared would frighten the children. She jumped out of bed, went into the dressing room, and seeing a man in the bathroom she didn't recognize, who was coming towards her, fired without hesitation. Seeing him fall, she ran to raise the alarm. Who would have thought it was Alceste and that, far from having left, the wretch had returned in secret to…."

At this point, Teresa fell silent, embarrassed, without knowing how to continue. Anna Maria smiled with a degree of sadness.

"Unfortunately, I know why he came," she said. "Alceste knew he was headed for his own tragic fate. Even if the countess hadn't killed him, he would've killed himself that night after declaring his crazy feelings and knowing that she would never satisfy them. He confessed it all to me in a letter, asking for forgiveness. I do forgive him, but you have to understand that I can't grieve forever for a man who didn't think of me, who would rather have killed himself over another woman regardless of whether she shot him first. I pity the countess more as she could've fallen victim to Alceste who had clearly lost his head, and she's had to suffer the consequences of what happened."

"You're right!" exclaimed Teresa. "In this house, we all knew about his emotional attachment, but you see, nobody thought he would go so far as to attempt anything so reckless. Even the countess had noticed his feelings towards her but hadn't wanted to say anything to Signor Sigrano for fear of causing a scene. She did, though, try to force Alceste to return home under the pretext of the saint's feast day celebrations, where he was supposed to write a letter of resignation to the lawyer, explaining that he wanted to stay with Uncle Tommaso and marry you."

"That was good of her," Anna Maria said in a voice seemingly veiled with emotion. "Ah, if only Alceste had done that."

"He pretended to accept and to leave, but he came back secretly, perhaps to get by force what he couldn't through imploring the countess."

"The wretch! Now I understand why, unlike me, being in this room has no effect on Signora Sigrano. Alceste doesn't deserve regrets or to be held in memory." Her voice was calm as she spoke. "But let's not worry about him anymore," she added with a certain vivacity. "These dear children are looking at us in amazement because they can't understand the language we're speaking. Let's go to another room, so I can talk to them."

The signora, who had returned home around six o'clock, found Anna Maria in the sitting room with Mina and Ottorino on her lap.

She was telling them a story, which they were listening to with evident pleasure. Teresa, too, was hanging on the words of the storyteller.

"Excuse me, dear Anna Maria," said Sultana, "for being so late."

"Time flew by, signora, looking after these sweet little angels."

"Mamma," shouted Ottorino, "I want Anna Maria to be with us always."

"Me too!" added Mina.

"Yes, yes, my treasures," answered the countess turning to the young woman. "I'm going to change my clothes. I'll be back in a moment. Teresa, come with me."

"I'll finish the story for the children," said Anna Maria.

She had noticed that Sultana, although trying to appear casual, looked very worried. Her blue eyes had a hard-set look, and her nostrils were twitching like a woman gasping for breath. Her smile was forced. Anna Maria wondered where she had gone that afternoon, neglecting her children as if they didn't exist. And the children, who clung to her as if they were afraid that she was going to leave, were so adorable.

Sultana had just left the room when Signor Sigrano entered. Anna Maria tried to get up to greet him but was stopped by Mina.

"Don't move. It's papa!"

"The little one is right. Just give me your hand, and I'll take it to thank you for accepting our invitation. I would've been home earlier, but even today, I had a lot to do at the office, so much so that I couldn't take my wife out, as she'd wished."

"Mamma is back now," Ottorino said.

"I know. She went to visit a sick friend," replied the lawyer while looking fondly at the group formed by Anna Maria and the children.

Sultana returned, startling the younger woman with her change in demeanor. Her attractive face had no sign of disturbance, her house dress was immaculate, and she had assumed an air of pseudo-innocence. What an amazing mastery over her own emotions, to transform herself so suddenly. Sultana approached her husband and, leaning towards him, kissed him on the forehead.

"How tired you must be, dear Bruno!" she said in a sweet, charming voice.

"Not at all, my love," he replied, looking at her with affection. "The tiredness fades when I remember I'm working for you and our children."

"I know, I know. It's so appreciated, and we love you too."

Anna Maria listened with her eyes lowered, her cheeks blushing, but with an indefinable smile on her lips. Sultana went to sit next to her.

"That's an exquisite dress," she said in admiration. "It certainly wasn't made in the village."

"But yes," Anna Maria answered, her eyes full of candor as she lifted her head. "We have a very good tailor, and he's got excellent taste."

"This lace trim, though, you must have bought that in the city!"

"No, I made it myself. My mother was very skilled in this kind of work, and she taught me well."

"Marvelous!" Sultana replied. "Look, Bruno, what intricate work."

"The signorina has fairy fingers."

Anna Maria's cheeks reddened once more.

"Please, don't call me signorina," she said in a sweet voice. "Let's be more informal, as your good wife wishes, then I'll be happy."

At that moment, Teresa announced the arrival of Count Herbert. Sultana was unable to hide a momentary display of delight while her husband went to meet the young officer.

"Come in, come in, my dear boy," she said with frank cordiality, extending her hand towards him. "We've been waiting for you."

"I apologize for being a bit late," he replied with some embarrassment, "but I've been on duty."

He came into the living room with Signor Sigrano, greeted Sultana but without exchanging glances, and then blushed somewhat as he bowed to Anna Maria, who was looking at him with an amiable smile. They all sat down, exchanging small talk. The young woman noticed that Signora Sigrano, although appearing casual, occasionally directed a piercing glance from the corner of her eye towards the count, who was paying her no attention.

On hearing that the meal was ready, the lawyer gallantly offered his arm to Anna Maria, which meant the officer was forced to do the same to Sultana. Before leaving the room as the first couple had, she turned to Mario in a low voice: "Are you decided then?"

Although she had spoken in a whisper, Mario was startled and looked around the room in a restless manner, as if the others might overhear.

"We'll talk about it tomorrow at four," he quickly replied, drawing her towards the neighboring room.

At the table, there were only four place settings, as the children were eating with their governess. At first, the young woman seemed embarrassed and confused, with Bruno Sigrano on her right and Mario on her left. After some encouragement from Sultana and her husband, she relaxed into confident conversation on art, literature, and music to such an extent that she managed to capture her audience.

Mario had not observed her closely at the previous reception, but now, at such close quarters, he was free to admire her. As a lover of the finer things in life, he realized that a man with such a companion by his side could not wish for anything more.

The lawyer was happy to see the young man's admiration, and even Sultana had regained her composure and sense of serenity, letting any notions of jealousy fade. She thought there was no way that Mario could make a mistress or a wife of her.

Anna Maria, now far from shy, was asked to sing. She chose, from the music available, a piece she knew and sang it with a sweet, harmonious voice designed to stir the emotions. The two men, who sat a short distance away, started to talk in low voices.

"What do you think of the girl?" the lawyer asked the young man.

"Wonderful!" replied the officer.

"You're right, my boy. Anna Maria has all the qualities you could wish for, of both body and soul. It's my wish, and Sultana's, that she should be happy and married well."

Mario shuddered.

"She deserves it," he answered in a slightly forced voice, "and I truly wish her all the best."

Bruno failed to notice the emotion as he spoke.

"And you, when will you start a family?" he said. "Your father and mother are keen to see you married, and I know that marriages made when you're young are the best. It's to my regret that I didn't know Sultana at least six years earlier. I would have enjoyed six more years of happiness, and the children would now be of an age to spend more time with me and their mother, who loves them a great deal."

Mario was on his toes, agitated as he listened, and completely unable to look him in the eye.

"I don't expect, at least for now, to get married," he answered in a stifled tone.

"I see! You like to play the field. But take care, my boy, because guilty affairs empty your wallet and leave you with remorse and regret."

The lawyer would have continued, but Anna Maria had finished singing and he had to applaud. Mario, consumed with embarrassment, stood up and approached her so he could pay a compliment instead. Their eyes met as she quickly turned to thank him. They both felt the same spark and sensed that their lives would now be entwined. That moment seemed to decide their entire future. Sultana was completely oblivious.

"Don't you think," she asked, smiling, "that my young friend has an enchanting voice?"

"Divine!" exclaimed Mario. "Have you been studying singing for a long time?"

"I haven't started yet," answered the young woman, "but that's why I've come to Turin, to study.…"

"And to go on stage," added Sultana.

Mario looked at her surprised.

"Really?" he said. "Would you like the life of a performing singer?"

"I'm not sure, but I have a great enthusiasm for music and faith in myself."

"But it's not the kind of world for someone of your age. Even if art can lift a woman in the eyes of the world, her private life will always be up for discussion, and it's true to say that the most honest of women will get lost in all this. Nobody believes in the virtue of theater performers."

"There are also deceitful women in the wider world," Anna Maria retorted.

"You're right," interrupted the lawyer forcefully, "and their dishonesty is more wretched, given that they can't use the excuse of the adoration of the crowd and the dangers an artist is exposed to. It happens in the sanctuary of the family, to the detriment of a trusting and ignorant husband, and the children whose lives should be sacrosanct. They are such despicable creatures."

As Bruno spoke, Anna Maria could see the embarrassment on the officer's face. Sultana, on the other hand, kept admirably cool.

"Signora Leberto is a prime example," she interrupted with a smile on her lips.

Mario was sickened by such an outrageous insinuation.

"Excuse me," he exclaimed abruptly, "I must defend the lady against that accusation. I can assure you that you're wrong. Signora Leberto is a very decent woman, worthy of the utmost respect...."

"Perhaps for you."

"For me and everyone else!" Mario fiercely disagreed. "You're judging her by envious gossip from the all-too-common mudslingers in our society, who blame her for not knowing how to conceal her impressions like so many others. They blame her sincerity. I swear to you, Signor Sigrano, that Signora Leberto is above all suspicion."

"I believe you, dear boy," observed Bruno, "but you, with the attention you pay her, could make people believe the opposite."

"The attention? If I gladly converse with her when I meet her at some friendly reception, it's because I enjoy her interesting conversation, as she's very intelligent and doesn't get involved in gossip, which is not always the case at our gatherings. If I accompanied her once, having met her by chance, I can tell you that it was her husband, who was with her but had to leave on business, who asked me to walk her to the carriage, which was to pick them up at the restaurant near the park. I have never allowed myself the slightest indecency towards that lady, nor spoken a word that she would find distasteful. I'm honored to be held in her high esteem."

"Well done, young man!" Signor Sigrano said with sincerity. "I know that, deep down, you're a decent fellow who wouldn't lower yourself to do such things."

Mario went pale, but it was Sultana who grabbed everyone's attention.

"Well now! Let's stop all this talk, which can't be very nice for Anna Maria. We should talk about something else."

It was around eleven at night when Anna Maria returned home, accompanied by Bruno and Mario. It was a cold but still evening. The lawyer had offered to get a carriage, but she had preferred to go on foot.

"I'm used to walking," she said, "and tonight is so beautiful."

"Indeed!" Mario exclaimed. "It's an enchanting night."

Once outside the Sigrano home, the young man's melancholy mood disappeared. He became expansive and enthusiastic while speaking to Anna Maria. Bruno caught his attention on several occasions and smiled in amazement. He seemed to be another person. She listened intently, her luminous eyes drawn to his, attracted by the sincerity of his words, sensing their heartfelt echo.

When the young woman found herself alone in her room, she mulled over the events of the evening. How could such a straightforward man deceive Signor Sigrano and become his wife's lover? Sultana must have set some trap, forcing him to be with her. Unlike Alceste, he shows no love for her and clearly had no thoughts of emulating him. There was some hostility, even hate, and it troubled him to be close to her husband.

Realizing that he was attracted to her, she knew that it would not take much effort to steal him away from Sultana. If, through avenging Alceste, she found a happiness that he was incapable of giving her, would it mean she was guilty? Surely, she deserved to be loved more than that dreadful woman?

Tears rose in her eyes as she went over and over these thoughts in her head. If only Alceste had not been so weak and cowardly, she could have been happy with him and would even have loved his memory now that he had died. No other man would have taken his place in her heart, she could swear to it. Yet, he had been the very cause of her change in attitude.

12

The following day Mario Herbert was sprawled out in an armchair waiting with a certain rancor for Signora Sigrano. The clock was ticking towards four. He was determined to end the affair at any cost. If Sultana did not want to finish their relationship, which now tormented him, he would ask for a change of garrison and move away from Turin. It was clear that things could not continue in the same manner.

Sultana's charm had ceased to affect him, and he was no longer won over by her ardent attention. Her kisses and caresses left him indifferent, even nauseated. Naturally, he had been sorry to leave her house, but it was due to Anna Maria, who had made a hitherto unknown impression on him. It was not the crazy desire that Sultana had once unleashed, but a deep feeling of wonderful tenderness. It took him to a world of idealized dreams reminiscent of childhood where only kindness prevailed. The women in those early visions were angelic, like his mother and sister, who was herself now a wife and mother.

Why did he not confide in Anna Maria? He thought, on reflection, that she would not understand. But was he mistaken about the young woman who was, after all, Sultana's friend? Could it not be the case that she had a similar character, that she had the same tendencies and was also aware of their relationship? The looks she had given him were so strange, so profound, almost as if she were trying to read his soul. But no, surely, he was mistaken. Anna Maria did not know anything. You could see in her face that she was genuine and sincere. Maybe he should leave and not see her anymore.

A loud ringing interrupted his thoughts. He got up in a rush and went to open the door. It was Sultana. She entered hastily, closed the door, and brushed past him. He had still not uttered a word by the time she reached the drawing room. He turned and followed her. She was wearing a black velvet dress that accentuated the pallor of her face from which she had lifted her lace veil.

"Well then...I'm here. Explain your decision to me," she said, letting herself fall into the armchair without removing her hat while nervously twisting her handkerchief. Mario sat down in front of her.

"I'm ready, signora," he replied, his voice taking a serious tone.

"Signora! You're calling me signora!" Sultana snapped, raising her shoulders, then adding more calmly, "Mario, why do you want to make me suffer!"

"You will never suffer as much as I do when I'm in your house with your husband."

"But you should have thought about that before you took me as your lover. And well, if that's all that is troubling you, let's just meet here or in some other bolt hole of your choosing."

Mario shook his head sadly.

"It's useless!" he said. "I can no longer bear a relationship that causes me such continuous torment and remorse. I've decided to end it, and if you loved me, you would understand why."

"But precisely because I do love you," Sultana interrupted, using the familiar language they were used to in private, "I want to keep you all to myself. In your selfishness as a man, you only think of yourself. You don't understand my anxieties at the thought that you might abandon me. No, you can't leave me, nor will you, as it's against my wishes."

Gradually she began to assume her usual imperious tone. She fixed her eyes menacingly on Mario. For the first time, the young man felt no fear or emotion, only a sense of rebellion.

"If you don't wish it, I do," he answered harshly, "and I've already asked for a change of garrison. If they don't allow it, I'll take a year's leave so I can get away."

"You're doing this because you've got someone else. Admit it!" Sultana shouted.

"I don't and if I loved someone else, I wouldn't try to leave Turin. I'm just tired of being so two-faced in front of your husband."

A burning anger rose to Sultana's cheeks. "And you're only thinking of that now?"

"I've always worried about it…and, if you remember, I mentioned it several times, but you stifled my conscience with your kisses and laughed at my scruples and fears. After the death of that man you killed, I swore I'd never go near you again, but you made me believe that I was almost culpable for the murder because of the letter that Alceste had stolen from me.…"

"And that's true."

"Hmm, no. It's not. I'm not to blame. And I now know how much was stifled for the sake of your husband and children: the very fact that you were Alceste's lover. Perhaps the young man, having discovered that he was sharing your favors with me, made a scene because of his jealousy, which you ended with that gun shot."

"You insult me!" she exclaimed.

"No, I'm defending my freedom, which you'd like to remove in any way possible."

"What if I tell my husband that you tried to seduce me and lured me here to trap me. Do you think he'd spare you?"

"I know full well that you can make him believe what you want, but I'd prefer death from his hand, which would be an atonement, rather than continuing with this numbing of my conscience, having you here and pretending that I love you. I can't stand it any longer because your audacity and the moral tyranny you exert has killed it."

Sultana felt her energy drain away. She wrinkled her nose as her eyes roamed the room, seemingly lost.

"Do you hate me so much?"

"I don't hate you, and if you had agreed to forget our past weaknesses, if you hadn't wanted to force my will, I would have treasured you for it, and I would have remained a devoted and faithful friend, ready to defend you."

Sultana eyes, veiled with tears, pleaded with him.

"So, is it really all over?" she stammered. "Will those heady days never return? Will I never hear you call me 'my angel' or 'my beloved' again? It is all over?"

She was trembling, but Mario resisted the temptation to take her in his arms and embrace her. He understood that the slightest weakness could see him chained once more.

"We must part," he answered in a firm voice.

"No, it can't be possible. A bond like ours can't break in this way," Sultana continued. "You must have other reasons, which you're not telling me. There must be someone else.… Maybe Signora Leberto."

"I will tell you again that Signora Leberto is an honest woman and that I love nobody else."

"But you will!"

"The future is in God's hands."

"What if I were to kill you?"

Mario had a fleeting smile. "Be careful," he said with irony. "This time they would pursue a prosecution."

Sultana quickly rose to her feet, indignant, and for a moment, Mario thought her temper would be uncontrollable. Signora Sigrano, however, knew how to tame her anger when it suited.

"Why do you mortally offend me? I'd prefer a shot from a revolver. And yet, I forgive you, just as I implore you to forgive me the delirium that took hold of me and made me forget my duties as a wife and mother," she muttered slowly, returning to the formal mode of address.

Sultana appeared so sincere that Mario, who had stood up, was almost embarrassed.

"Signora,…" he hesitated.

"You're right, we must no longer see each other alone, but please, don't give my husband any reason to be suspicious by ceasing your visits, and swear to me that nobody will ever know what has happened between us."

"I swear to you on my honor as a gentleman," Mario answered. "I would be the vilest of men to betray such a secret."

"Thank you," Sultana said. "May the memories of the past vanish like dreams. I will try, if I can, to forget, just as you already seem to have forgotten. I've experienced the madness of loving you, so I must have the courage to suffer and get on with life. Come here, give me a kiss like a sister, and let's part."

Mario went to her and was about to kiss her forehead when she suddenly threw her arms around his neck. With her face raised to his, she broke into tears.

"Mario, Mario, has it all ended between us, forever? I love you so much, and I will continue to love you for as long as I live. Look at me! Aren't I the most beautiful of women, the most desired? Will you ever find another who can give you the love that I've given you? Mario, don't leave me!"

Sultana was still hoping to entangle her prey. He found it difficult to resist her beauty, the sight of her suffering, and the warmth of her kisses. Yet, he freed himself from the coil of her embrace.

"We must part," he simply repeated.

Faced with such resistance, Sultana drew back, her face reddened. She abruptly lowered a veil over her face.

"Goodbye!" she said resentfully.

"Goodbye!" Mario said, without trying to hold her back. And when he heard the sound of the door closing behind her, he let out a long sigh of relief, rubbing his hands together. "Free! I'm happy to be free!" he repeated to himself.

He thought it almost impossible that he had mustered the courage and been able to resist her bewitching allure, charms that others his age would have been happy to possess. He knew that he had done what was necessary, his duty, and shook his shoulders as if he had freed himself from a serious burden. He had been repelled by betraying a man like Signor Sigrano and would never have done it had Sultana not thrown herself into his arms.

He questioned whether he had been too austere towards her, particularly since he had enjoyed many delightful moments in her company. In reality, though, he knew that if he had given in once more, he would have been lost forever, and the chain binding him would have remained unbroken. He thought a change of lodging would make sense, realizing that if she returned, he might not have the strength to refuse her again.

In his heart, Mario had no regrets, but he felt a degree of rebellion nevertheless. Dismissing these thoughts with some violence, he recognized that he was softening his own opinions. Instead, he centered on Sultana's constant danger to his stability and the fact he no longer loved her.

"What I did was necessary," he repeated to himself.

Count Herbert needed some form of distraction, so he donned a civilian suit and went out with the intention of eating at the restaurant below Anna Maria's lodgings although he had no hope of meeting her. By now night had fallen and nobody passing by would have recognized him. He had the air of a student and had never felt happier or more cheerful. While he was walking along Corso Vinzaglio, despite the deserted hour, he heard a female voice behind him, which jolted him as he seemed to recognize it.

"Have you not yet understood, sir? You've got this wrong. Go about your own business and stop following me."

Mario turned abruptly and, with an exclamation of happiness, rushed to the young woman who was a few steps away from him.

"Signorina Anna Maria!" he said, respectfully removing his hat.

"Count Herbert!" she replied, extending her gloved hand, "I'm glad I met you at the right moment."

"Can I be of any service to you?"

"Yes, yes. Your presence has been enough to frighten off that man who's been following me."

The persistent person in question, an elegantly dressed man in his fifties, seeing Mario meet the young lady, had prudently disappeared. The pair could now see the funny side of the incident.

"Will you allow me to accompany you home?" the count asked.

"Happily. I understand how, in the evening, it's rather unwise to be alone on the streets. But you know what, I wouldn't have recognized you in civilian dress?"

As they spoke, they started to walk again. The weather was cold but dry.

"I dress like this sometimes in the evenings. I feel freer," Mario said. "I confess that I have simple tastes, and when I'm in uniform, I don't always feel comfortable. I like long walks along lonely avenues, and I enjoy eating in rustic restaurants, feeling free, incognito, among people and things I'm not familiar with. Tonight, though, I had an ulterior motive, I'm looking for accommodation because mine no longer suits me. Besides, I'm too far from the barracks in Viale Stupingi from where I live in Via San Quintino."

"I'm not sure where that is, but I don't think this is the right time to go in search of accommodation."

"I don't mean that I'm going to go inside. But, here, in Turin, they usual put rental signs on the doors of the houses. If I see something that I like, I'll go and visit the property tomorrow. And you, signorina, will you continue to visit to the Sigranos?"

"I just went to see the signora to show her a lace design she wanted, but she wasn't at home."

Anna Maria raised her clear eyes to look at Mario, and although the avenue was dark, she could see the embarrassment on his face. She pretended not to notice and continue with a feigned air of naivety.

"What a decent lady the countess is! She's like a real mother to me and to think that she's responsible for the greatest misfortune in my life. But I could never hate her as the poor lady has suffered more than me."

Mario didn't understand and was curious to know more.

"So, what did she do to you?" he asked immediately in spite of himself.

"Sorry? You don't know?" Anna Maria exclaimed, showing her eagerness. "Did Signora Sigrano not tell you who I am? Didn't her husband?"

"No. They just told me that you were from the same place as the countess."

"Nothing else? And my name, didn't that remind you of anything? Weren't you in Turin when Signora Sigrano killed her chauffeur by accident on that fatal evening?"

"Yes, I was in the city," he replied, "but I don't understand what you have to do with that unfortunate incident."

Anna Maria held her head high as she answered: "Alceste Bianco was my fiancé."

Mario's eyes widened. "Your fiancé?" he repeated in a constricted voice.

"Yes, count!" Anna Maria added, her beautiful face now pale. "Perhaps it will seem strange to you that a young lady of good standing, and I was introduced to you as such, was engaged to a simple chauffeur. But Alceste and I grew up together. He was only a few years older than me and, I can assure you, he would've lived at ease happily back at home, if he'd not been drawn to the city and not enjoyed an adventurous life at the center of things."

"So, signorina, he can't have loved you then?" Mario reluctantly murmured.

"He thought he loved me," answered Anna Maria slowly, "as indeed, I felt bound to him by the oath we'd sworn over a gravestone. Yet, my innocent affection wasn't enough to keep him. He wanted to leave, to go to the city. I waited without any impatience for the day he would return and we'd get married. Instead, I should have broken things off."

A moment of silence followed. The pair, while talking, had not noticed they had taken another route and were moving away from Anna Maria's house. Cold gusts began to blow, but they failed to notice them, entranced as they were in the middle of sharing a confidence.

"After he missed the train home, fate wanted Alceste to go back to the Sigrano house that night and enter in secret," continued Anna Maria with sweet ingenuity and a moving frankness. "Perhaps he'd drunk too much and entered the signora's apartment without realizing it."

She fell silent again and looked towards him. Mario appeared to be deeply affected by her naivety since she seemed unaware of the rumors that had swirled around about the countess. She had put her trust in Sultana. He was both moved and disturbed at the same time. Not knowing what to say when confronted with the quizzical but trusting look from her sparkling dark eyes, he stammered a reply with some difficulty: "Of course…it was a mistake…a misfortune."

"When I heard what had occurred, I could hardly believe it. It seemed such a frightening and unlikely thing to have happened. But then I had to acknowledge the evidence, yet as I was mourning the sad death of my fiancé, I tormented myself by thinking of the good countess and how she'd killed him by mistake, thinking him a thief. She must have been in despair and such pain."

Mario felt annoyed at hearing praise and pity for Sultana coming from her innocent mouth. He shuddered at the thought that she might one day discover the truth.

"But did you know her well, Signora Sigrano?" he asked almost unconsciously.

"I'd seen her a few times when she was still young, in church or at the village's public gardens. Frankly, I have to say that, although she was beautiful, I didn't like her, nor did the other girls of my age. She was very haughty and didn't deign to glance in our direction or speak to us, even though, in reality, we all had more money than she. But her background was different from ours, and she was a dozen years older. Perhaps that's why she didn't care for us. Then she got married, and we only saw her in passing, occasionally in the fall, when she came to the countryside with her children. Back home hardly a good word was said about her. My friends told me about the men she had led to ruin and who had died. I never believed it because Uncle Tommaso said it was all slander.

"Alceste, himself, when he started working for Signor Sigrano, told me that the countess was a decent wife and mother, something he always repeated in his letters. So much so that when I came to see my fiancé's body and accompany the funeral cortege home, I no longer saw her as guilty but as an unhappy person, more so than me because she would always regret Alceste's death. I cried as she held me, and although I was in pieces, I consoled her."

"You're an angel!" Mario exclaimed, looking at Anna Maria with admiration.

By now she realized that they had taken a wrong turn and told him. Retracing their steps, they fell silent for a few minutes, simply exchanging smiles.

Mario then began to speak about himself, of his childhood, the time spent at the military academy, of the joy he felt at receiving his epaulettes and learning that he had been assigned to a cavalry regiment in Turin, a city all his companions called Little Paris. He mentioned how they had intended to spend many pleasant hours off-duty, adding however that, unlike some others, he was not a lover of every frivolous pleasure.

He had a romantic nature and was a dreamer, loving solitude and a deeper contemplation of his surroundings. He felt great affection for the beauty and heartache of nature and art. He would have liked to live a life of the mind, abandoning himself to the sweetest flights of fancy. He then explained how his family had recommended him to Bruno Sigrano, speaking of him with real admiration. There was not a single mention of Sultana.

"And what about the signora?" Anna Maria asked innocently.

"She is a very well-mannered lady," he replied indifferently, "but I prefer her husband."

Anna Maria did not reply, having, by now, reached her front door.

"Because of me," she eventually said, "you've forgotten to look for new accommodation."

"It was more pleasant keeping you company," the officer replied with a lightness of tone. "And since the walk has made me hungry, I'll eat in the restaurant," he added, pointing to the nearby glass door with its embroidered curtains behind which you could see the tables full of customers, mostly boarders.

"Really?" laughed Anna Maria. "Then I'll recommend you to the owner, a countryman of mine and a distant relative of my godmother. By now, he'll be preparing food for us while waiting for poor Camilla, Uncle Tommaso's old servant, to appear. She arrived this morning and will be staying with us. Come in through my door, if you don't mind, and I'll let you in from the kitchen side."

Mario followed her, fascinated by her graceful movement and her candor. He realized how much he had misjudged her, speculating that she might be another Sultana. Secretly, he was alarmed by the thought that Anna Maria, both gullible and decent, might one day learn that Sultana had been his lover. If only he could distance her from Signora Sigrano. Yet how could he achieve such an aim without arousing suspicion?

Anna Maria introduced the young man to Matteo Ferpio, asking him to treat him well. She also added that he was looking for affordable accommodation nearby so that he would have good access to this part of town.

"There's a very elegant apartment for rent in the building opposite, which comes with use of the stable," said Ferpio, "but the price is quite high."

"Well, that doesn't matter as long as it suits me," answered Mario. "When could I view it?"

"Right now if you want to come with me. The accommodation is empty, and the doorman eats here and is a friend of mine."

"Let's go. Let's go now!" said Mario, eager to rent the rooms.

Anna Maria left the two men alone after shaking the count's hand and thanking him again for having rescued her from the prowler.

"See you soon," she said.

When she went up to her quarters, she found the table laid with both Orsola and Camilla waiting, somewhat worried due to the lateness of the hour.

"I thought that Signora Sigrano had delayed you this evening as well," added Orsola.

"No," replied Anna Maria, "I spent a while with Teresa and the children and then, on my way home, I met Count Herbert, the lawyer's friend, who was kind enough to accompany me to the front door."

"Good girl," added Orsola. "With these dark, cold evenings it's not advisable for you to walk the streets alone. We're not in the country here, where everyone knows and respects you."

"You can even get respect in Turin," the young woman retorted. "I have no fears, and as I told you, dear godmother, I came here for a reason, which you'll only know about when I achieve what I've set out to do."

"I'm not questioning that," said Orsola, "because I know you, and I know that, whatever it is, you'll be doing it out of a sense of duty and honor and that you'll do nothing to stain the good name of your parents."

"On that score, you can rest assured," exclaimed Anna Maria, embracing the older woman.

The meal passed cheerfully with Anna Maria chatting in a lively manner, buoyed by the thought that Mario was in the building. Without being vain, she knew that she had made a great impression on the young man, which indeed was what she had intended. However, such an easy and fleeting victory was not enough. She needed something more.

If only Mario had not been that woman's lover, she could easily have fallen in love with him. He was decent and sincere with a delicacy of personality that Alceste lacked. But Mario, too, had succumbed to Sultana's charms, and although she bore the brunt of the guilt, the very thought was enough to calm Anna Maria's heart and engage her brain, which she would need for the project to succeed.

The two young people met the following day. Count Herbert had taken possession of the new accommodation opposite to where she lived. Mario Ferpio had been instructed to send him breakfast and an evening meal, which would only be served by the officer's orderly since he didn't want other servants or strangers around him.

Anna Maria introduced him to her godmother and, since Mario knew she was studying singing, he had asked to accompany her on the piano, which she happily accepted. He soon became a welcome guest of the house and spent his free hours close to her. His friends no longer saw him at restaurants and social gatherings, nor did he appear in Signora Sigrano's box at the Regio. Nobody knew what to make of this change.

Almost by tacit agreement, the two of them ceased to speak of the Sigranos and even abandoned visits to the household. Both seemed amazed that they had heard nothing from Sultana, and Anna Maria could not understand how Signora Sigrano had lost interest in her.

One morning on leaving the house, she came face to face with Sultana. Feigning confusion, she noticed that the countess looked ashen and rather disturbed. She stretched out her hand to the young woman.

"I was coming to look for you. Why haven't you been coming to see me anymore?" she said.

"Forgive me," answered Anna Maria, "I've failed in my duty, but my godmother has been somewhat indisposed."

"I've not been well either," added Sultana, "otherwise I would have come earlier."

"I'm sorry, if I'd known before, I would have rushed to see you. I can't believe that Count Mario didn't warn me."

Sultana gasped, her bewildered eyes fixing on the girl.

"Have you seen Count Mario?"

Anna Maria blushed heavily but replied with an admirably naïve tone: "Yes, signora, almost every day. He's been so kind to me, showing me where to go to hire a good piano, where to buy music, and he asked my godmother's permission to come and spend some evenings with us. Isn't he just marvelous, the count! He plays cards with us, plays the piano when I sing.... He's really nice."

Anna Maria's every word was like a slap to Sultana's cheek. She flushed hot then cold as she pressed her lips tightly together in an effort not to scream out, but her eyes gave away the anger inside.

"Now I understand why he hasn't been seen around either," she said between gritted teeth, "but it's not right that he's abusing your trust. You, dear girl, don't know our count very well. You're not aware that he's a dreadful lothario."

Anna Maria turned to Sultana, her eyes full of surprise: "You mean, a seducer?" she asked. "But you must be mistaken, signora! He's shy and decent, almost like a boy, and has never spoken a word to me that my godmother couldn't hear. He only talks to me about art, music, and poetry."

"He's smart! He's doing that to attract you," Sultana replied dryly. "Didn't you hear, that day in my living room, how they talked about it, about him courting Signora Leberto?"

Anna Maria's smile was radiant. "But you must also remember, signora, that the count defended himself against those rumors when we dined together. He affirmed that Signora Leberto is an honest woman, and I believe what he said."

Sultana was shaking. "As you're little more than a child, you know nothing of life," she replied impatiently, "but I will never allow Mario to flatter you and lead you to ruin."

"And why would that happen, signora?"

"I can't explain myself out here in the street."

"Well, come up to my rooms. We're just a few steps from the house, and my godmother will be happy to receive you."

"Ok, let's go."

Anna Maria was happy to accompany the countess back to her accommodation, and Sultana was convinced that the young woman had told her the truth, a conviction that took the sting from her hostile thoughts. The same could not be said for Mario, who had made fun of her torment by seeing someone else. But what was he expecting of Anna Maria? He was not so stupid as to think that he could make her his lover…much less his wife. Did he think that, once she had trodden the boards, he would have more of a chance of seducing her?

Irrespective, Sultana felt an intense, blistering anger. To think that Mario, after their separation, had no longer bothered with society and had left the lodgings where they had spent many happy hours over the past two years. She had not known his whereabouts and had even believed he was no longer in Turin. During the two weeks following their parting, she had felt ill, feverish, and the pain of their separation troubled her deeply.

Two days prior to meeting Anna Maria, she had pulled herself together and resolved to resume her social life, to take another lover as an act of revenge on Mario. During the two weeks, she had never thought of the young woman, except to say to her husband, who had queried her absence, that perhaps her godmother was ill and that she ought to pay her a visit.

Orsola now received the elegant lady with much courtesy. Almost immediately, talk turned to the count. The old woman was frightened by the ugly portrait Sultana painted of his behavior and morals.

"Who would believe, seeing him and hearing him speak, that he was such a dangerous young man," she exclaimed. "My Anna Maria had assured me, dear lady, that the count was almost like a son to you and your husband. It was this that induced me to receive him, to show him all kindness, to let him talk with my goddaughter. But now, quite frankly, I'll tell him to stop his visits. Isn't that right, Anna Maria?"

"I'll do whatever you and my benefactress suggest," replied the young woman in a gentle voice. "However, I don't think we should suddenly close the door in the face of someone who has, so far, shown himself to be so kind and has treated us decently."

"This is also true," murmured Orsola.

"Instead," continued Anna Maria, "when Signor Mario comes tonight, I'll tell him that you, countess, have been here and have been surprised to learn that he's been paying us daily visits without informing you while ceasing to visit your house."

"Very well!" answered Sultana. "And you should add that, on behalf of my husband, I must speak to him. I'll be waiting for him tomorrow afternoon at four o'clock."

"Yes, signora, I won't forget, you can be sure."

Relieved that she could prevent the burgeoning relationship, Sultana took her leave.

Anna Maria embraced her godmother with a curious smile on her face.

"Don't worry, Signora Sigrano is wrong about Count Mario. He has never uttered any words of affection to me, but I've already guessed that he's in love with me. You'll see. He'll take the opportunity to tell the countess, who's like a mother to him. I think I'm going to be his wife."

"If only that were true!" exclaimed Orsola unreservedly.

"It will be," she said with a vigor that astonished her old guardian. Anna Maria surprised her more every day, and she wondered who had given her so much presence of mind, so much energy, when she had spent most of her time living modestly surrounded by the wilds of the Alps.

13

The feelings that Anna Maria had instilled in the young cavalry officer were, indeed, noble and virtuous. From the first moment he approached her, he seemed a transformed character. He anxiously awaited the next time he would see her, and when close to her, all his moral dilemmas and sad memories disappeared. He had returned to a child-like state precisely because he loved her. Although his feelings seemed to suffocate him, he did not dare address a less than respectful word to the honest young woman. He was content to admire her and observe her kind heart simply through her conversation.

That evening, he also visited Anna Maria, happy to see her again, given he had been unable to call the day before due to his military commitments. When he knocked on the door of the apartment, his heart rate began to speed up and his head was whirling with pleasant thoughts. Usually, it was Anna Maria who opened the door and welcomed him with a large smile, but on this occasion, the elderly servant Camilla appeared, her back a little bent with age.

"Good evening, lieutenant!" she said with simplicity.

"Good evening!" he answered, somewhat perturbed. "Are the ladies at home?"

"Yes, yes. Give me your cloak and sabre and go on through. They are in the dining room."

When Mario entered, Anna Maria, who was sitting next to Orsola, stood up and extended her hand to him in a rather sad manner.

"Good evening, Signor Mario!" she said.

"Good evening to you both! Why are you so upset? Have you received any bad news?"

"No, no," answered the young woman, "but we have had a visit that has stunned us somewhat. Take a seat, Signor Mario, and I'll tell you everything."

Rather agitated, he took a seat, nervously twisting the cap he was holding in his hands.

"A visit?" he repeated. "From whom?"

Anna Maria looked fixedly at him, her eyes both marvelous and sincere.

"From Signora Sultana Sigrano," she replied.

Mario's felt prickles of heat on his skin, but he made no gesture that betrayed his emotion.

"Her!" he said coldly. "What did she want?"

Orsola remained silent, letting her goddaughter speak.

"Firstly," Anna Maria exclaimed, "she scolded me for failing to visit her recently. On which account, she is right. However, when she learned that you were coming to visit us, she was scandalized and told us that we were wrong to receive you without warning her beforehand and that you weren't right to keep your visits secret. She made me promise to ask you to go to her house tomorrow at four o'clock because she simply must talk to you."

Mario had listened carefully, trying not to give away the distress he felt.

"And she didn't say anything else? Please don't hide anything from me."

Orsola was unable to keep quiet.

"I'll tell you the truth," she exclaimed. "Signora Sigrano made it clear to us that your perseverance will compromise my goddaughter, and she also added that I absolutely must not allow things to continue."

"It's true," Anna Maria murmured, her countenance pale and troubled. "And she painted an unflattering picture of you, but I came to your defense because I can't believe you have such dubious aims. Nonetheless, certain insinuations have unsettled me."

The young officer was assailed by feelings of anger and pain, even desperation. He took Anna Maria's hand with tears welling up in his eyes.

"Thank you, thank you for not believing such deceitful insinuations. I can't tell you at this moment why Signora Sigrano hates me and is trying to damage my reputation, but one day you'll know and will forgive me. Right now, Signora Sigrano's accusation has destroyed any vestige of hesitation or delay that I might have felt. I had wanted to wait before revealing to you, Anna Maria, the true affection that I have felt towards you since we first met. I was afraid of being rejected because of your memories of Alceste, but now your tears tell me that you're not indifferent to me. Here, in front of your godmother, I ask you to be my wife."

Anna Maria gasped.

"Me, your wife?" she repeated. "But you're from a noble family, and I'm just the daughter of a schoolteacher!"

"Well, do you think that's an obstacle for me?" said Mario.

"Maybe not for you," added Anna Maria in a low voice, "but for your parents?"

"My parents will agree. A word from Bruno Sigrano will be enough to assuage them. So, I won't visit Signora Sigrano tomorrow but will go direct to the lawyer and talk to him. I know how to convince him of my love for you, Anna Maria. But I must know if you'll allow me to take this step, if my love is reciprocated and you want to sacrifice your theater ambitions for me."

Anna Maria did not appear remotely distracted by the sparkle of Mario's dark eyes staring at her.

"Are you serious in asking me such a question?" she said in a gentle but firm voice.

"I swear on my mother's life."

"And I, in the presence of my godmother, agree that I'll be happy to share your life and that, from this moment on, will be nobody else's but yours."

Mario let out a cry of delight and brought the girl's hand to his lips and kissed it.

"Your eyes have not deceived me," he exclaimed. "Do you love me, Anna Maria?"

The girl smiled, looked at her godmother, who was beginning to cry, then at the handsome young man who was staring at her with anguished expectation. "I love you, Mario," she replied simply, without embarrassment.

The rest of the evening passed in a flash. What seemed to separate them had, instead, united them. Mario made a thousand plans for the future, which Anna Maria answered calmly but with admirable finesse, while showing her innocent nature, something he found irresistible.

They parted company at midnight, exchanging their first innocent kiss in front of her godmother.

"See you tomorrow, my dear fiancée," Mario said. "Think of me! I can't wait for the day when we'll no longer be apart."

When he had left, Orsola turned to Anna Maria.

"You were right, and the signora was wrong. Count Mario is a gentleman, and you can now be sure that you'll be his wife. Think of your parents' happiness had they been alive! But why do you look sad now? Surely you must be happy. Are you thinking of Alceste? You must realize that he didn't deserve you."

"I'm thinking that it's due to her that I find myself engaged to Mario," replied the young woman, "and I can't smile at my happiness being based on the death of someone else. It was my duty to be happy in front of Mario, but with you, I can also be sad. I'm going to bed now as all this emotion has tired me out. Good night."

"Good night, dear. God bless you!"

Alone, in her own room, Anna Maria wept. She thought about the little charade she had just enacted with Mario in order to avenge Alceste and crush Sultana and what he would do if he knew. She had sworn to hate him but could not bring herself to do so, just as she could not love him because she knew he had been that woman's lover.

The sinister vision of them together refused to leave her and stifled her tender emotions. Nevertheless, she had promised herself that he would be her husband and she would go through with it. She mouthed these remaining thoughts almost audibly with dry eyes and trembling lips. Then, defeated and feeling martyred to the core, she broken down in tears once more.

The following day, at four in the afternoon, Sultana was waiting for Count Herbert in her living room. The lawyer was at the office and would not return until seven for the evening meal. Teresa had taken the children to a toy fair, and Caterina had orders to send anyone except Mario away.

Sultana had spent a terrible night thinking of Anna Maria and the count together. Perhaps, though, if he had found out that she had been Alceste's fiancée, his enthusiasm would have waned. As for the young woman, Anna Maria was disposed to do what she and her godmother wanted, so she did not need to worry about her.

The countess bore the traces of a sleepless night on her face. She looked as if she had aged, with a leaden circles around her menacing eyes. But she had kept her beauty, wearing a simple sky-blue dress that fitted her to perfection. Sultana was suffering through her own sense of self-worth and pride. No, she could still not believe that Mario could abandon her or even be horrified by her. He had, after all, once knelt before her as if she were a goddess.

She blamed Alceste, cursing him as the avenging obstacle who had risen between them. Then, on second thought, she realized it was a pretext and that Mario had evoked the shadow of Alceste because he was fed up with her. But there would be hell to pay if he tried to seduce the dead man's fiancée.

Sultana had prepared a speech in her mind that she would deliver to the count with the gravity of a mother who wanted to prevent her son from doing something crazy. Given the last conversation she had had with the officer, she knew she could no longer act as a lover. Had she not told him herself to forget the past, to forgive her for her madness, and to just remain friends with her? She, therefore, had to behave with a degree of consistency, although her intense character and her feverish thoughts could lead her to lash out with recriminations and threats.

Sultana, deep in self-absorption, thought neither of her husband nor her children. It was possible that she did not even love Mario. If the young man had been smarter and had feigned the love he did not feel, she would have been the first to tire of things because her whims were short lived and another would have taken his place.

However, his resistance had inflamed her guilty passion, and she had tried everything conceivable to take him again. On the surface, though, despite her personality, Sultana had managed to maintain the appearance that she was indifferent to men, which led people to think she had a spotless character.

Four o'clock passed, then five, and Mario made no entrance. She sat there waiting nervously, in the throes of real anxiety. Had he not visited Anna Maria the night before? Was he avoiding the temptation of being alone with her again? If he did not show up, she would go and seek him out. Although Mario had changed his residence, it would be easy to find out his new address by phoning the barracks. She now had a good excuse to go and find him.

More time passed, and Sultana remained motionless in the armchair, distraught and nervous. Tears began to well in her eyes as she muttered to herself. Suddenly she heard the voices of her children coming home and galvanized, stood up. By now it was useless waiting anymore, and she was determined to visit Mario the following day.

Once she had made this decision, she was able to calmly embrace the children and respond to their chatter, so much so that when Bruno returned home, he found her laughing, with Mina on her knees and

Ottorino sitting on a stool at her feet. The lawyer was in a cheerful mood.

"Good evening, Sultana," he said to his wife, who had stood up to hug him. "Didn't you go out today?"

"No…I didn't feel like it, but I sent the children to the toy fair."

"And we had a lot of fun," Ottorino shouted.

"I won a doll!" Mina added.

A smile lit up the lawyer's loyal face as he kissed his wife and children. Caterina announced that dinner was ready, and while Mina and Ottorino followed her, Bruno and Sultana moved into the adjoining room and took their seats at the table.

"Today," said the lawyer, "I had an unexpected visit and a question that I expected even less, but which, nevertheless, made me very happy."

Sultana, not imagining what it was about, listened with a smile. "You never miss out on a meeting."

"That's true," replied Bruno, whose mood seemed very buoyant.

Caterina served the soup then withdrew. He took a few spoons of the minestrone, continuing to talk.

"Today's visitor, however, should have come to you instead, but he didn't dare, having neglected us for a couple of weeks. So, you can easily guess who I'm talking about."

Sultana understood and stiffened her nerve against showing any emotion.

"It's only that reckless Mario who neglects us so," she replied with a smile.

"Yes, you guessed it, but I can assure you that you'd never recognize the dear boy anymore. He's become serious, thoughtful, and spoke to me like a son to his father.…"

Caterina came back to change the dishes and serve another course.

"I have little faith that he's changed," added Sultana. "In any case, let's hear what he wanted from you."

Bruno handed the tray to his wife so that she could take some food first.

"He confessed to me that he was in love with Anna Maria and begged me to persuade his father to agree to the marriage."

Sultana let out a thunderous peal of laughter.

"Mario's making fun of you!" she exclaimed when she had calmed down. "The husband of Anna Maria, him? It's absurd."

"No, my dear, no, because, you see, in a letter that I've kept from Mario's father, the good man confides in me that he'd like to see his only son married. He says that at his age and in his position, it's easy for him to fall into the hands of some adventuress. He even adds that he's not worried about a daughter-in-law's nobility or wealth, simply that she come from an honorable family of equal virtue.…"

Sultana interrupted him rather violently. "And you're happy to be Anna Maria's guarantor? Remember she was Alceste's fiancée, and they were often alone together in the freedom of the countryside. Besides, if she was whiter than white, she wouldn't have tried to attract Mario or hide his visits from me, especially since I treat her like a daughter."

The lawyer, now paying serious attention, listened in silence. "Perhaps you're right, but neither Anna Maria nor Mario thought there was any harm in being together in the presence of her godmother. Mario swore to me that he'd never said any words of affection before last night. He had simply wanted to approach her, to get to know her character, and to guess her intentions. Anna Maria has not hidden anything from him about her past life or her engagement to Alceste. He swears that there is no young woman who could be more honest and loyal and that he wishes to make her his partner in life. And I believe him. Only last night, when her godmother begged him to cease his visits, did he declare his love and ask Anna Maria for her hand in marriage. He added that he would come and talk to me today, sure that I'd help him persuade his father."

Sultana couldn't help but grind her teeth. "And you? What was your answer?"

"I approved of his plan as I, too, hold Anna Maria in great esteem. After all, you've also always said that it was your wish to see her married and happy, which would fulfil a duty you felt towards her."

"Yes, I did say that, and I'll be delighted to repeat it," Sultana replied, "but that libertine Mario surely can't satisfy my requirements or yours."

Bruno frowned, prompting a deep wrinkle to appear on his forehead.

"You're decidedly averse to Count Herbert," he said with a harsh edge to his voice. "I've noticed it before, but it seems worse now. Don't you think this is rather an injustice?"

From these words and even more from the tone with which Bruno had spoken them, Sultana understood that her hostility could betray her. She bowed her head to him.

"Yes, I could be wrong. But what do you want me to say?! It seems impossible that such a vain and frivolous young man could suddenly acquire good judgment."

"He's always had it," added Bruno, finding a smile, "despite his jocular manner, which makes him appear the Don Juan. However, having talked to him seriously, I see something else in him. Mario has heart and feeling, all of which means that he dreams of domestic happiness and healthy children to dance on his knee, who reflect, as ours do, the virtues of their mother.

"It's not a passing whim that attracts him to Anna Maria, but love, an honorable sentiment that can't end in anything but marriage. He told me that he felt like a castaway and, with tears in his eyes, that Anna Maria was his lifeline. I, therefore, promised him all my support.

I told him that I'd write to his father, giving him a good account of the young woman, who is not without a reasonable dowry.

"Sultana, dear, you should go and visit Anna Maria tomorrow, since she doesn't dare come here, fearing that she may have unintentionally offended you. You can gauge her feelings and where her heart lies, thereby making sure she's really willing to be Mario's wife. You'll be able to help her find future happiness."

Sultana felt her rebellious streak break free. Several times during Bruno's monologue she had been tempted to shout at him, unleashing her real thoughts, questioning why he had not yet understood that Mario was her lover, that he had stolen her away, that she still loved Mario even though she hated him, and that she would never allow him to marry Anna Maria.

Yet her lips remained sealed. However daring she was, she could not confess all to her decent if credulous husband, who had placed her on a pedestal, not for fear that he, in the heat of the moment, might kill her, but because she would lose the halo of honesty that made her proud and envied by other women.

She also understood that her confession would not be enough to get back at Mario because Bruno would have spared him. The part her husband wanted to play in Anna Maria's marriage struck her as ridiculous, even awful, but she had to accept it. The idea that it was only the young woman herself who could destroy the proposed union and ruin Mario's dreams quickly came to mind. Anna Maria had such trust in her that she would believe it if she told her that the officer was unworthy of her and that, while he swore undying love, was in a relationship with someone else who was entitled to his fidelity. With this plan in mind, she replied to her husband with a marked change in tone. "You're always right Bruno, dear, and you know how to see things in a clearer light than I do. I will go to Anna Maria, and you can be sure that, if it's up to me to make her happy, I will do it with all my heart."

The lawyer felt a surge of emotion. "Now that's better, my darling!" he exclaimed. "You'll see. By talking to her and then to Mario, you'll be persuaded that it would be difficult to find a better matched couple. After which, you'll be willing to join me in helping them find happiness."

Sultana remained silent but found the strength to smile as if she fully approved.

14

Now hopeful, Sultana spent a peaceful night. Around ten in the morning, wrapped in a fur cloak and wearing a velvet hat adorned with a feather, she walked towards Anna Maria's house. Under her light veil, she took deep breaths of the crisp air, which expanded her lungs and gave her a sense of well-being. She kept her hands hidden in an otter fur muff and walked swiftly with her head held high like a young woman of twenty. In fact, she seemed little older with her golden locks, her creamy pink complexion, and her shining eyes. She was beautiful and had herself noticed it when looking in the mirror that morning, a feeling that made her face appear calmer and gentler.

Behind the windows of Matteo Ferpio's restaurant, she saw that the tables were prepared, waiting for his customers and boarders. She thought about how Alceste had dined at one of them on the last evening of his life. She felt a slight shiver and looked away from the tables immediately entering the hallway of the house and climbing the stairs. However, she stopped for a moment in front of the door to the small set of rooms inhabited by Anna Maria and her godmother. Her heart had begun to beat rapidly, and for a moment, she felt the anguish of the night before.

Quickly regaining her composure, she rang the bell with a steady hand. There was the sound of footsteps inside, and the door opened to reveal the smiling figure of Anna Maria. The young woman was wearing a simple house dress made of grey wool, with a high neckline, similar to those worn by schoolgirls, over which she had a gold chain with an icon of the Madonna hanging from it. The simplicity of her appearance gave her a fascinating innocence.

On seeing Signora Sigrano, Anna Maria expressed her delight. "You! It's you!" she exclaimed. "Come in. Come in. I've been expecting you."

"You've been expecting me?" Sultana replied warmly as she followed the young woman into the living room where they were alone. "And who told you of my visit?"

"Nobody, but I guessed that you'd come to see me once you'd heard from your husband about his conversation with Mario.... But, please, sit down."

Sultana was startled to hear the name of the count spoken with such sweetness and familiarity, but sitting down on the low sofa, she tried to be casual.

"You guessed correctly. As soon as I heard about their chat, I wanted to talk to you, but I want to ensure we're alone without any prying ears."

"You've chosen the right time," said Anna Maria, sitting on a chair in front of the countess, "since I'm alone in the house. My godmother spends her mornings at the house of a lady who is not very well. She keeps her company. Camilla is in the courtyard helping Matteo's wife do the laundry. So, do speak freely, because I'm the only one who can hear."

"That's what I was hoping for," Sultana replied. She threw the muff on the sofa, lifted her veil over her forehead and removed the fur that was too warm for the room, where a stove was lit. Her demeanor changed and became serious. "First, I would like to know why Mario went to my husband rather than coming to me, since you must have told him."

"Yes, signora," answered the young woman gently. "My godmother and I repeated exactly what you'd asked us to say. Yet, when Mario, who had never before uttered affectionate words, felt that his visits here had to cease, he confessed, with tears in his eyes, that his intentions were honorable. Given the opportunity, he revealed in front of my godmother that his feelings were both noble and honest. He asked if I was willing to become his wife and then said that he would talk to Signor Sigrano before you, because he could help with ensuring his father's consent."

"What a cad!" Sultana exclaimed between gritted teeth. "And did you believe him?"

Anna Maria managed to summon up an admirable surge of astonishment. "Why shouldn't I believe him? What interest would he have in deceiving me? I've done nothing to encourage his declaration, and the trust he's inspired in me has been such that I've hidden nothing from him about my past, about my engagement to Alceste, about the love I had for him, which was cut short by his tragic end, or about the motives that led him to such a sad destiny."

Sultana was trembling and had turned pale. "Is Mario equally sincere with you?" she said in a tone full of irony.

"Yes, signora. He hasn't hidden the fact that he had been leading a rather dissipated life until now, that he'd been led astray by casual relationships, even if such ephemeral pleasures had only led to bitterness and despair. He said that it was only from the evening of our first meeting that he really understood how things could be different and that his newfound feelings could ennoble even the most abject of men and make their lives worth living. I, too, have felt that it was our destiny to be together, and last night, when Mario came to tell me that Signor Sigrano had approved of his choice and was sure of obtaining his father's consent, I had all the proof I needed of his sincerity. We swore our mutual fidelity and sealed it with a kiss."

Anna Maria spoke with naivety, but firmly, refusing to lock eyes with Sultana's burning gaze.

"You must break that oath!" Sultana exclaimed, no longer able to contain herself. "No, you must not marry Mario. He's unworthy of you."

"Unworthy of me?" the young woman replied in a shrill voice. "What on earth has he done?"

"Mario has a relationship with someone else that he can't break," Sultana replied resolutely.

"Does he have a wife, then?" Anna Maria said with incomparable candor.

"No," answered Sultana, "but he's seduced another man's wife, and this woman, who has sacrificed everything for him, who loves him madly, will not give him up for you or anyone else."

The young woman lifted her head with pride. "Is that all? I was beginning to worry. Well, I can tell you that she's deceiving herself. Mario doesn't have the makings of a lothario, and almost certainly, the woman you're talking about must have seduced him instead. She's to blame if she had the temerity to deceive her husband, who probably loved her and still does. In any case, it's likely that Mario, by ending this relationship, has swapped such a heavy chain for a lighter one, less tangled with barbed wire. And I'm delighted to help him disentangle himself from such an unwholesome bond."

Sultana wanted to hurl insults at Anna Maria but resisted the temptation, suddenly changing to becoming gentler and milder. She caught her eye and began to speak. "What if that woman were me?" she murmured in anguish.

"You? You? Repeat that so I'm sure I heard you right. You, Count Mario Herbert's lover?"

"Yes," repeated Sultana in a choked voice. "May God preserve you, my child, from certain passions that overwhelm your existence, that make you trample on the most sacred of duties and forget those dearest to you. The love that drew me to Mario has upset my spirit and reason, has eaten away at me, and makes me long for death."

She started to sob, then extended to her arms to Anna Maria in a desperate gesture.

"My dear girl, would you comfort me?" she asked. "Tell me you'll reject him...."

Anna Maria began to laugh, a seemingly unrelenting laugh bordering on the manic.

"You're amused?" stammered Sultana, both fearful and surprised.

"Yes, I am," answered the young woman, raising her head proudly. "I'm laughing at the thought of what an admirable trickster you are and at how far your audacity will go. Did you also spin the same sentimental line to Alceste so that the poor unfortunate gave up his claim, handing you meekly to someone else?"

Sultana gasped, turning pale. The countess now understood, in the young woman's words and stare, that she knew a great deal about her and was an enemy ready to take revenge at the right moment. She had no time to answer, though, because Anna Maria continued talking. "Come on. Throw away that mask that covers your face and show yourself as the cynical, dishonest, and evil woman you really are. I'm not the least bit frightened of you at all. I've known for a long time just who I'm dealing with, but I wanted to hear the shameless confession from your own lips. But you're not going to achieve the end you want because I won't give up on Mario. No! And you, yourself, will tell your husband that you're happy with the marriage, and you'll accompany me to the civic ceremony and the altar."

Sultana lost all restraint.

"Never!" she cried. "After all, what can you do to hurt me? Nothing!"

"Are you sure? Well, I'm sorry but you're wrong. Wait a moment."

Anna Maria got up and disappeared into the next room leaving Sultana feeling destroyed. Was this all possible? Not only did the girl know everything, but she had evidence in her hands that could ruin her. Were these proofs the very items that had induced her to kill Alceste?

Anna Maria returned with a sheet of paper. It was a copy of Alceste's letter.

"Read it!" she exclaimed, handing it brusquely to Signora Sigrano. "I'm not giving you the original as I know what you're capable of, but I can tell you that, together with this letter, I have the objects that Alceste talks about, and they won't leave my possession unless they are passed to your husband or the king's attorney, which I'll do if you try to get in my way, if you prevent me from getting what is rightfully mine. You took my fiancé from me, and I'll take your lover away from you, but not on a whim, to make him my legitimate husband instead."

Sultana's anger overcame her anguish and fear. "This still doesn't take away from the fact that Mario loved me before you, more than you. You'll never be able to make him forget my kisses."

Anna Maria lost the color in her cheeks but kept her head high.

"I'm not looking for Mario's love or affection," she said, "but I do want his name, and I'll have it!"

Sultana did not answer. She was reading the letter, a letter which could drag her name through the mud, reveal her shamelessness, her infamy, and reopen the doors of the prison from which she had been able to walk free. And to think she had believed in Anna Maria's naivety and thought her a docile puppet in her hands. Nevertheless, she would lay a bet that the girl did not know what to do with Mario, apart from wanting him for a husband in order to avenge herself and Alceste. Had she told Mario of her plan? No, the officer would not have believed it, but then, Anna Maria could produce Alceste's letter, something which could lead to her disgrace.

The more she read, the angrier and more uncontrollable she became. The dead man had taken a terrible revenge. He had judged his fiancée well by choosing her as an instrument of retribution. She was finished! If she did not find the strength to avert the worst, things would end in catastrophe. Maybe it was enough to give her consent to the marriage, to approve of it…then she would be safe. Otherwise, the young woman would be totally unforgiving. At that moment, Sultana had flashes of her past life in her mind's eye, all her dishonorable actions, of which the wider world had not the slightest suspicion. And she must have seen her well-designed edifice of lies tumble, all because of her insane passion for a young man who no longer loved her, who in fact, now despised her.

But how could she admit to being beaten in front of Anna Maria? Sultana was in utter turmoil, in a fate worse than death. Yet she had to decide. Her hands holding the paper began to shake with nerves, and her eyes widened with anxiety. She bit her lip in a convulsive manner, and her face appeared disheveled, full of anguish.

"I shot your fiancé, it's true," she said in a broken voice, "but he's taking revenge by slinging mud in my face. A fate I don't deserve. He's lying to you as a way of excusing himself for having betrayed you."

"Don't insult the dead as well as the living!" replied Anna Maria, maintaining her calm sense of superiority. "The letter you wrote to Count Mario is plenty enough to judge you in a poor light."

Sultana pressed her dry lips between her teeth.

"Be that as it may, I'm not here to discuss the love lives of Alceste and Mario," added the young woman, "but to claim my rights in front of you. Are you willing to go back to your husband and say that you're truly convinced that my happiness depends on my marriage to Mario and to admit to him how glad you are with the choice Mario's made?"

"Well, yes!" Sultana replied. "But in exchange for my compliance and agreement, you'll give me the original of this letter and the other objects left by Alceste."

Anna Maria laughed, full of sarcasm. "Do you really think that's going to happen? Alceste's letter and the other items are my guarantee, my defense, and I've kept them secret for these past two years. They will remain a secret unless you retaliate or if you continue to betray the decent, generous man whose name you bear. He has such faith in your love and the nobility of your sentiments. On the other hand, if you die before me, I swear that I'll destroy the evidence of your crime and infidelities so that your children are not tarred with your brush."

Sultana reflected for a moment. "It's my atonement," she murmured as if speaking to herself, before raising her head. "You're merciless, and I realize that nothing can shift you from the resolution you've made. So be it! I give in. But beware that one day you don't regret this marriage since Mario isn't a man to remain faithful to you for long. He will abandon you, just as he's abandoned me."

Anna Maria remained calm with a smile on her face.

"You don't have to concern yourself about me, signora," she replied, "since that's for me to worry about. So, are we decided then? When you return home, you'll tell your husband that you believe me worthy of Mario's love and that you're delighted with the marriage. Tonight, I'll inform Mario that my benefactress, for whom I have so much affection and veneration, came to visit me to congratulate me on my fortune and happiness and that she was delighted."

Sultana listened, motionless, to the wheezing of her breath. "Can you swear to me," she said through clenched teeth, "that Mario is unaware of the existence of Alceste's letter and the other items?"

"I swear to you, signora, as I also swear that my godmother and those close to me know nothing about them. They just think that I have a deep esteem for you, like a daughter for a loving mother."

"And you still swear that Mario never told you about the relationship between us?"

"I do. He must've been afraid of offending me, and perhaps even losing me, by telling the truth."

Sultana felt a momentary choking sensation once more. She jumped to her feet and then, with a totally altered voice, started to speak, a bewitching smile now on her face. "Go ahead, reach for your dream, Anna Maria. I will help you because I know you're worthy. I admire you. Tell Mario that tomorrow evening I'll be waiting for you so we can celebrate your engagement with the family, which will become official as soon as he gets his parents' consent, something that won't be long in coming."

"I hope so. And thank you, signora," Anna Maria answered. "You can be sure that we'll obey you and be there, grateful for your kindness and sensitivity towards us."

Her voice was gentle, but the meaning of the words made Sultana turn ashen faced.

"See you tomorrow evening. Could you let me have the copy of Alceste's letter?" she added, trying to be casual.

"Keep it. The original is enough for me."

Sultana hastened to hide the sheet in her handbag and put on her fur. Before lowering her veil, she brushed the young woman's cheek with her lips. "No bitterness," she said, smiling, before walking towards the door.

Anna Maria accompanied her to the landing and watched her go down the stairs. Sultana turned to look up and saw her leaning over the railing.

"See you again," she added, then disappeared through the hallway. Anna Maria went back inside her apartment.

She was now sure of victory, yet her face expressed pain rather than anything triumphal. She could not believe in Signora Sigrano's indulgence and knew she had to be very careful with regard to herself and Mario. In thinking of the count's name, she was overcome with sadness. Sultana's insinuation about their marriage had aroused a degree of anxiety. She realized her victory would be worthless without his true affection but was equally aware that her deception would lower her to Sultana's level. She would fight to win with a smile on her lips, naïve or provocative, depending on the circumstances.

Anna Maria knew that she would always hate her rival, the killer of poor Alceste and someone who was capable of killing Mario just out of vengeance. This time, however, she would be there to intervene between Sultana and the potential victim.

When her godmother returned home with Camilla, she found Anna Maria in a singularly happy and lively mood.

"She's been here. Signora Sigrano!" she said. "And she wasn't the same as yesterday. Now that Mario has explained himself, she's delighted and wants us to visit her tomorrow evening to celebrate the happy event together. You'll come with me, won't you, godmother?"

"Of course, I shouldn't and won't let you go alone in these circumstances," replied Orsola. "My legs are a bit weak, but seeing you so happy and glad, has helped me regained a bit of my strength. If only your parents were around, they'd be so pleased seeing you become a countess. They'll all be amazed back in the village. And you owe everything to the good lady, Signora Sigrano. Don't forget that."

"I won't, you can be sure of that," replied Anna Maria with the hint of a mysterious smile.

Matteo Ferpio and his wife were also delighted to hear the news.

"I didn't think the girl would forget poor Alceste so quickly," said Matteo somewhat inevitably.

"Well, it's the right thing," observed Marietta. "What comfort did your friend bring her? If he'd loved her, he would've stayed close to her and wouldn't have lost his mind over some other woman. It wasn't because of Anna Maria that he got himself killed. I think you've mourned him enough. What's more, she would've been daft to refuse that cavalry officer since, besides his illustrious name and wealth, he's a nice man who sincerely loves her."

"You're always right," Matteo concluded.

In the evening when Mario came to Anna Maria's, she told him about Sultana's visit with words of affection and gratitude.

"If you only knew her as she really is. She's happy with our marriage. She regards me as a daughter so her only fears were that your intentions towards me were less than honest. Now, however, she's convinced of your sincerity and feelings. She will also help us achieve our dream as soon as possible. She wants us to come to her house tomorrow evening."

"I've also received an invitation from her husband," Mario replied.

The prospect of appearing as Anna Maria's fiancé in front of Sultana did not appeal to him in the slightest. It seemed impossible that she had adapted so quickly to their split. Maybe, though, it was possible she could be sincere and repentant, given she had acknowledged that her feelings had made her neglect her duties. Sultana must have understood that the relationship could not continue. After the initial acrimony, perhaps she had tried not only to forget, but also to appear generous with them both in an attempt to gain their gratitude. This idea reassured him because his own feelings for Anna Maria, along with his youth, had encouraged him to search for the decency in others.

Hearing his fiancée's praise for the signora, he added some warm sentiments, so much so that the young woman stared at him with a restless gaze, gripped by anxiety. Surely Mario was not still in love with the witch? No, no! His face showed no sign of turmoil, and his eyes reflected nothing but loyalty. Comforted, she laughed happily.

15

On returning home, Signora Sigrano knew her husband would already be at the table with the children waiting for her.

"I'm coming now," she said. Her eyes felt clouded, and her mind was a whirl of uncomfortable thoughts. After freshening her face with cologne and putting on a dressing gown, she appeared transformed. She had managed to hide the hard expression on her face, and the blood had returned to her cheeks. The old sparkle lit up her eyes, and she managed a gentle smile.

"Here I am," she announced, appearing on the threshold of the room. "I know I'm late."

"You're already forgiven," her husband replied, while the children rushed to kiss her. "I know where you've been. Well?"

"Well, my dear Bruno, Anna Maria is beside herself with contentment and doesn't know how to express her gratitude to us for the help we're offering in making their dream come true."

"So, Anna Maria loves you?"

"More than I would have thought. The dear thing, she opened up entirely to me, and I was very moved. She then happily accepted the invitation for tomorrow evening."

"I'm really pleased to hear it. I'll be sure to appear pleasantly surprised for Anna Maria and Mario."

A shiver ran down Sultana's spine. "How so?"

"This morning I received this telegram from Count Herbert in reply to my letter."

Sultana hesitated to read the sheet her husband had handed to her.

My wife and I accept your hospitality to meet the young lady who, chosen by you, will doubtless be worthy of our family. Don't warn

Mario, we want to surprise him by personally giving our consent to their engagement. We will arrive at noon tomorrow.

Herbert

Sultana suddenly felt the heat of anxiety on her face, but the smile remained on her lips.

"Excellent!" she exclaimed. "It's clear that the count is not unappreciative, and to please you, he's willing to trample on the family's aristocratic traditions, allowing his son to marry a simple bourgeois."

"Nowadays, more is thought of the happiness of the couple than titles!" he replied good-naturedly. "You, yourself, who could've aspired to marry an aristocrat, preferred the modest professional who fell in love with you. Have you ever regretted that marriage?"

"Truthfully, no, and you know it," Sultana answered hugging him.

They sat down at the table and, while they were eating, Bruno continued to talk about the couple and the preparations for the following evening.

"I won't leave the house for the rest of today," Sultana said, "as I want the apartment for the Herberts to be tidied. We'll give them a bedroom, drawing room, and the bathroom that gives on to the winter gallery so that way they'll feel totally at ease."

"I'll leave it to you, dear, to arrange everything as you see fit. Shall we both go in the car to pick them up from the station?"

"Of course!"

Signora Sigrano had not met Mario's parents before and was surprised to find them younger than she had anticipated, given that they already had a married daughter. Count Herbert, Senior was a handsome man, tall, with a mustache and dark hair that had kept the grey at bay. Accompanying his aristocratic grace was an amiable character without any sign of haughtiness.

Countess Jolanda Herbert was the image of her son, blonde like him, with dark eyes and a gentle gaze. She possessed a charm that displayed the kindness of her character in the most natural of ways. It was easy to see that she was one of those sincere people who had never been affected by the shadow of life's worst aspects, whose existence could be summed up in duty and love for her children and husband. They were an exemplary couple.

Sultana and Jolanda hugged like two friends, and the lawyer exchanged a genuine embrace with the count. In the car on the way to the Sigrano palazzo, there was time for them all to scrutinize one another.

"Well, do you know, countess," asked Sultana in her most appealing voice, "that nobody would believe you were Mario's mother? You look more like his sister!"

"Yet I also have a married daughter, two years older than Mario, and I've been a grandmother for five years," Jolanda answered with a radiant smile. "Though you, signora, also seem young to me and, without overly complimenting you, I have to say that you're much more beautiful than the picture that you were kind enough to send me."

"You're too kind," Sultana replied.

"My wife is right," exclaimed the count in turn. "I congratulate you, my friend. Just like me, you've chosen a beautiful, decent, and intelligent companion. Among all these modern women, we have two rare pearls."

"We can, indeed, be proud about that," agreed the lawyer with enthusiasm.

Not a muscle on Sultana's face twitched as she continued to smile along with Jolanda.

"Let's hope our Mario is equally lucky," added the count.

"I hope so," Bruno answered firmly. "Signorina Anna Maria Tosingo-Belgrado is an affectionate and gentle girl with the face of an angel and the heart of a dove. She's like a daughter to Sultana and me, isn't she, dear?"

"Very true," Sultana replied, "and your Mario fell in love with her from the first day he met her."

"She's an orphan, didn't you say that in your letter?" observed the count.

"Yes," replied Bruno. "She lives with her godmother and guardian, an elderly moneyed woman, and Anna Maria is her only heir. However, she already has a dowry of about one-hundred-and-fifty-thousand lire. It's true that her father was a simple schoolmaster and her mother modestly middle class, but nonetheless, the daughter has a solid education and very decent manners. Her dowry came from an uncle, a very rich farmer."

"Oh!" Jolanda exclaimed with a winning, almost childish smile. "My husband and aren't worried about questions of nobility or money, we just need to know that she's an honest girl and that she sincerely loves our Mario and will make him happy."

"I can guarantee that," Bruno replied gravely.

The car had stopped in front of the house, and the conversation was subsequently cut short. With her usual skill and good taste, Sultana had already arranged everything for the reception of her guests and for the evening. Nobody was to warn Anna Maria or Mario of the arrival of the Herberts, who would appear at just the right moment.

The closer it came to evening, the more Sultana became agitated. At times, she felt as if she were suffocating, or her heart was about to give out. She made a great effort to think only about her duty to others but was troubled by the idea that Anna Maria had triumphed and that she would have to bow, defeated, before the girl whose indomitable will, cunning, and hypocrisy in exacting her revenge was unknown to everyone except herself — it was a feeling that induced feverish thoughts that made everything swim before her eyes.

Would she have the strength to face the blooming couple, their mutual affection? Nonetheless, the need to remain calm was imperative. No one could know the storms in her soul. Sultana wanted to keep her good name and supposed moral integrity in the face of the world. Anna Maria and Mario would pay for these feelings of hers later on.

Signora Sigrano had never been as striking as she was that evening in a low-cut velvet dress that highlighted her pale complexion and golden hair. But even her beauty was not as arresting as that of Countess Jolanda, whose attraction was chiefly in her kind smile and grace, whereas Sultana's blue eyes could not hide an arrogance nor her smile a sense of high-handedness and resentment.

When Caterina announced Signora Orsola Martin and her goddaughter, Signorina Anna Maria, the Herberts disappeared behind a door leading to an adjoining drawing room, but in its lee, they could easily see the young woman enter in the company of her godmother. The impression she made was immediately favorable. The couple were fascinated by her whole demeanor, one of rare elegance and integrity, by her fresh-faced youth, her chaste and dignified air, and the intelligence and loyalty she projected.

"She's enchanting," Jolanda whispered in her husband's ear.

"Oh yes!" he added. "That rascal Mario has good taste."

In fear of being discovered ahead of time, the couple withdrew. Sultana had stepped forward to meet Orsola and Anna Maria, kissing her on the forehead and shaking her godmother's hand. She then invited them to sit down.

Orsola had worn a black silk dress, which the young woman, herself, had modernized and which gave her a distinguished appearance. She also wore a black lace bonnet over her white hair, which, still thick, was and parted above her forehead.

"You can't believe, dear Orsola, the pleasure you give us by accompanying your goddaughter," said the lawyer affably, "especially on such an occasion."

"I would have come before now," said Orsola, "but my poor legs can hardly hold me up, and I've had to give them a rest. Tonight, however, I would've felt like I was failing in my duty by staying at home. And I must take this opportunity to express my deep gratitude to you and your good lady for what you have done for my goddaughter."

"Oh yes!" Anna Maria added with a sweet naivety. "I owe my present happiness to you, signora, and to you, Signor Sigrano. I'll never forget it."

"It was my duty to ensure that you're happy," Sultana replied.

Count Mario was then announced. Anna Maria looked at Sultana and noticed she was very pale but was managing to hold her head high despite an unpleasant sneer. Mario entered, appearing to be deeply moved. After greeting his fiancée and Orsola with a smile, he bowed to Signora Sigrano.

"I thank you," he said, a red tinge rising rapidly to his cheeks, "for your kind invitation and for the interest you and your husband have taken in me."

"Not so much in you," answered Sultana laughing and holding out her hand, which he brought to his lips, "but in this dear girl, whom I love like a daughter. In truth, you didn't deserve our indulgence for having acted in secret...."

"I assure you, signora, that I don't deserve your reproach," Mario swiftly replied, "because I've done nothing that could offend you or your husband. My visits to Anna Maria, with her godmother present, were most innocent, and I would never have revealed how I felt to the young woman, fearing rejection, if it hadn't been said that my attentiveness towards her could end up compromising her. At that point, I didn't hesitate, asking her if she wanted to be my wife. She said that she'd be happy to do so, and therefore, I went straight to Signor Sigrano, knowing that he could intercede with my father, and begged him to plead my case."

"It's true," confirmed the lawyer, warmly shaking hands with the young man, "and, moved by your loyalty and the high esteem in which you hold Anna Maria, I immediately wrote to Count Herbert eager to contribute to your happiness."

"Go and get your letter and the reply," interrupted Sultana, turning to her husband, smiling.

"The answer? You've already got it?" Mario exclaimed eagerly.

"Yes," added Sultana, while Bruno, exchanging a knowing glance with his wife, left the room.

"Come on, Mario. Sit down with your fiancée, because I know you're dying to, while I talk to Orsola."

How could he now be suspicious of Signora Sigrano? At that moment, Mario reproached himself for having doubted her decency, her repentance, and answered with obvious emotion.

"Thank you, signora," he said. "Anna Maria is right to tell you that you're kind and generous."

"Anna Maria understood me better than you!"

The young woman had not said a word, remaining calm, and when Mario sat next to her so he could take her hand, she smiled at him in an ineffable manner, both captivating and laden with feeling.

The two young people had not yet exchanged a word when a door was opened and the Herberts appeared with Bruno Sigrano. Mario, surprised, rushed towards them.

"Father, mother! You're here!" he exclaimed in a voice choked with emotion.

"We've come to bring you the answer in person and to meet your fiancée," the countess answered softly.

Briefly, the three devoted family members exchanged affectionate greetings, then Mario, with tears in his eyes, ran to bring them the young woman who had stood up in response, feeling somewhat intimidated. As she tried to stay her trembling, he introduced her to his parents.

"This is Signorina Anna Maria Tosingo-Belgrado, about whom our good friend, the lawyer, has spoken to you. I hope you won't blame her for stealing away a part of my heart that belonged to you before I met her. I'm sure you'll love her like a daughter when you get to know her."

Countess Jolanda drew the girl towards her warmly and kissed her on the forehead.

"You already have my affection," she told her with the frankness central to her character, "because you've made my Mario wise and happy. Also, when I give someone my love, I never take it back."

Anna Maria's eyes clouded with tears.

"Countess," she murmured, "I don't know how to express my gratitude. I can only say that, from this moment on, I'm at your disposal."

"Then, I, with the full consent of my husband, give you permission to marry my son," added the countess, who smiled, hiding the emotion she felt.

"And, trust me, I'll know how to guard her jealously," said Mario, hugging his father, mother, and even Bruno several times, not knowing how else to show his joy and gratitude.

It was then Orsola's turn to meet the Herberts, and Anna Maria was moved to say that they owed all their happiness to Signor Sigrano, but above all, to the countess. Sultana, during the entire proceedings, had barely been able to contain herself, but it was only the occasional grimace that betrayed the violent passions beneath the surface. Finally able to impose her indomitable will, she managed, when her turn came, to kiss Anna Maria with feigned effusion.

"It's not just kindness that makes me love you," she said, "but the seductive influence you have over those around you, my dear."

"It's true! That's right!" said the others.

"What you're saying is what we all think, Sultana," added Bruno.

"Thank you," murmured the young woman.

She had lost the color from her cheeks owing to a singularly distressful thought, namely that Sultana was not alone in pretending at that moment. She, herself, was also not revealing the truth because, although she loved Mario, she could not forget that he had been her lover. She feared that the flame could be rekindled, even if she could make him happy, he might not be able to commit himself.

She, too, was therefore an unworthy creature just like Sultana. It was dishonorable to marry Mario without the corresponding passion he currently felt or any thought of having those feelings in the future. Yet, they had made her suffer so much that it seemed only right that they should also suffer. Nonetheless, in front of good and trusting people like Mario's parents, the lawyer, and her godmother, she had to conceal this at all costs and carry out the part imposed on her, however odious it might seem.

That evening, Anna Maria made a great deal of her talents, singing various romances with a voice that touch the heart, conversing on art, literature, and domestic matters with Countess Herbert, thereby displaying her education, but also her enchanting simplicity.

A superb dinner brought everyone together in a more intimate setting. Seated close to each other, Anna Maria and Mario, while taking part in the general conversation, occasionally exchanged glances and smiles that, when noticed by Sultana, felt like lashes from a whip. Despite these lacerations, she was able to maintain lively conversation.

After the meal had concluded, they all returned to the living room where the lawyer turned to Orsola. "For Count Mario Herbert and in the name of Count and Countess Herbert, I ask you for the hand of your goddaughter, Signorina Anna Maria, given that the young lady has still not reached the legal age to marry without your consent."

The old woman was shaking and had tears in her eyes. "I give it to you with all my heart," she stammered. "Anna Maria will one day have my nest egg, which combined with what she already has will make a nice inheritance."

Mario wanted to answer, but his father made a sign to stop him so that he could reply. "Dear lady, my wife and I don't consider financial interests when it comes to the marriage of our son. In giving our consent, we're only thinking of the happiness of the couple. The wedding, however, can't be held immediately, because you can't ignore the formalities required for the marriage of a cavalry officer. This, though, will all be taken care of by our good friend, Bruno, who'll get things done as soon as possible. Meanwhile, Mario, here is the ring that your mother and I have chosen for you to give your fiancée."

On saying this, the count handed a small white box to his son, who in turn gave it to Anna Maria. The young woman blushed but let out a gasp of delight as she opened it.

"How beautiful! Look, Signora Sultana, look Signor Sigrano, and you too, Orsola, look! It's wonderful!"

"Yes, it's really splendid," they all exclaimed.

The ring had a pearl and a diamond that was larger than most.

"We're glad to have met your taste," said the countess.

"And mine too!" interrupted Mario. "Oh, Mama, Papa, how can I thank you?"

"By loving each other, dear boy," said the count, "and, I should also say that, to please your mother, I've decided to spend the winter in Turin where your sister will also be shortly. So together you can all sort out the trousseau and the house. Anna Maria will have all the help she needs."

"You're so kind to me," said the young woman.

"That'll be marvelous!" exclaimed Mario. "I'll put my apartment at your complete disposal, which is too big for me. I'll rent the other floor of the building, which is currently empty. It's a new, very elegant property, with its own garage and stable. There's even central heating.

It also has the advantage that it's not far from the barracks and right in front of my fiancée's house."

"Ah, that's my boy!" said the count laughing. "We'll come and see you tomorrow and take up your offer by the end of the week."

"Don't you want to stay here?" said the lawyer.

"My friend, it's already been too much of an imposition for us to accept your hospitality for a few days," answered the count.

Sultana did not say a word, but her face was so pale that the countess noticed.

"Are you feeling ok, my dear?" she asked in a gentle voice.

The blood rushed back to Sultana's cheeks.

"No," she replied brightly, "I was just feeling slightly dizzy, but it's already passed, and I'm much better now. It would be such a shame if the engagement was disturbed by my slight discomfort."

She laughed in a frank, if youthful manner, which seemed to dispel any unease among the others, but it startled both Mario and Anna Maria. He understood that he had assumed too much about the strength of his ardent former lover and that she could not remain indifferent to all those displays of affection for someone else. Anna Maria felt the irony of her words and the anger that was hidden beneath the laughter. She stood up and approached Sultana for the first time.

"We have abused your kindness, please allow my godmother and I to retire as it must be very late," she said with affectionate good grace.

"Yes, yes, Anna Maria is right," added Mario. "It would be inappropriate to stay any longer. I'll accompany Signora Orsola and my fiancée. I'll come and see my parents in the morning to arrange everything. In the meantime, dear mamma and papa, I thank you very much for the affection you've shown me, and I must also thank you, Signor Bruno and Signora Sultana. You all have my complete gratitude."

The party exchanged compliments as they embraced and kissed each other by way of saying goodbye. Mario then offered his arm to Orsola and left the room, followed by Anna Maria, which prompted the Herberts, who were tired, to excuse themselves so they could retire to their rooms. Caterina offered her services as a maid, which were gratefully accepted, but the couple soon found themselves alone in their bedroom.

"What do you think of Signora Sigrano?" Jolanda asked her husband.

"Extremely attractive," answered the count, "and what do you think?"

"Yes, she is beautiful, but I have to say that I don't like her. She's got a wicked look about her and a cruel smile."

"Funny you should say that. She had the same effect on me."

"And there's something else...."

"Tell me."

"At times, when her eyes lit upon Mario and Anna Maria, they seemed to express an intense dislike."

"I can't say I noticed that," added the count, "but she certainly doesn't have the sincerity and loyalty of her husband. The lawyer was really pleased to see the happiness of his protégé and our son."

"Yes, he's a decent man, and Anna Maria truly does deserve his affection and ours. What a sweet girl!" added the countess with a degree of real enthusiasm. "Bruno didn't exaggerate when he called her an angel, and I'm convinced she'll make our Mario happy."

"He really is in love with her," said the count, "and I'm absolutely sure that if we'd denied him our consent, he would've been desperate. Dear boy, I hope his happiness lasts as long as ours, as you, my love, have been the greatest comfort throughout my entire life."

The count hugged his wife, gently kissing her forehead with genuine emotion.

16

The following morning Mario was dressing to go to see his parents, singing happily, when his orderly entered to say that a lady was asking for him.

"Did you let her in?" he said, thinking it must be his mother.

"Yes, lieutenant, she's in the living room."

"Very good. You can go now. I don't need you at the moment. Come back this afternoon and tidy up my room."

"Yes, lieutenant."

After saluting him, the orderly left. Mario put on his jacket, looked at himself in the mirror, and went into the living room. His visitor was seated in an armchair and stood up as he entered, lifting the veil that covered her face. It was not his mother, but Sultana, pale as a corpse. Mario almost took a step backwards.

"You?" he said, caught between fear and disillusion.

She looked at him with a fierce sarcasm then sat down again.

"I guess you weren't expecting me?" she said with a bitter smile.

Mario remained standing

"No, signora," he replied, trying to regain his composure, "I thought I'd find my mother here."

"Your mother is still asleep and won't be going out this morning. Neither will your father. They'll both be waiting for you. I'm used to going out every morning, and now knowing your new address, I've come to talk to you. Sit down."

Mario obeyed reluctantly, biting his lip.

"I thought we had nothing more to say to each other. You promised to leave me alone, to return to your husband and children, to forget the past, to forget everything."

"And you believed that? Well, I'm here to tell you that I can't, that I don't want to give up on you. I love you. I need you more than ever...."

"I will say again, even if I wasn't engaged to Anna Maria, who now has my heart, I would have broken with you because our relationship unsettles me greatly. The shadow of a dead man hovers over us." Mario interrupted with venom.

"I curse the moment I killed him!" snapped Sultana. "If that wretch had still been alive, Anna Maria wouldn't care about you, she wouldn't pretend to love you in order to be your wife."

"You offend my fiancée by believing her capable of such a vile calculation."

"You'll soon realize that I'm telling the truth."

"Prove it!"

However, Sultana understood that in trying to undermine Anna Maria she was undermining herself. Having no evidence, while the young woman had Alceste's letter, was more than enough to reveal her lies. She kept quiet. Mario made a gesture indicating his anger but also striking a triumphal note.

"You know you're making a false accusation against an innocent girl whose fiancé you've already taken away, and now you'd like to strike for a second time against me."

"Why not since you're now in my way. Mario...once more, I beg you to take pity on me, on the person who loves you and doesn't have the courage to see you with someone else. Call me vile, weak, evil, but don't reject me, please!"

Mario was losing his equilibrium and felt the blood rise to his head.

"Remember what I told you before," he answered abruptly, "I'm no longer yours. The memory of all this will inexorably distance me from you. Tears, threats, or prayers, they're all useless. Accuse me in front of your husband, in front of Anna Maria if you believe what you say. I'll be able to endure everything. On the contrary, I'll gladly accept the punishment they'll want to inflict on me — it'll be an atonement — but speak no more of our love as you make me embarrassed with the shame of it. I'd rather kill myself than betray your husband's trust again and deceive the young woman who believes in me."

Mario's words fell like cuts across Sultana's angry face. She understood that Mario was not lying. She could read it in his eyes, which had a firm and certain look.

"I don't want to take your life," she answered harshly, "but I will sacrifice my future to prevent your marriage to Anna Maria. In my room, I've left a sealed note for my husband, in which I confess that you're my lover and to please you I got rid of Alceste because of your jealousy. And, since you now reward me by wanting to get married, I've also said that I've come here, unable to accuse you in front of anyone else, to prevent you from such a monstrous hypocrisy. He'll know that I can no longer put up with acting as your accomplice. If I don't return home, he'll realize that it means you've killed me because I got in your way. In fact, I will kill myself, so you'll have to answer for my death in your house."

A cold sweat beaded Mario's forehead, although he tried to hide his anguish.

"But you've gone mad, signora!" he told her starkly.

"You think so? Well, I'll show you quite the opposite."

Mario saw her take out a shiny object and hold it in her right hand. He realized what she was doing and rushed towards her, grabbing her wrist with such force that in a spasm of pain she dropped the revolver on the carpet. He immediately bent down to pick it up.

"No, I won't let you kill yourself here in this house," he said with resolution. "I'd rather blow my own brains out to escape your despicable trap and ask God to forgive you because your victims never will!"

As he said this, he brought the revolver to his forehead, but then Sultana threw herself on him like a madwoman.

"No, no, don't do it. Forgive me! Mario, forgive me, I won't harm you anymore. I swear."

She collapsed on the floor. Mario lowered the weapon and looked down, stunned, at the woman who lay at his feet, motionless. He was touched by her reaction, his hatred towards her fell away. He saw nothing more than the woman, however guilty or badly motivated, who had loved him, who still loved him to such an extent that she was prepared to dishonor herself before the world. His decency led him to be struck by pity.

Kneeling on the carpet, he freed her motionless body from her hat and cloak and, lifting her in his arms, laid her on the sofa. He then went to get some cologne to wet Sultana's temples to bring her round. Signora Sigrano was not long in opening her eyes and seeing him bending over her, pale and anxious, she burst into tears.

"Forgive me! I'm wretched, but it was my last madness. No, I won't try anything else as long as you live. Be happy," she said.

"I will be," Mario answered softly, "when I've seen you regain a degree of peace, which I've upset without wanting to. I realize now that I've been harsh by showing up at your house with my fiancée, displaying the happiness I feel, but I thought that you'd forgotten things, and that, for the sake of your family, you would've been happy to see me married to a girl who is very fond of you and who you're fond of too."

"Yes, I should've been happy about it," murmured Sultana, "but my heart couldn't help rebelling, nor can I now explain how I felt at that moment."

"I do understand, but this can't be repeated. After I entrust Anna Maria to my parents, I'll find an excuse to go away until my wedding day. After that, you won't see me again."

"Oh no, Mario!" Sultana said in desperation. "Don't do it. It might give rise to suspicion, but more importantly, seeing you gives me the courage I lack. I won't make you suffer anymore, I swear, and I won't ask you to write to me, but you can't stop me loving you or living for you. From these depths, I'll find a way to ease my pain and get the courage to carry on with my life, to make those around me happy. Don't you want that?"

"I do," replied the young man, "because I trust that you're sincere and because I hope you don't want to see me die."

Rather than throwing her arms around his neck or kissing him, she gave him a look of anguish and bewilderment.

"Live your life with Anna Maria…and thank you for your forgiveness," she said hesitantly, but with a smile. "It's strange how weak I feel, but it will pass. Please send for a carriage, Mario, if you'd be so kind. I don't have the strength to walk home."

"I'll get the carriage myself."

"Thank you. In the meantime, if you'll permit me, I'll freshen up my face and put my hat and cloak back on."

"Go ahead, the bathroom is over there."

As soon as Mario had left the apartment, Sultana opened a balcony window and leaned out, letting her hair down, a triumphant smile on her lips. She knew that behind the shutters of the house opposite, which could be clearly seen among the lifeless trees, Anna Maria would be standing there. When Sultana had entered the building, she had seen the young woman at the window and was sure, despite her veil, that she had recognized her.

Anna Maria had already pulled the shutters, a sure sign that behind the slats she was spying on her. Indeed, before returning to the sitting room, she saw them move slightly as if a nervous hand was uncertain whether to open them or close them completely. Sultana did not need to dally any longer. Once she had achieved her aim, she withdrew from the balcony, closed the window, and went back inside to freshen up.

When Mario returned, she was ready to go with the veil lowered over her face.

"The carriage is at the door," he said. "Excuse me if I don't accompany you, but you must understand why."

"Oh, I do, my friend," she answered in a gentle but subdued tone. "Pardon me for the trouble I've given you. It will never happen again. Will you forgive me once more?"

"I've forgotten it all," Mario said, shaking Sultana's outstretched hand.

Before getting into the carriage, Signora Sigrano quickly glanced again towards Anna Maria's window. The shutters were wide open, the window now closed, but a white hand was holding part of the curtain up. Sultana gave the coachman the address, and as soon as she was in the carriage, the horse began to move. She could not resist a sardonic laugh, musing on how her plan had worked to the best effect. She wanted them to suffer as a married couple. Through that, she would find her vengeance.

17

Anna Maria had slept badly, agitated by various feelings. The affectionate welcome by the lovely Countess Jolanda Herbert, the count's acceptance of her as his only son's fiancée, the gift of the ring that now bound her to Mario, the words of affection and the kisses they had exchanged at the door of the house — the emotion of it all had caused her to lose sleep.

Where had her desire to take revenge on Mario gone? Was it only because he had been Sultana's lover? Was it right to blame him for Alceste's offence, given that, in her fiancé's letter, he had not hidden his passion for Signora Sigrano, even admitting he was prepared to die and could not live without her?

When Mario had been fatally snared by Sultana, he wasn't aware that Anna Maria existed. He had neither betrayed nor deceived her, so why should she make another's sins weigh heavily on him? She had been persuaded that he hated Sultana, loved her, and wanted to spend his life with her. She had a certain remorse beforehand at the prospect of dealing him such a blow after their marriage by revealing how she knew of his relationship with Sultana and that she had become his wife as an act of vengeance for both herself and on behalf of Alceste.

"No, I won't. I can't," she repeated to herself. She knew that the weapon she had chosen for her revenge had turned against her as she had fallen in love with Mario, but equally she knew how to keep things a secret and to reveal nothing. She would not let that woman take him away from her.

These feelings ended up comforting her, and towards the break of dawn, she eventually fell peacefully to sleep with Mario at the front of her thoughts. She woke when the sun came streaming into her room because she had left the shutters open. Getting out of bed, she dressed quickly and opened the window to breathe the fresh morning air and to glance at Mario's apartment. The shutters were all wide open, a sign that he was already up and had perhaps left the building. He had to visit his parents that morning to see them before they left in the afternoon for the countryside. They were planning to return the following week when they could settle in Turin and take care of the wedding preparations.

She was reassured by their affection towards her and knew she would return it, which again prompted her to feel bad about the thoughts she had entertained regarding Mario. She was about to retire when she spotted a tall, lithe-looking lady on the opposite sidewalk wearing a fur cloak and hat that she recognized. It was Sultana. Her heart rate rapidly increased as she pulled the shutters to, convinced that Signora Sigrano had not yet seen her. Where was she going at this time of the morning? Not to see her as she was on the opposite side of the road. Had she covered her face with a thick veil because of the cold or so she was not recognized?

A burst of anger crossed her face when she saw her stop at the door of Mario's building. What a nerve! Sultana had boldly defied any sense of danger by going directly to find him, to try and seduce him again, perhaps hoping that she could break their engagement. She could only hope he was not at home or, if he was, that he would reject her unworthy advances.

Anna Maria saw that Sultana, before disappearing into the hallway, had turned to look briefly at her windows, but she could not have thought that anyone was spying on her. She waited with pent up emotion, hardly aware of the cold that whipped across her face. Sultana did not reappear, so Mario had to be at home and had let her into the apartment. She could hear the blood pump in her ears and felt a stabbing pain in her head.

Anna Maria remembered that Sultana had wickedly suggested that Mario would never forget her kisses. What if this were true? Could Mario really betray her in this way, almost at the very moment when he had officially become engaged to her with the full permission of his parents?

Dressed in her white flannel robe, her hair still hanging over her shoulders, the young woman looked lifeless, only her eyes showed a lively spark. Time passed, and Signora Sigrano was nowhere to be seen. Anna Maria, in her misguided imagination, saw Sultana in Mario's bedroom, in the arms of the young man who was now swearing his undying love for her despite his forthcoming marriage. She felt such a compulsion to run over to the house and surprise them, to deal them a mortal blow by denouncing them to the signora's husband, to Mario's parents, and to the king's attorney and to reveal their complicity in Alceste's murder by producing the evidence he had left her.

In lashing out at them, however, she would be hurting herself. Mario would never marry her, and she could not make them suffer for a sufficient period of time. How foolish she had been to briefly regret the plan she had conceived and, instead, to feel remorse! Yet, deep down, she had believed in the feelings Mario had for her and that he would not prove as weak as Alceste when confronted with the witch. Now, though, all her illusions about her fiancé had collapsed. He, too, had turned out to be the same as other men, maybe even worse, because this was almost like an insult thrown in her face. Why had he fallen in love with her?

She raised her hands nervously to her feverish head. So many thoughts and scenarios were whirling around her brain, but her eyes never left Mario's windows. Suddenly, she had to reach out to her own window frame to stop herself from falling. Mario had rushed from the building, and almost immediately, Sultana had appeared on his balcony, looking disheveled, a triumphant smile on her lips. She leaned out for a moment to follow him with her eyes, then hastily disappeared inside.

The sight of her, terrible as it was, raised Anna Maria's spirits and brought her to her senses rather than having the opposite effect. She was horrified by that shameless woman who was making such a show of her behavior. And Mario, the young man who had fascinated her with his charming personality, well, now she hated him. In all candor, Anna

Maria could not accept the fact that while Mario might love her to the point of giving her his name, he was prepared to fall into the arms of someone else, who above all, was the wife of a decent, upstanding man like Bruno Sigrano. She was repelled by such despicable behavior.

Her mind turned again to Alceste and to the thought that she had wanted to forget the oath she had made to exact revenge for them both. She knew he was right and that they deserved no mercy. She had to continue her duplicitous part in this tragedy, which had stained her soul and left her with the unfortunate understanding that life was nothing but a horrible comedy and a shameless lie. Nevertheless, she would carry things through and see who ended up the victor.

She smiled bitterly, threw open the shutters, and closed the windows while remaining in front of them with a part of the curtain raised. Her gaze was hard, contemptuous, laden with hatred, even menace. She saw a carriage stop in front of the building, Mario got out and disappeared into the hallway. Shortly afterwards, Sultana appeared alone, in furs and veiled. She stopped for a few seconds to give the coachman the address and got into the carriage, which then pulled away.

Anna Maria dropped the curtain and moved back into the room. There was a knock at the door.

"Who's there?" she said without bothering to go and open it.

"It's me," replied her godmother. "Aren't you up yet?"

"No, I didn't sleep much last night, and I'm still tired. If anyone comes, please don't bother me."

"No, I won't. Get some rest."

Orsola's steps receded, and Anna Maria dropped into the chair near her bed, leaned forward, and buried her head in the blankets. She sat there for the best part of an hour, thoroughly agitated. The delusional thoughts running through her brain were an understandable reaction. When she eventually stood up, she was very pale, but her face was still striking in its beauty. In her large dark eyes, set against her ashen face, there was a certain indomitable energy, even a peculiar zeal. Her mouth, a fierce red, parted in a curious smile revealing her perfect teeth.

She passed into the adjoining bathroom and took great pains to apply her makeup and style her hair. She chose a black dress that fitted her figure and accentuated her graceful neck. She knew that she would be seeing Mario and his parents in the afternoon before his father and mother left, and they would all visit the rooms that Mario had promised to them. She wanted to be ready for the occasion. When she picked up the engagement ring to put it on her finger, she winced, briefly biting her lip. She was aware that she had to stiffen her emotions and not betray the deep wound she felt inside.

Anna Maria threw the window open again to air the room, busying herself by making the bed whilst humming a tune. Her godmother, on hearing this, entered the room.

"Already dressed?" she said somewhat surprised. "You didn't manage to get back to sleep?"

"I couldn't."

"I understand. All this happiness and excitement makes it difficult to sleep."

She hugged Orsola.

"Yes, I'm very, very happy!"

"You don't need to tell me. I can see it on your face. I've never seen you look so cheerful and beautiful."

"It's always going to be like this from now on."

She finished tidying up the room while Orsola went to close the window.

"Don't you notice the cold?" she said.

"Not at all," Anna Maria answered laughing.

"Oh, what it is to be young! You're always warm. Anyway, come and sit at the table. The coffee is ready."

"Ok, I'm coming."

By now, Anna Maria had regained her composure and felt able to receive Mario or find herself in Sultana's company without displaying signs of anger or disgust. No symptom of her inner struggle was apparent apart from the pallor of her face, something that, while beautiful, could also be attributed to feelings of happiness.

In the afternoon, Mario was beaming, his demeanor one of a young man in love meeting with his parents and fiancée. Anna Maria, after ushering them into the living room, tried to kiss the countess' hand, but flushed with confusion and emotion, was instead taken into the smiling signora's arms and hugged.

"My dear girl, treat me like a mother now!" she was told with great attentiveness.

"Signora, you're so very kind-hearted," Anna Maria replied with apparent feeling, kissing the older woman in turn. The count limited himself to a smile and a handshake. Mario kissed her on the forehead.

"Hello, my love," he said to her. "I hope you slept well last night?"

"Not really," she replied with a naïve, but lovable smile. "I was too full of pleasant thoughts and as soon as I got up, I ran to the window to see you."

"But you couldn't have seen me," Mario interrupted sharply, "because at ten I was still in bed."

"So, you weren't the officer in front of the entrance to your building?"

She stared at him with a look full of candor and a childish grin. Mario's face began to show his embarrassment, but he did not hesitate in replying. "In truth, no. You must have mistaken my orderly for me since I sent him to get a carriage for the journey to my parents."

He turned in mid-sentence to the count and countess, who had remained standing. At that moment, Orsola entered, greeted them, and asked them to sit down.

"We can't stay," replied the countess. "We want to leave today, and we've just come to pick up Anna Maria, as we agreed last night, so she can come and visit the apartment that Mario will let us have on our return."

"Alright. If you'll permit me, I'll go and put my hat on," said the young woman, "and I'll be at your disposal."

Entering her bedroom, Anna Maria suddenly felt giddy and had to lean on the chest of drawers. Her eyes began to feel watery. He had lied to her with such ease, but the reddening of his cheeks was worthy of a confession. She was suffering but vowed it would be for the last time. She would arm herself against any emotion. Hurriedly, the young woman put on a small coat the same color as the dress and a velvet hat, returning to the room with a modicum of serenity.

"You look lovely!" a besotted Mario remarked.

"Flatterer!" Anna Maria exclaimed, keeping close to the countess who had taken her arm.

"Mario's right," said the signora. "However, beauty, despite its charm, is but a passing phase if it's not accompanied by a decent heart. And you're already loved as part of the family, precisely because I feel you aren't only beautiful but also a nice person."

The compliment made Anna Maria start, but she brought Jolanda's hand to her lips.

"I will always be there for you, countess," replied Anna Maria.

"And for the rest of us too?" Mario said jokingly.

"Yes, I'll be there for all those who love me and who are sincere," she answered adopting a serious tone. "I hate but one thing in the world: lying."

"Good!" shouted the count. "Your loyalty makes you worthy of being my daughter. You'll find my family to be the same. Right. Let's go."

Mario had smiled approvingly when Anna Maria fixed her dark eyes on his. He didn't have the slightest suspicion that she doubted him, and his moment of embarrassment had passed quickly enough. He followed them all to go out after cordially taking leave of Orsola.

Crossing the avenue, the young man explained to his father that the concierge had told him that the owner of the building was going to sell it because he was short of money due to some business venture that had failed. He suggested that it would be a good moment to buy the property rather than rent it.

"But you'll not always be stationed here," observed the count.

"I think, father dear, that I should resign my commission," replied Mario, "and settle in Turin to be with you and my wife. In the summer, we could retreat to our land in the country and visit Anna Maria's holdings, then in the winter, we'd all be together, especially since you say that my sister would like to come and settle in the city with her husband."

"It's something to think about," added the count. "We'll talk about it again. In the meantime, let's deal with the matter at hand and visit the accommodation."

Mario played the host, laughing and chatting, as he showed them around. He failed to notice that Anna Maria, on entering the building, had pulled away from his mother's arm and had lost her color, becoming even more serious. The apartment had been tidied, but the heating had allowed the scent of violets to permeate the air. The furniture was very elegant, the carpets thick and soft.

"It's a honeymooner's nest!" exclaimed the countess. "You certainly have refined taste, my dear boy. Ours are simpler, but I think it'll be fine for us."

"I'm sure," replied the count gallantly, "and all the more so in your company."

"And you, what do you think of it?" asked Mario, approaching Anna Maria to put his hand around her waist. She smiled, raising her bright eyes to look at him.

"I'm like your mother," she replied. "I have simple tastes, but this is lovely."

"It's only like that because you're here," Mario whispered to her sweetly. They were in the living room where he had received Sultana. Anna Maria, releasing herself with a graceful turn, began to pick up the ornaments and statuettes placed on the surfaces. She examined everything with the curiosity of a child, occasionally letting out a cry of surprise.

"How beautiful! This group of women at a fountain is so charming. What about those little *putti*! Delightful.... Look, countess."

"They are beautiful artistic reproductions," agreed Yolanda, "but do they belong to the owner of the building?"

"No, I bought them all," Mario replied.

"Even that hand-embroidered photo frame?" Anna Maria asked.

"Yes, that too," answered Mario, blushing. "Please sit down for a moment. I'll be back in a couple of minutes."

The count was busy leafing through an album of landscape photography, while the countess was looking at the photographs of a group of cavalry officers, which included her son. Anna Maria, who had already walked to the sofa to sit down, called over to her.

"Look, countess," she said with an enigmatic smile that struck Yolanda as naïve, "look what I've found here, down the side of the sofa. These must belong to a woman...."

She produced a light-colored hairpin encrusted with small diamonds, and a rather crumpled lace handkerchief. The countess quickly took the objects.

"They're mine, dear. I put the handkerchief down a while ago when you were looking around. The hairpin must have fallen off without my noticing. Thank you so much," she replied in a rather unsteady voice. She immediately hid the items in the muff she had been wearing, but a small flicker crossed her ashen face. Anna Maria continued to laugh, which persuaded the countess that the young woman had not realized she had been lying.

Mario returned followed by his orderly, who carried a tray full of pastries and another with drinks. The two women took a pastry, but the men had a glass of grappa. They continued to explore the apartment, and while the count was talking to Anna Maria, Yolanda pulled her son to one side.

"I need to speak with you alone before leaving today. Once we've finished here, we'll take your fiancée home, and I'll send your father back to the Sigranos to wait for me. I'll tell him that I want to stay a bit longer so I can recommend a few things to you."

Mario was shocked by the look his mother had given him since he had never seen her so serious or upset.

"Yes, yes, of course," he replied mechanically.

Everything went according to the countess' plan. The count avoided making any comment when he was about to leave, but smiled ironically, thinking that his wife, so she could rest easy, wanted to grill the poor boy to see if he had any dubious relationships or debts that he had dared not tell his father.

When Anna Maria learned the countess was staying and sending her husband back to the Sigranos, it was easy for her to guess the reason why. She felt secretly pleased since it allowed her to tread more easily the path she had mapped out without anyone suspecting her intentions. In the eyes of her fiancé and the countess she would remain this naïve, virginal creature unaware of the iniquities of life. This much was apparent when the countess took her leave. Embracing her and repeatedly kissing her, she told the young woman that she was grateful God had sent Mario such an angel who could save him from all the dangers open to a rich, carefree, young bachelor.

"The luck is all mine," Anna Maria answered good naturedly, "in finding a husband like your son and parents, like the count and yourself, who are so kind. God will reward you all. For my part, I'll try to make you as happy as possible."

Eventually Countess Jolanda found herself alone with Mario in his living room. She sat on the sofa where Sultana had perched while her son sat on a stool at her feet.

"Mamma," he said in a melodic voice, resting his folded hands on the countess' knees, "now will you tell me what's happened and why you're suddenly looking at me so intently rather than with your usual kind demeanor."

Jolanda produced the two objects given to her by Anna Maria and handed them to her son.

"Here's my answer! Do you recognize them?"

At first, Mario did not understand. He seemed surprised at the shiny hairpin and unfolded handkerchief, which had Sultana's name embroidered in one corner.

"Where did you find them?" he stammered, turning white.

"I didn't find them," insisted the countess, "but Anna Maria did, on this very sofa a little while ago, and she gave them to me."

Mario was panicked, almost defeated.

"My God! Anna Maria knows...."

"She doesn't know anything," interrupted the countess, "because I told her they were mine, and she didn't have time to check the handkerchief. Naïve as she is, she didn't doubt anything at all."

Mario sighed with relief.

"Oh, mamma, thank you!" he exclaimed.

"I wouldn't be so happy if I were you. If I managed to deceive that angel of a girl, you won't find it so easy to deceive me. I want to know why these items are here and what kind of a relationship you have with Signora Sigrano. Don't lie. If you don't give me a straight answer, I'll go and see her."

The countess had never spoken with such severity. Mario, like a child caught doing something wrong, burst into tears, his head resting on his mother's lap. Jolanda was moved but did not let her maternal authority slip. She placed a hand on his head.

"Listen, Mario," she said. "If I demand the truth, it's because I alone can save you from this predicament. If your father knew that you've deceived a man who's like a brother to him and to whom we owe the wealth that you're now enjoying, he would never forgive you. I can't believe you're the main one to blame for this, because if that were the case I, myself, would disown you as a son."

"Oh, no, mamma, no!" he said, lifting his handsome face now distorted by the emotion. "I'll tell you everything, and you alone, mother, can judge me and save me from all this."

Mario was sincere in his sentiments. Knowing his mother truly loved him, he poured out his heart eager for some kind of understanding. As a gentleman, he found it difficult to accuse Sultana, but he realized it was his duty not to keep anything hidden about her depraved behavior and the part she had played in the life of Anna Maria, who fortunately, seemed to be unaware of anything. She considered Signora Sigrano to be a benefactress and that Alceste had been guilty and deserved his fate. Mario could not remain silent about Sultana's threats, about her repentance, or about the last conversation they had had in the same room that morning.

The countess heard him confess with apparent calm, but inside she was seized by nausea, even panic. Was it possible that a lady of Signora Sigrano's ilk, with a husband who loved her, two innocent children, and respect in society, was capable of such monstrous actions? Despite these feelings, she believed her son, believed that his intimate yet appalling story was the truth. And she realized that, had it not been God's will to put Anna Maria and Mario together so she could watch her as a daughter, the innocent girl would have been another of Sultana's victims.

Everything Mario had said about Anna Maria had only increased her affection for the young woman, orphaned as she was. On the other hand, she felt a real repugnance for Sultana, the dishonest wife and unworthy mother. She had guessed from her behavior that she was far from the virtuous woman everybody believed her to be. She had not forgotten the flashes of hatred that had passed across her eyes when they focused on her son or Anna Maria believing that everyone's attention was elsewhere.

"Look me in the eye, my son," said Jolanda once he had finished speaking, "and tell me the truth. Have you really gotten over your guilty passion for that witch? Or are you such a coward that you still want her?"

"No, mamma, I swear that she horrifies me. Ever since last year I would've resigned and moved from Turin, but the wretched woman came after me with threats. In fear that Signor Sigrano would end up learning the truth and curse me for staining his reputation, I stayed."

"And you did the right thing. Precisely because of Signor Sigrano, we must act with a great deal of prudence. I'll continue to treat Sultana as a friend to keep a better eye on her. My gut reaction tells me that her repentance is far from sincere."

"I'm doubtful as well," said Mario, "but Signora Sigrano is too fond of your esteem and that lavished on her by high society, so I don't think, despite her infernal audacity, she'll do anything imprudent that would end up in a compromising situation. The world once considered her a victim of that young man's folly, despite that fact she killed him, but I doubt it would believe her any longer, and her reputation would be trampled underfoot."

"Even so, just in case, I think it's better not to harbor too many illusions about her. Leave it to me. I'll return to Turin sooner than I'd have liked, and Anna Maria will never go out or approach Sultana without me. I won't be able to relax until this marriage has taken place."

"Oh, mother dear, I'll take all your advice. Please tell me you forgive me. I know I've sinned, but I've suffered so much, and I really do repent."

He looked at his mother with tearful eyes. Jolanda opened her arms, uttering words of forgiveness as she kissed him. When mother and son left the building, Anna Maria was spying on them from her window. She noticed they were unflustered, as they calmly looked up at her house before walking away arm in arm.

She was shocked, even angry, and could not help turning her thoughts to the conversation between Mario and Jolanda. She believed it likely that he had deceived his mother just as he had deceived her and was more than worthy of Sultana. She dismissed such thoughts, though, as unimportant as long as he became her husband. A mocking smile concealed her turmoil and sadness. She was far from calm.

18

A month had passed after Mario Herbert's engagement to Anna Maria, and nothing out of the ordinary had happened. Mario had purchased the building he lived in and then sold the first and ground floors to his parents, who had not been absent from Turin for more than a week. He had set up the second floor for his bride, just keeping a room, bathroom, and small living room for himself.

Sultana had regained her ease and vivacity of spirit. She seemed to participate happily in the wedding preparations, passing opinions on the countess's purchases. Jolanda, although a shrewd judge of character, came to the conclusion that her apprehensions were ill-founded and that, if Sultana had a thing for Mario, she was now cured of it and was no longer worried about the couple, wishing them instead a happy marriage, something that would save her from any scandal.

If only the countess could have read her thoughts. Sultana, now convinced that Anna Maria had always believed her to be Mario's lover, did nothing to dissuade her of the idea. With consummate treachery, when she noticed Anna Maria looking at her, Sultana would approach Mario and whisper in his ear that she was looking happy.

Anna Maria could not hear her words but saw him smile and nod his head. In her mind, the two of them were daringly arranging assignations right in front of her and the countess. She shook with anger at the thought, remembering Sultana's assertion that she would not be able to make him forget her kisses. She remembered her reply, saying she wanted his name above all else.

However, it was an emotion of a different sort that was now disturbing her. Mario's name was no longer enough for her. She wanted to be loved, she wanted him to feel a burning passion for her, and she wanted to take him from Sultana for good. Yet how could she succeed in this? Could she shout from the rooftops about their betrayal, showing the evidence she had against her? Could she crush her and make her lose her reputation?

In doing so, she would only hurt herself as well because she would never become Mario's wife, not to mention the damage she would do to innocent people in the process. No! However much Anna Maria struggled with her emotions, she did not hate Mario enough to ruin everything around him. No, she loved him and wanted to be loved in return, to defeat her rival.

Anna Maria had ceased to believe in his words, his passionate looks, his smiles. She could only see deception and thought herself ridiculous, while harboring the occasional false hope. But if Mario was not in love with her, why was he marrying her? She had arrived at the conclusion that the pair of them had colluded so that no suspicion of their relationship would arise in the minds of the Herberts or Signor Sigrano. She, therefore, saw herself as the victim immolated on the altar of their guilt.

Even Mario's insistence in wanting to resign from the army so he could reside in Turin, his eagerness to buy the building, was clear proof to Anna Maria of the two lover's complicity. She, alone, wallowed in her pain, which left her dejected, washed out, and feverish.

The countess had noticed the alteration in the young woman's demeanor, and one evening, while she and Anna Maria were gathered at Mario's along with Sultana, she could not help but comment.

"Aren't you feeling well, my dear? I've never seen you so gaunt."

"I've been thinking the same thing," added Sultana wickedly, "but I'm not surprised. As a fiancée, I also lost my complexion and was always agitated and nervous. Too much happiness can have that effect."

"You're right, signora," answered Anna Maria.

Mario, next to her, took her hand and forced her to turn and look at him.

"Is it true, then, you're happy?" he whispered with much affection.

Anna Maria saw Sultana looking at her with a malignant smile. Wanting to take revenge, she bent her head to Mario's shoulder.

"I am, yes, too much and that's what's worrying me. I'm afraid it won't last."

"Why? I adore you. I live for you and only you. I'm happy to share my whole life with you."

The young woman raised her eyes to his, trying to gauge his innermost thoughts.

"Are you in any doubt?" Mario asked, rather agitated.

"No, no, but...."

"Believe me, my angel. From the day I met you, I understood the real nature of love, the kind that strengthens you and makes you forget everything else. I treasure your tenderness and kindness and want nothing else but to make you happy. You're my angel."

Mario appeared sincere, and she would have liked to believe him, but she could see nothing but Sultana on her fiancée's balcony and hear nothing but Sultana's words saying that she would never be enough to make him forget her. While Anna Maria seemed to be listening in rapture to his declarations of love, in reality the same refrain was hammering away inside her brain — "He's lying. He's deceiving me!" She tried to smile, not wanting to give herself away in front of Signora Sigrano.

Countess Jolanda looked on with maternal indulgence at the young couple seemingly so united in their shared affection. Perhaps she was recalling when, under the watchful eyes of her own mother, she exchanged similar words, the epitome of true feeling.

From her seat, Sultana could only see Anna Maria's attractive face sparkle on hearing Mario's words. She bit her lip in annoyance, her nostrils flaring as if searching for air. Eventually, she could not contain herself any longer and stood up.

"Dear countess," she said to Jolanda, "I have to go since I forgot that I have an appointment with the seamstress. When shall we see each other again?"

"Tomorrow will be a bit difficult," she answered. "Around nine in the morning, I'm going out with Anna Maria and her godmother. We've got various things that must be done. In the afternoon, since Mario is free, we have to go to city hall to send some papers to Rome."

"Well then, come over to ours in the evening."

"I can't promise, but if possible, we'll call on you."

"Ok, that's that then."

Mario and Anna Maria, absorbed in their own conversation, made no indication that they had realized Sultana was leaving. Nonetheless, Sultana approached them.

"See you again, my dears," she said with a sarcastic smile. "I don't want to disturb your idyll any longer."

"You never disturb us, signora," Anna Maria replied, challenging her with a calm stare.

"Really? In which case, I would kindly ask Mario to accompany me to the street. There is something my husband would like him to do. I'll send him back to you straight away."

A forced smile contorted Anna Maria's lips, and she felt frozen to the spot. Nevertheless, she mustered an apparently calm response.

"You can keep him as long as you need. Go ahead, Mario."

Countess Jolanda intervened at this point, approaching Signora Sigrano.

"Excuse me, Sultana," she exclaimed, "but can't you explain in front of us what Bruno wants? I'll take you to the street myself."

The young couple turned with much gratitude to face Jolanda.

"It's all the same to me, but my husband recommended that I only speak to Mario. Don't be worried. It's only a bill to be collected," replied Sultana.

Mario rose to his feet.

"I understand," he said. "It's from Captain Silvestri. I acted as his guarantor. Sorry, mamma and you too, Anna Maria. I'll accompany the signora and tell her what to say to her husband."

Mario went out with Sultana, who took her leave of Anna Maria with an air of insouciance and smiled at the countess. Jolanda, upset and agitated, did not have time to compose herself in front of the young woman, who, unable to contain herself, had placed her head on her knees and started to cry.

The countess immediately guessed what was going through her mind. She had been suspecting as much, given she had been observing her recent change in attitude, and found it most upsetting. She bent down to speak to her.

"Tell me the truth, my daughter. You're jealous of Signora Sigrano."

Anna Maria raised her shocked face and met the countess's kind eyes. She saw so much care and affection that she felt overwhelmed. With a final deep sob, she threw herself into the woman's arms.

"Oh, mamma, mamma, save him, save him. That woman will ruin him. She'll kill him as she did poor Alceste!" she stammered as if unconscious.

The countess held her tightly.

"What? Do you know that Mario?…" she replied hesitantly.

"I know everything. And she won't leave him. She told me herself. I won't be able to make him forget her."

"The wretched woman," the countess said indignantly.

"Why didn't you tell me before? Mario thinks you no nothing about it.…"

"Let him think that. I'll tell you everything, but only you. I can't bear this secret any longer. It's tormenting me, tearing me apart, and driving me to the grave."

"Oh, poor Anna Maria! But shush…I hear Mario coming back."

"Don't tell him anything for pity's sake. He'll know everything later on."

Mario, on returning, found his fiancée and mother intent on looking at some lace. He failed to notice their agitated state since he was also upset. Sultana had only talked to him about the bill and other trivial matters but was happy that she had achieved her intention of making Anna Maria believe her fiancé had wanted to spend time with her, perhaps even to arrange a meeting.

When she got home though, Signora Sigrano ran to shut herself in her room where she could vent her anger and jealousy, which was becoming more virulent every day. She could not bear him getting married. Mario would come back to her without Anna Maria's evidence, she was sure. Suddenly, an audacious thought flashed through her mind and made her smile.

Sultana was almost sure that Anna Maria kept Alceste's letter and other objects with her. Given that the young woman would be going out with her godmother the following morning, as the countess had said, Camilla would be alone in the house. She thought it would be easy to dismiss the maid.

The idea haunted her all evening and during the night took deep root in her mind to such a degree that when she woke, she was fully prepared to put it into practice. When her husband left for his office, Sultana dressed to go out.

"If Camilla, Anna Maria's servant, comes here in my absence, will you give her the box of embroidery samples I left on the dresser in my room. They're for her mistress. Also, try and keep her for a while to see if Anna Maria really loves her fiancé, and if she still thinks of

Alceste. It would also be interesting to see if you can find out what she thinks of me and my husband," she said to Teresa.

"Yes, signora, rest assured, I'll get the news. Camilla is very talkative. I couldn't pass Tommaso's house back home without the old woman calling out to me so she could tell me all her gossip."

"Good. Look after the children, and if my husband calls, tell him I'm out shopping for Anna Maria."

"I understand, signora."

Sultana left the house a little before nine, wanting to make sure that the young woman and Orsola had gone out with the countess. The foggy day, full of drizzle, acted in her favor, as she could hide beneath her umbrella and go unnoticed. She had put on a simple, dark gray cloth dress that had not been worn in company before and had pinned a heavily designed black veil with a high edge to her velvet hat, which masked her face perfectly.

On her way, she came across several people she knew but, keeping the umbrella lowered, managed to escape being recognized. When she reached Mario's avenue, she saw from afar a car parked outside the entrance. Crossing the road, she reached a street recently opened to vehicles that was still cluttered with piles of timber. It was deserted, the ideal place to shelter and observe the comings and goings from Mario's building.

Sultana soon saw Anna Maria crossing the avenue slowly with her godmother, while at the same time, the Countess Herbert appeared at the entrance door, coming to meet the two women. She was able to see them exchange greetings and words but was not able to catch their significance from her position. All three subsequently got into the car, which immediately departed.

Signora Sigrano left her hiding place, closed the umbrella because it had stopped raining, and with her head held high, strode purposefully straight to Anna Maria's house. She entered the hallway without even turning her head towards the concierge. After quickly climbing the stairs, she rang the bell. Camilla opened the door. Sultana had raised her veil to the top of her forehead.

"It's you, signora," said the old woman. "How sorry Anna Maria will be when she hears of your visit. I'm afraid she's out."

"So, she's not here?"

"Sorry signora, no, but come in, please. You must be needing a little rest."

"Well, that's true, plus I need you to do me a small favor."

"At your disposal, signora. I'm happy to help."

They had entered the living room as they were speaking. Sultana, sitting down on the sofa, looked up at Camilla: "Yesterday, I promised Anna Maria that if I went out this morning, I'd bring her some embroidery that she wanted. But the box is rather large, so I thought I'd ask you if you'd mind getting it."

"Gladly, signora, but I'll go when the signorina returns. She told me not to leave the house unattended."

Sultana smiled.

"It won't be unattended. I'll stay here until you get back. It means I can also wait for Anna Maria as well. Will she be back for lunch?"

"Oh, I think it'll be sooner than that."

"So much the better! Don't tarry with my errand. You can be sure that I'll keep an eye on things and won't leave this room."

She laughed so hard that the old woman felt compelled to join in.

"No doubt," exclaimed Camilla.

The servant soon left, leaving Sultana to bolt the door so she wouldn't be disturbed. Entering Anna Maria's room, she began to rummage through everything. She opened drawers, delved into her linen, clothes, even checking all the furniture, yet she found nothing. She then realized she had not noticed a small cabinet desk to the side of the curtains between a pair of windows. It seemed designed to hold trinkets rather than a secret, but she went over to examine it.

She realized that it had a drawer masked by an artistically designed frame, but it was shut tight. Perhaps the mysterious drawer held the items she was searching for. She bent down to check out the lock, seeing that it was quite complicated. Grabbing a pair of scissors, she tried without success to force it. It was not going to be easy. The key to the little cabinet was not a common one. Instead, Sultana looked to see if there were any screws on the lock, again without success.

Persuaded that the drawer must hold the dangerous evidence, she knew she had to get hold of it at any cost. She started to breath heavily, biting her lip. Lifting up the desk to better examine it, she stuck the scissors in the gap between the lid and drawer, pressing with all the strength she could muster. There was a loud crack. The lock had come apart and the lid had sprung backwards revealing the inside of the drawer. Staring at her was the portrait of Alceste, as if mocking her. At that moment, she heard Anna Maria's voice.

"I thought you were smarter than that, signora. One doesn't keep certain precious objects in the house."

Sultana cried out in alarm, letting the little desk drop, which broke as it hit the ground. Turning with a shocked face, she saw Anna Maria at the door, still wearing her hat, and staring at her with a stern if stunned expression.

"You? You?" Sultana stammered, convulsed, unable to believe who was in front of her.

"Yes, it's me," replied the young woman. "Camilla warned me that you were waiting for me here. It's fortunate that I bumped into her on the corner when the car was forced to stop to let a carriage pass. She told me why she had left the house, and I didn't want to keep you waiting too long. Thank God I came back in time to prevent you from vandalizing all my poor innocent furniture. I couldn't get in through the landing door, but I had the key to the kitchen, and so I'm here to defend what's mine, to defend my rights!"

Sultana, who had been in the grip of violent emotion, began to collect herself. The color returned to her cheeks.

"Your rights?" she shouted boldly. "It's you who are trampling on mine. I'm not denying why I'm here, and I'm not going to leave without you handing me the things that belong to me."

"They're no longer in my hands, signora," Anna Maria answered coldly. "As you have forgotten your promise, I'm no longer bound to mine."

Sultana gestured furiously, approaching her with menace.

"What do you mean?" she asked with venom. "Explain yourself."

"I warned you," she said slowly, "that in the event of your retaliating, or if you betrayed the decent man whose name you bear, I would use Alceste's letter and the items he left to me to unmask you, to prevent you from harming anyone further."

Sultana was consumed with anger, her eyes bloodshot. She grabbed Anna Maria's arm violently.

"And have you done it? Have you?" she said in a hoarse voice.

Anna Maria held her gaze resiliently: "I'm sure you intended to challenge me," she replied, "by going to see my fiancée, appearing on the balcony as if you'd just been intimate with him, knowing full well I was behind the window spying on you?"

"Well then, wasn't that enough to open your eyes to the man you thought you'd stolen away from me but who's still my lover?" Sultana interrupted. "If Mario's given you to understand the opposite, he's a coward and a liar."

"You're the coward and liar, signora," Anna Maria retorted without losing her composure, "because you're accusing the victim, just like you once accused poor Alceste of trying to rape you. But the truth always comes out, and now, not only are you being blamed by the dead but also by the living, by the man who's ashamed that he once believed in you, who would rather kill himself than approach you again."

Sultana had lost control completely.

"So, you gave him Alceste's letter and the objects?" she asked, outraged. "Answer me!"

"And what if I did?" Anna Maria responded boldly.

"You miserable, hateful creature. You're all alone here with me. Don't you think you might be in trouble?"

"I'm not afraid of you, signora, even though I know you're a killer."

"You should be!" Sultana replied, hastily grabbing the scissors that had been used to force the lock on the desk.

The stern figure of Countess Herbert, who had just walked in, stopped the blow that Sultana was about to strike. The scissors fell to the ground with a dull thud, and Sultana, livid, unsteady, and with wild eyes, backed herself up against the wall.

"You?" she said, staggered.

"Yes, signora," the countess answered in a slow, emotion-laden voice. She went up to Anna Maria and hugged her. "I heard everything, and I still feel like I'm in the grip of a dreadful dream. I can't believe your utter depravity despite my son's confession, dragged as he was by you into this whole guilty business, and despite the evidence of this dear young thing who asked for my help and who's been subjected to the cruelest torment. I thought it impossible that you, a noble woman, esteemed, even adored, could sacrifice a man like your husband for a passing fling, a guilty intoxication — the very thought of which makes an honest woman and mother sick. Yet, it seems I must surrender to the evidence.... For your sake, it makes me cry."

Indeed, tears were beginning to well in the countess' eyes. Despite, trying to avoid any ostentatious show, she could not, however, hide her distress in the face of such monstrous behavior. The tears mortified Sultana more than any verbal recrimination. She lowered her eyes to the floor, trembling.

"Yes, I've been dishonorable…and I still am! But I have the devil in me and often against my will. I know I'm wretched."

"That very devil," added the countess in a more measured tone, "pushed you to kill poor Alceste after you'd thoroughly corrupted him. Despite my son's pleas to break free from the relationship he feels so remorseful about, that devil compels you to try and compromise him and, in so doing, to torture the heart of his fiancée, the self-same person who'll be my son's redemption."

Sultana's face contracted in a pained expression.

"Yes," she replied, "he heightened my senses, armed my hand, and made me the foulest of women. Yes, the very devil inside intended Anna Maria to believe that Mario was still my lover. I hated his happiness. I felt compelled to try and steal the evidence for my sins… and the devil would have driven me to kill Anna Maria. It was your presence alone that saved her. I don't deny any of it! I'm shameful, and I deserve your contempt, your retribution. Anna Maria has already punished me by unmasking me in Mario's eyes."

"Mario isn't aware of anything," Anna Maria said impudently. Although, she was minded, once again, to take seriously the woman's act of repentance.

"It's true," added the countess. "It's only thanks to this dear girl's pleas that I too have kept silent and not told my son about her revelations. I've put all the compromising items in a safe place, and that way Mario will think that you've forgotten everything and only wish him and Anna Maria happiness."

"You're too kind. I don't deserve this," sobbed Sultana. "Don't spare me! But, out of pity, spare my husband and my innocent children. I will end it all, if needs be, but they don't deserve to hear the truth."

Sultana seemed in the throes of utter dejection. Her hands together, she pleaded with the countess and Anna Maria.

"We're not your judges," said Jolanda gravely. "God alone will punish the guilty. We don't wish you dead precisely because of your decent husband. We'll keep silent for the sake of your innocent little ones. Are you in agreement, daughter of mine?"

"Yes, completely!" exclaimed Anna Maria.

"I really want to believe that your repentance is sincere," continued the countess, "and if you're truly feeling remorse that devil inside will never rise again. In the meantime, however, until my son's marriage, you must find some pretext to move away from Turin."

Sultana could not hide her alarm.

"I'll gladly do it, but what possible excuse could I find?"

The countess had no time to answer as she heard the sound of a car stop at the door.

"Maybe it's my godmother who's come back for us. She must've been waiting impatiently," said Anna Maria, running to open the window and leaning out to see what was happening. She drew back almost immediately.

"It's not her, it's the lawyer, Signor Sigrano."

"My husband!" shouted Sultana, horrified. "What's he doing here at this hour?"

"Compose yourself, signora. Let's move into the other room," the countess said quickly. "Anna Maria, why don't you pick up that picture from the floor and put the pieces of the desk to one side. Then come and join us."

Just as she finished speaking the doorbell rang.

"One moment," said Anna Maria, who had already carried out Jolanda's advice. "I'll get the door myself."

When Signor Sigrano appeared, he saw his wife and the countess sitting next to each other on the sofa. They seemed to be talking amicably, but as he entered, they jumped to their feet in surprise.

"You're here, at this time?" said Sultana rather mechanically. She noticed that Bruno was pale and serious.

"Yes, my dear," he said. "I've come to take you home."

"My God, what's happened?" she interrupted, "Is it the children?"

"They're fine. I'm sorry, countess, Anna Maria, please forgive me for being intrusive, but I'm here out of necessity. Half an hour ago I received a telegram from my mother-in-law warning me that her husband, who's been ill for a few days, has suddenly deteriorated and wants to see his daughter and grandchildren."

Jolanda caught the eye of Sultana, who seemed to intimate that her pretext had been found. Jolanda in turn insinuated that God had sent a sign, and her innocent children would be none the wiser.

"Oh, my poor father. Yes, I must leave today. I'm sorry, countess, and to you, Anna Maria, but we'll no longer be able to finish the preparations together."

"Duty must come first," said the countess. "Anna Maria and I will pray, in your absence, that God will come to your father's aid."

"And Signor Sigrano will pass on any news," added the young woman.

"My husband will keep Bruno company while you're away," assured the countess.

"Thank you, thank you for your kindness. See you again, my friend, and you, my dear, stay happy."

"Yes, yes, I will, and I owe a lot to you," replied Anna Maria. "Although you thought you'd done wrong, being such a kind soul, in fact, you've opened the doors of happiness for me without even knowing it."

Only Sultana and Countess Jolanda understood the profound irony of this sentence, which the lawyer attributed to the death of Alceste. Mario's mother remained calm though, and Sultana betrayed no emotion other than a slight flushing of the cheeks, which disappeared as she replied: "Your words are precious. Your forgiveness eases my conscience."

She held out her hand to Anna Maria and embraced the countess, who was unable to avoid her. She then followed her husband as he moved to leave. He was clearly upset by the scenes he had witnessed and by his beloved wife's concern.

As soon as they were alone, Anna Maria threw herself into the countess' arms: "That's dispelled all my doubts," she said. "I believe in Mario, but for heaven's sake, he must never know how much I doubted him and wanted him to pay for that wretched woman's sins."

"The best we can do now," answered Jolanda, kissing her, "is to feel sorry for her and then forget her. And you, to atone for having misjudged my Mario, must love him even more. Rest assured, though, that my son and husband will never know the secrets you've told me. They'll die with me, but only if that treacherous woman doesn't try to harm you or Mario again. If she does, I'll have no compunction That'll be the end of any indulgence or pity."

19

The departure of Signora Sigrano and her children from Turin had restored peace and tranquility to Anna Maria's life. Confessing to Countess Herbert had already been a great relief. She had unburdened herself of everything from the moment she had read Alceste's letter and sworn to fulfil his wish until her meeting with Mario. She mentioned her joy when she thought he loved her, but also the pain when she was convinced that Mario, despite his promises, did not know how to make a definitive break with Sultana. Finally, she admitted to the jealousy that had torn her apart, reviving her sad intention to take revenge on Mario for her torment once she had married him even though she loved him and felt sorry for him.

The countess had listened to her with care and attention, sensing the young woman was not lying and was hoping for words of comfort. At the end of her explanation, Anna Maria could not contain her tears.

"No, Mario doesn't love me…. When he's with me, he's thinking of someone else. But I don't want to lose him, no!"

Jolanda comforted her, holding her tenderly.

"You won't lose him," she replied, "but you've accused him unfairly."

She looked at the countess, bewilderment in her watery eyes.

"How? I saw Signora Sigrano myself on his balcony, looking half-dressed."

"Sultana did that on purpose because she realized that you'd spotted her entering the building. I swear to you, as his mother, that Mario is innocent."

"What about the things I found on the sofa?" Anna Maria replied hesitantly, her face reddening rapidly.

"Those things made me question my son, and he told me all about his relationship with Sultana. Mario may have innocently fallen under her spell, but the day he learned of Alceste's death, he did everything he could to escape her clutches. Signora Sigrano threatened to tell her husband and denounce him as her lover and accomplice in the murder. In fear of a scandal, the poor boy yielded to her once again. But when he saw you, he began to fall in love, knowing you could be his redemption. Her pleas and threats weren't enough to stifle his rebellion or stop him from splitting with her forever.

"It was then that she made a scene that forced him to move house, hoping to avoid her altogether. Seeing that she was having no success, Sultana changed tactics and feigned sincere repentance. Mario believed her, but it was your engagement with the help of Signor Sigrano that led her to think she could still control him. However, realizing she could no longer bend my son's will, she turned her fire against you, hoping that you'd break off the engagement. She didn't succeed because, by then, I was watching out for you and my son."

"My God!" Anna Maria exclaimed. "And to think I, sure that Mario was deceiving me, was going to hurt him. If he knew, he'd never forgive me."

"He won't find out, my dear. And now that I've told you everything, trust that he loves you and try to make him happy."

The echo of the countess's words reassured her. The desire to retaliate, which had once taken hold, had turned into a deep love for Mario. Her ashen face and tremulous thoughts, the doubts and melancholy, they had all gone. Her beauty and the sparkle in her eyes gave away her newfound happiness.

Sultana had written to her husband to tell him that her father had been getting worse and there was no hope of saving him. When his death came, the lawyer left Turin for a few days. The Herberts and Anna Maria felt sorry for Signor Sigrano and wrote moving letters of condolence to his wife, allaying any suspicions that would have otherwise come to the fore in Bruno's mind. The correspondence also gave a renewed vigor to Sultana.

When the lawyer returned to Turin because of work, he told them that his wife would remain behind and spend the next few months in mourning with her mother.

"My poor Sultana has suffered so much," added Bruno, "that she really needs a calm period of rest. Although being apart is difficult, I think it's necessary for her health. I'm only sorry for Anna Maria who'll have to get married without my wife by her side, especially since she loves her like a mother."

"It's a shame," said the young woman warmly, "but what can be done? It's better that she stays, and the fresh mountain air will help her feel better. I know I'll have her blessing from afar."

The countess and Anna Maria were pleased with Sultana's decision since her presence would have upset their happy mood. Mario was in high spirits, opening his heart to his fiancée in a lively and joyous manner without the fear of Sultana's jealous eyes following his every gesture or her thoughts second guessing his every word.

Time passed quickly despite the endless preparations that always precede weddings. Mario's married sister had arrived in Turin and, like the others, was enchanted by Anna Maria, judging her most worthy of her brother's affections and those of the family. The young woman, living in a manner she could only have dreamed of in the past, felt it was almost impossible to feel so happy.

The only cloud on her horizon was the occasional thought that her current contentment was due to Sultana's crime. Surely though, Alceste would be enjoying the revenge she had taken on Signora Sigrano and would bless her marriage to Mario without begrudging her cheerfulness.

Anna Maria had received many gifts from her soon-to-be in-laws and Mario, but also from her godmother and fellow villagers. Sultana had asked her husband to give her a gold bracelet in the shape of a snake, with emerald eyes and a ruby tongue. A note was attached to it in which Sultana explained that the snake was a symbol and a talisman that would bring the bride luck. The countess and young woman exchanged a brief glance because they both understood the hidden meaning: the snake they had crushed could still bite. Her poison, though, had ceased to cause them any anxiety.

The wedding day finally arrived, and in accordance with everyone's wish, it was an intimate affair with relatives and a few of the couple's friends. Anna Maria was pale with emotion during the church and civic ceremonies. Mario, on the other hand, could not hide his delight and would have been glad to shout to all and sundry how happy he was feeling.

After receiving everybody's good wishes and attending a splendid wedding breakfast at the Herberts' residence, the couple set off on a honeymoon to a villa owned by the count some three kilometres from Nice where they would be looked after by two groundsmen and a cook. All three of them were ready and waiting for the couple. Neither Anna Maria nor Mario had wanted any other servants.

The Herberts accompanied the newlyweds to the station where they boarded a first-class carriage.

"May God bless you, my dear daughter, for making Mario so happy," the countess whispered in Anna Maria's ear.

"Take care of you wife. Make her happy. She deserves it," whispered Count Herbert in turn to his son. "God has given you an angel like your mother. Remember how to treat her…and be as good a husband as you've been a son."

Mario, with much emotion, kissed both his parents. When the couple were alone as the train left the station, Anna Maria burst into tears. Mario was surprised, frightened even. He moved closer to her and held her gently in his arms as you would a child.

"Why are you crying, my love? What's the matter?" he said softly.

"I've been horrid to you," the young woman answered sobbing.

"You? In what way?"

"I doubted your love for me."

"My love! When? Why?"

"I thought you still loved Signora Sigrano."

Mario could not hide his embarrassment. Nevertheless, he managed to ask,

"Why would you think that?".

Anna Maria pressed herself nervously to his chest. "I saw her enter your house one day," she whispered, "and saw her leave in a carriage. The following day I found some objects belonging to her on the sofa in your living room. I gave them to your mother, who led me to believe they were hers, but I'd seen that shiny hairpin in Signora Sigrano's hair, and I'd made the lace handkerchief myself and given it to her.…"

Mario's embarrassment deepened.

"My dear," he stammered, "I swear to you.…"

"There's no need to swear anything," she interrupted. "You don't need to because I know you're innocent. Although I was carrying on as normal, your mother understood that I was suffering and feeling depressed. One day, she caught me crying and wanted to know why. I told her all my doubts and jealousies. She explained how I'd got it wrong about you and confided how Signora Sigrano, driven to lose her senses by some temporary delirium, had fixated on the fact that you couldn't marry me because I'd been Alceste's fiancée.

"She'd come to see you to plead with you to leave me. Your mother added that you'd tried to calm her down, saying that neither you nor I were offending his memory since it wasn't our fault that Alceste had died, and even if he deserved to be mourned, this was still no reason to sacrifice our happiness — especially as he could never have loved me, given that he harbored such passion for his mistress. Signora Sigrano had then collapsed on the sofa, which is when she lost her belongings.

"When she came to, she apparently felt like she'd woken from a bad dream. She put pressure on your feelings of loyalty so you wouldn't let on what had happened, adding that she approved of the marriage and wished us all the best. It was then she begged you to call a carriage so she could go home. You can imagine my relief at your mother's words. Even if I still had doubts, when the signora left Turin and you knew she wasn't coming to the wedding, the relief you showed was enough to dispel any negative thoughts. Now, I just feel bad for having doubted you, hence my tears and this plea for forgiveness."

When she was speaking, Mario had run the full gamut of emotions, secretly thanking his mother for having hidden the truth from his naïve wife who had always believed in Sultana's honesty. However, he was startled on hearing her final words and felt a twinge of guilt.

"You? You're asking me for forgiveness, my angel? Yes, it's true that I'm innocent, and I swear that from the day I met you there's been nobody else for me. I adore you, and I've never been unfaithful to you, not even in my thoughts. But…unwittingly, I've made you suffer. So, it's you who must forgive me," he said almost breathlessly.

Anna Maria threw her arms around his neck.

"But I feel absolutely fine now," she replied with passionate intensity. "I'm happy, very happy, and I really love you, Mario."

Like soul mates their lips touched, and for the first time, it was a kiss full of desire.

20

Many changes had taken place in the four years since Anna Maria's marriage to Mario. Six months after the death of her father, when Signora Sigrano was still away with her children, she suddenly became a widow. Her husband had died in a car accident when he and some friends were on their way to visit her. It was a Sunday, and Sultana had received a telegram explaining they were coming. She put on a light crepe dress that suited her blond hair and then decided to wait on the villa's terrace overlooking the valley to watch for the vehicle's approach.

The hours passed, but the car never arrived. Instead of the open-topped vehicle, another car drew up outside the gates of the villa. Sultana came down from the terrace to see who it was, but even before she had reached the hallway, she started to hear anguished cries, then she saw two men carrying her husband, who was already dead. About a kilometer from the village, the driver had swerved abruptly to avoid some oxen, which made the car overturn. Two of the passengers were thrown from the vehicle along with the driver and ended up on a nearby embankment, a little stunned but unharmed. The lawyer had remained in the car and was trapped underneath. With a great deal of difficulty, it took half an hour to remove him. Although he had several broken ribs and head injuries, he was still breathing, but when they tried to lift him, he died uttering Sultana's name.

Signora Sigrano showed such grief that she inspired compassion in those around her. In reality, though, she was not crying for her husband, but for the thirty thousand lire a year she had lost. It was true that Bruno, in addition to the income from his practice, also had some personal wealth, but this had been greatly reduced by the construction of their home and the money given to support his wife's luxurious lifestyle, a lifestyle she could not and would not give up.

It was at this point that she received some luck from an unexpected direction. The signora had an uncle, her father's brother, Count Daniele Flaminio. Although something of a character who had started off as poor as a church mouse, the count had managed to achieve immense wealth within a couple of years through land speculation and the stock market. He had turned thirty thousand lire into a fortune of twenty million.

He had always lived like a recluse, receiving no visitors. Nor had he forgiven his brother for refusing to take part in his land speculation scheme. He had voiced the opinion that he did not want money from such a daring and exploitative action. The land that Daniele sold at exorbitant prices was bought from poor people for derisive sums. They had no idea that their properties would acquire considerable value because of certain work that needed to take place on their land.

Nobody knew anything about Count Flaminio's private life. The only servant who lived with him, who had been his confidant, died a few days before his master. Daniele had suffered an attack of angina at a café and was carried home in serious condition. He had rallied enough at one point to ask his doctor to help him call Sultana, his niece. She was in Turin where she was in the process of trying to liquidate all the assets from her inheritance. She rushed to her uncle's bedside who, until then, had never wanted to see her.

She barely knew the man but was left alone with him. Their conversation lasted thirty minutes, but nobody ever found out what the dying man had said to her. In the end, Sultana had to shout for assistance when her uncle was afflicted by another attack. The doctor came running, but he had already passed away by the time he approached the bed.

Daniele had not made a will and had no heirs except his niece, therefore Sultana suddenly found herself in possession of twenty million lire, which dried her tears after the death of her husband. Her first concern was selling the building built by Bruno. She bought an attractive modern property located in one of the city's most aristocratic avenues. She kept the first floor entirely to herself along with the ground floor, a separate entrance, the vast garden, and the courtyard.

She rented the second and third floors with a splendid terrace to a wealthy financier and his wife.

Signora Sigrano soon sent her children to boarding school, her secret motive was to be free to enjoy the life that had fallen into her lap in the most auspicious manner. The Herberts had sent their condolences on the death of Bruno. As soon as Sultana had returned to Turin, she had gone to visit them and had wept in Jolanda's arms. Being as decent as she was, the countess had taken Sultana's grief at face value, especially since she now believed in the signora's repentance and her wish to see Mario happy.

Two months after his marriage, his regiment had sent Mario to Tuscany. He was happy with the move, hoping the distance would cure Sultana of her fixation and because Anna Maria was content to get away from Turin. He no longer spoke about resigning. Their life was a newlywed's haze, and at times, they were so wrapped up in each other's company further considerations seemed unimportant. Their relationship was an example to the rest of the regiment. Everyone loved Mario for his inexhaustible spirit and joie de vivre. Anna Maria was admired and respected.

They heard of Signor Sigrano's unfortunate death from Jolanda, and both mourned him as if he were a relative. Anna Maria sent their condolences to Sultana, and she had replied with a simple business card. They then learned of her inheritance, of her new home, but attached little importance to it because Anna Maria had just become a mother. Mario was madly happy, declaring that he loved her a thousand time more because she was not only his beloved wife but also the mother of his son and heir. Moved, she had smiled in reply. Motherhood had made her more beautiful, and with the past completely forgotten, she was totally at peace. She wanted to breastfeed the baby, and Mario was in complete agreement.

The following year, Mario learned that his regiment would be posted to Sicily. Reluctant to move so far away from his parents and tired of the kind of military life that prevented him from enjoying his home and family as he wished, he resigned his commission with the full agreement of his mother, father, and wife. They decided to settle in Turin with the Herberts. When Sultana heard of their arrival, she went to see them.

The signora looked younger and more attractive than ever. She shook Mario's hand in a carefree manner, leaving him somewhat disconcerted, kissed Anna Maria, and payed enthusiastic attention to the child. She spoke straightforwardly of her unexpected inheritance, remembered her husband with much affection, and detailed how she proposed to move on with her life. She wanted no more ties except those to her beloved children, hoping to have fun, while at the same time, dedicating herself to those less fortunate.

"You'll be amazed," she said to Anna Maria, "that I've put my children in boarding school, but they're growing up, and I want them to have a good education. I've put Mina in a school run by French nuns where my mother was educated and Ottorino is in the same school that his father attended. I'll be able to visit them often and have them with me during the vacations. I'm happy for them, and it means I'm following Bruno's wishes. I did much that could've hurt him, but I'm trying to atone for that now.

"Yes, my friends, I have to confess that if I could go back a decade or so I'd be a different woman. I understood too late what you, Anna Maria, and you, Jolanda, must have realized immediately, namely that the best life is one with duty at its heart. It's true, even with such a raison d'être, you can still suffer or feel tormented, but at least you're free of remorse."

As she spoke, her face was lit with intelligence and energy, but a painful smile parted her lips. Her eyes settled expressively on the two ladies who sat in front of her. Jolanda and Anna Maria sincerely believed that she was sorry for past follies. They pitied her condition.

"There are still many nice things in life," the countess added with kindness, "and with your children's affection and your charity work, you'll discover how to forget."

"I hope so," replied Sultana.

She had avoided Mario's gaze as if he were not there, whereas he, on the other hand, sure that his wife and mother were paying no attention, started to observe the woman who had once been his, who had been deeply in love with him. There was no comparison with Anna Maria, who he had already put on a pedestal, but he could not help but admire Sultana. He remembered their affectionate words, hearing her honeyed voice whispering to him. He saw her red lips eagerly seeking his. And was she really now repenting this passionate past, precisely when she was free to indulge any whim that came to mind? He could hardly believe it, and although he had no intention of putting her to the test, he briefly felt a frisson of desire.

In the meantime, Sultana was taking her leave.

"I hope you'll come and see me regularly now," she said to Anna Maria and her mother-in-law.

"I'd like that," the young woman answered gently, "but my son takes up most of my time."

"But if he's weaned, walks by himself, and is chirping away,…" observed Sultana. "And since your governess seems to be a very serious young woman, he'll be fine with her."

"And then you've also got me, his grandmother," interrupted Jolanda. "I love being with the little boy. Believe me, Sultana, ever since Gino was born, my son and Anna Maria rarely go out and when they do, it's always with the child."

"That's very admirable," Sultana exclaimed, turning her head towards Mario, who seemed embarrassed. She then looked directly at Anna Maria and smiled sweetly. "I don't want to distract you from your duties as parents, but on the occasional evening, when your son is asleep, you could give me an hour or so of your time, especially as I'm hoping to hold some evening receptions and concerts. I intend to have my dearest friends there, so you must also come, Jolanda, along with your husband."

"We'll do our best," they replied.

"Thank you, and see you again."

She kissed the two ladies, casually shook Mario's hand once more, then went to leave, leaving a trail of violet perfume behind her. Once she had shut the door of the car, which was waiting for her outside the building, a treacherous, triumphant smile crept across her face. She had no intention of letting Mario escape this time. She wanted them to pay dearly for her humiliation, and today was just the start. There was an intensity in her eyes as she leaned back voluptuously on the soft cushions in the back seat. Her eyes narrowed in a glorious daydream.

21

Neither Jolanda nor Anna Maria had the faintest idea of the shock Mario had felt at seeing his former lover again. They spoke of her with kindness, without any envy or suspicion. They were convinced that she had changed, believing her to be sensible, thoughtful, and truly repentant of her past carelessness.

"It's such a shame that poor Signor Sigrano died so young," remarked Anna Maria.

"Bruno's tragic death will have made her come to her senses," Mario replied, although to try and silence his guilty thoughts he adopted a mocking tone. "However, I don't think she'll be a widow for too long, assuming someone hasn't already replaced her dead husband."

"Mario!" Jolanda and Anna Maria disapprovingly said in unison. In response, Mario hugged his wife. "Besides, what does it matter to us?" he said with a nervous laugh. "Signora Sigrano can do as she pleases. We don't have to worry about it, do we, my dear?" He embraced her once more. Anna Maria smiled happily.

"You're right," she replied with her naïve frankness, "but as I haven't forgotten that it's she I have to thank for meeting you. I, for my part, wish her all the best. I don't want to dwell on her past faults which, in any case, aren't up to me to judge."

"Well said, Anna Maria!" exclaimed Countess Jolanda. "You're of the same mind as me. And, my dear boy, since God has given you this angel as a wife, you could at least be indulgent to the woman who helped you in the process."

"With you two around, it's difficult to speak out of turn," Mario concluded jokingly. Nevertheless, he remained uncomfortable with his own thoughts. Next to these two homemakers, Sultana, with all her perfidious charm, seemed more beautiful than ever. Her artfully styled hair, curvaceous figure, and fresh incomparable complexion were all too evident. Her violet perfume had gone straight to his head.

Close to his wife and son in the subsequent days, Mario managed to forget Sultana. On Saturday, though, while they were all gathered for lunch, they received an invitation card from her addressed to Count Giorgio Herbert. Mario's father read it aloud: "Countess Sultana Flaminio, widow Sigrano, asks Count Giorgio Herbert, Countess Jolanda and their children, Count Mario and Countess Anna Maria, to do her the honor of attending a concert that will take place at her residence on Thursday the 6th at 9 pm."

"Oh, how boring!" Mario exclaimed. "Father, you and mother go along. Anna Maria and I will stay at home."

"Signora Sigrano might be offended," replied the count, "and it seems more sensible to me that I should stay at home with my wife. Our absence would be more excusable."

"I think," observed Jolanda, "that it might be better for everyone if we all go to this first invitation, then we can refrain from accepting others in the future."

"Your mother's right," added Anna Maria, "and I don't understand why, Mario, you're so against attending a concert when you love music so much. Is there any reason why you want to avoid Signora Sigrano?"

The young woman had spoken simply with a smile, but Jolanda, who understood the veiled motive behind the question, looked at Mario just as Anna Maria did.

"What reason could I have?" Mario added brusquely to hide his consternation. "I thought I was doing you a favor by deciding against it, but if you're of the same opinion as mamma, well, we'll go!"

Anna Maria did not reply, nor could she find the words. Mario was ignorant of the fact that she knew all about his past. He had not spontaneously confessed the truth to her, even when she had offered him the opportunity as soon as they had found themselves alone after their wedding. Indeed, Mario had confirmed the story that she had pretended to have learned from his mother, which made him appear innocent. Even Countess Jolanda, begged by Anna Maria, took care not to reveal that his wife knew about his former relationship with Sultana.

Of course, by now Anna Maria was sure of his love for her, as she was of Sultana's change in attitude. However, she felt a certain apprehension at the rapprochement, fearing a looming danger hanging over her husband's head.

On Thursday at around nine in the evening, Anna Maria, already dressed, was in the room where the governess usually slept with her child. Little Gino had fallen asleep, and she was looking at him tenderly. Mario entered with a top hat and gloves in his hand.

"Are you ready? he asked.

"Yes, but I just wanted to kiss our little boy again."

Touched, Mario went over to the bed and looked at his son, who was asleep with a smile on his face. He bent down to kiss him as well.

"You look lovely, my dear!" he exclaimed. "Come here. Let's have a look at you."

Anna Maria went over to him. Wearing a white satin dress embroidered with pearls, she looked enchanting, full of grace and youthful beauty. She wore no jewelry other than two very large pearls in her ears and a string around her neck.

"Do you like what you see?" she asked him.

Mario held her tightly and kissed her passionately. It more than answered her.

"I'm convinced," he said, "that everyone will envy me tonight."

"Flatterer."

As they kissed again, they were surprised by Countess Jolanda and her husband.

"Good for you both!" exclaimed the count. "And to think we've been waiting for you for a quarter of an hour."

"Well, here we are," replied Mario. "We just wanted to kiss our son before leaving."

"It would seem that Gino had nothing to do with it," said the countess as they all enjoyed the joke.

By the time they reached Signora Sigrano's palazzo, many guests had already arrived. Sultana went over to greet them enthusiastically. She was dazzling in a light lilac dress, which was boldly low-cut to show off her sculptural figure. She was wearing a few rows of pearls in her hair, and her lips were blood red in contrast to her immaculate white complexion. Brown eye shadow lightly rimmed her blue eyes.

"Thank you so much for coming," she said, embracing Countess Jolanda and Anna Maria. In turn, she shook hands with the count and Mario.

"It's strange to see you in civilian clothes," she said to Mario. "You look like someone else."

"Really, signora," said the young man with a slight start, "but is that a good or a bad thing?"

"Not so good, at least in my opinion. Sorry, excuse me, but my duties as a hostess are calling me. Please, make yourselves at home."

She left them alone so she could greet some other guests who were just arriving. In the large attractive room, chairs had been arranged for the concert, and on an improvised stage, a grand piano had been set up along with music stands complete with scores.

Anna Maria and Countess Jolanda took their seats in the second row where two chairs were still free. Mario and his father had already said they would stand. Mario decided to approach a group of young men he knew who welcomed him with cries of surprise and delight.

"You! Here in Turin? Since when?" they asked.

"For a month or more."

"And yet you've never made an appearance? Is it true that you've taken a wife? Have you left the army?"

The questions flew over each other like crossfire. Mario answered them in turn, rediscovering his former vivacity.

"Did you expect to find Signora Sigrano a widow, rich as Croesus, and a hundred times more beautiful than before?" one of the men whispered to him in a low voice. "If only you knew how many flies are buzzing round her. For now, her favorite seems to be young Duke Farelli, the handsome guy now talking to the signora's mother."

"Is Signora Sigrano's mother here?" asked Mario with some vehemence.

"Yes, she's been around for two days, and it's said that she'll stay with her daughter. As we know, Sultana pays a lot of attention to her appearance even though she's free to do so, but with her mother around she'll take on some little deserved respectability."

The young man smiled and winked at Mario, who moved to one side rather brusquely.

"I don't pay attention to such tittle tattle," he answered harshly. "I've always known the signora to be a lady worthy of respect. She's my mother's friend and my wife's, therefore I won't hear her talked about so frivolously in my presence."

He turned away from the group. In truth, he felt anger and spite on hearing that Sultana had many suitors. He felt nothing but dislike and jealousy towards the young duke although he had never met him.

Driven by feelings stronger than his willpower, Mario crossed the room to where he could see Signora Sigrano, who at that moment, was next to her mother and Duke Farelli. Seeing him, she called out with a degree of familiarity: "Mario, come here. Come and introduce yourself to my mother. She's really keen to meet Jolanda and your wife. Mamma, this is Count Mario Herbert. I've already told you about him and his marriage to the teacher Tosingo's daughter. Mario felt he was under the spotlight as the elderly Countess Falminio, tall, stiff, and typically aristocratic, stared at him through her eyeglass. Eventually, she held out a hand.

"I'm pleased to meet you. I've noticed with pleasure your wife, who used to come up to the castle to bring us produce from the garden and chicken coop. She was very pretty."

The allusion to Anna Maria's humble birth acted like a slap across Mario's face, especially as Duke Farelli had overheard the conversation. Anger inflamed his cheeks, but he managed to control himself.

"The countess, my wife, will be happy to see you again, as indeed, my mother will be delighted to meet you."

Bowing low to the elderly lady, he tried to walk away only to be stopped by Sultana.

"One moment, count," she said in a dulcet tone of voice. "I'd like you to do me a favor."

Forgetting his annoyance, Mario turned.

"At your service, signora," he answered, heady with enthusiasm.

"Please stay and help my mother with her hostess duties. You'll know most of the guests. I have to look after the performers who are waiting for me in another room."

"Certainly, signora."

"Bravo, Mario," Sultana replied cheerfully. "I'm putting my trust in you. Come along with me, duke."

She leaned languidly on the handsome young man's arm, pulling him away. Disheartened, Mario looked after the couple who were walking away smiling. Was Sultana trying to make fun of him? The most absurd ideas flashed through his mind. He immediately regretted coming to the party and decided to leave but, understanding the ridiculousness of such a notion, was drawn back to his duties by the arrival of several guests.

In the end, what did it matter if Sultana was paying attention to others like the duke? If she thought she could irritate him, she was mistaken. He loved his decent, trustworthy wife, and it was reciprocated. This thought calmed him, letting him play with ease the part Signora Sigrano had given to him.

With the space full, the concert began. Sultana sat in the front row with her mother on one side and another elderly lady on the other. Mario, who had been circulating around the room, glanced around to see if he could spot the duke. With surprise, he saw him a short distance away from where his wife and mother were sitting next to the wall. He was speaking to his father. Driven by curiosity, he approached only to be stopped by Count Giorgio himself: "Come! Let me introduce you to Duke Alessandro Farelli's son. Alessandro is a dear friend from my school days. We met him last year in Switzerland during the month I spent there with your mother."

"I was there too with my father," added the duke, "and it was a nice surprise to see you here tonight. But I haven't had the honor of meeting your son although I recognized his name when Signora Sigrano introduced him to her mother, Countess Flaminio. I didn't have time to ask because the signora led me away, but I'm now happy to shake your hand, and I hope we can become friends just like our fathers."

Duke Giorgiano Farelli expressed himself in such a charming manner that Mario felt his feelings melt away and shook his hand enthusiastically.

"Oh, yes, I hope so too."

At this point, they fell silent when they saw an attractive young woman appear on the stage who was about to play a piano piece. She immediately won over the audience with her agile playing and feeling for the performance. A true artist, projecting the power of the music, she was followed by a talented singer, then an eminent violinist.

Mario, next to his new friend, seemed intent on listening to the artists, but his eyes honed in on Sultana. Several times his gaze caught hers as she looked to one side, but he was unable to tell if the glance was meant for him or Duke Giorgiano. During an interval, Mario, despite himself, turned to the duke.

"Have you known Signora Sigrano for long?"

"For a week," the duke replied candidly. "I was introduced to her by Marquise Campi, with whom I'm staying because she's an old friend of the family and a distant relative."

"So, you're just passing through?" Mario asked.

"Yes, I won't be here long unless circumstances change."

"What do you think of the signora?" said a somewhat surprised Mario.

"Very beautiful," replied the duke, "however, she's one of those beauties who overwhelm the senses but leave the heart rather empty. I'm not looking for just physical attraction in a woman," he added in a lowered voice.

A cloud lifted from Mario.

"That's exactly what I think."

He then turned to look at his wife with affection, just as she glanced up at him smiling. It was already clear, he thought, that Sultana's coquetry was doing her no favors with the duke. He was cheered by this conclusion.

After the concert, Mario introduced his wife and mother to Giorgiano. Farelli was clearly enchanted by the young countess's wonderfully clear complexion and graceful behavior. Anna Maria, with her simple beauty and uncomplicated manner, had eclipsed Sultana. He also passed comment on Countess Jolanda. "Your mother," he said to Mario with sincerity, "really reminds me of my own, of whom I'm very fond. And your wife is one of those ideal women we were talking about earlier. I can see why you're so happy."

"Yes, indeed!" Mario exclaimed eagerly, proudly appreciating the praise directed at his loved ones.

It was at that point that Sultana approached with her mother, the countess. After an exchange of introductions and compliments, the elderly Countess Flaminio stared at Anna Maria with her eyeglass.

"I wouldn't have recognized you, my dear. Never would I have thought you could wear the crown of a countess in such a worthy fashion," she said with an insincere smile.

"My Anna Maria would not be out of place on the steps up to a throne," replied Jolanda quickly, seeing the effect the old woman's humiliating words had had on her daughter-in-law. "The nobility of her character trumps nobility of birth, and I'm proud of my son's choice."

The light returned to Anna Maria's eyes, and she smiled.

"Thank you, mamma," she whispered gently.

"You're absolutely right, and I can't help but approve," said Countess Flaminio in a gentler tone.

Sultana had failed to notice the incident as she was intent on talking to Count Herbert and Mario. She was astonished to hear that the count knew Farelli's father. Giorgio, however, had heard the old woman's sarcasm and his wife's response, which only served to increase his pride in his family.

After the concert, Signora Sigrano's more intimate friends were brought together for a dinner in the winter garden of the palazzo. Sultana was seated between Count Herbert and Duke Farelli Snr. Mario took up his place between his wife and Countess Flaminio, whereas Jolanda found herself close to the young duke. There were no more than twenty around the table, mostly men. The table itself was splendid, like something from the Thousand and One Nights, with abundant flowers and silverware, all lit by electric bulbs.

Sultana had never been livelier, ensuring she attended to everyone but paying special attention to the duke next to her, who appeared to have fallen under her spell. At least, so it seemed to Mario, who was once again piqued by jealousy. Indeed, his wife was beautiful, decent, even angelic, but she lacked Sultana's inexhaustible spirit, her fire and passion.

The assembled gathering was hanging on her every word, and she reigned supreme. And to think, he mused, that such a woman, desired by all, had once belonged to him. She had been so in love with him that she was prepared to commit a crime. Yet now, she had ceased to care about him at all, as if he'd ceased to exist. She barely looked at him and didn't talk to him in the way she did to the others.

He was irritated by her attitude, and it made him tense. To dispel the dark thoughts swirling through his brain, he started to drink heavily. Anna Maria noticed but had no idea of the cause, given she was now utterly convinced that Sultana was no longer bothered about her husband.

"It's not going to do you any good, drinking so much," she shyly whispered to him.

The young man shrugged his shoulders.

"I'm absolutely fine. Why don't you have some more?" he replied smiling, almost as if he wanted to deceive himself.

Anna Maria made no response. The coffee and liqueurs had been prepared in a nearby room, and most of the guests filed through after the dinner was over. Some of the men remained in the garden to smoke, and Mario remained with them. His wife, after asking, went back to the piano to play, and Duke Giorgiano stayed with her so he could turn the sheet music. Several groups had formed in the coffee room. Countess Flaminio and Countess Jolanda sat next to each other and started an animated conversation. Sultana went back into the winter garden to make sure everyone had been served some coffee, then disappeared through a door to her private apartment.

She felt the need to be alone for a few minutes. Despite the *joie de vivre* that she had projected, she was not happy. She had heard too much praise for Anna Maria and had noticed the duke's admiration. Considering herself more attractive, she had no idea how she could be compared unfavorably. She threw herself into an armchair and tried to pull herself together but was startled to see a door opening and Mario appear. Sultana held back her emotion and stood up.

"You?" she said harshly with a disdainful frown on her lips.

"Yes, it's me," he replied, ignoring her attitude. "I wanted to be alone with you for a moment."

"Are you crazy? Are you trying to compromise me?"

"Nobody will notice. All the men are busy talking about politics, and the ladies are listening to music."

Sultana was barely able to suppress her impatience.

"Right, what do you what from me?"

The copious quantities of wine Mario had drunk made him reckless, enflaming his thoughts.

"I have to tell you, Sultana, that you're so beautiful you would tempt a saint…and I'd give an arm and leg to still have you."

Sultana burst out laughing.

"Would you care to repeat that in front of your wife?"

The observation brought a moment of sanity, but nevertheless, he wanted to maintain an air of confidence.

"Of course not," he replied, "for your sake. I wouldn't want to take away the esteem that Anna Maria has for you."

Sultana laughed again.

"Esteem? Really?"

"Certainly. I'm sure. Why? Are you in any doubt?"

"Well, no! And it's precisely to keep her respect that I'm telling you to go away. Keep a rein on your feelings even if they're useless. Arm and leg or not, there's no going back to a past I've buried forever."

"Sultana!"

"Go away, I tell you. I don't know what to do with you. Since you're here, I'll gladly tell you to your face — I hate you!"

"Because you love someone else."

"So what? I don't have to answer to you for my actions. I'll say again, leave me alone."

Sultana was so beautiful in her animosity that Mario forgot himself once again.

"No, don't push me away!" he pleaded. "Sultana, don't say you hate me. It's not possible that you feel nothing for me…after all you did." He repeated the same thoughts, thoughts that had been flooding his fevered mind. Sultana collected herself.

"Well, indeed, you've just said it. It was for you, for you, that I killed Alceste, for you I turned to murder. And what did I get in return? You squashed me, humiliated me, and treated me like a common streetwalker. You were impassive to my cry for help, and moreover, you married the very person who loved the man whose life I'd taken for you. Anna Maria knows all about this as well. I told her myself precisely to make her end her relationship with you."

Mario was shocked to such an extent that it brought him to his senses.

"So, Anna Maria knew? No, you must be lying."

This provoked Sultana's biggest explosion of laughter.

"Ah, you've been putty in her hands! I'm lying? Ask her to her face, and you'll see if she has the courage to deny it. Yes, Anna Maria has known everything since Alceste's death."

Mario put his head in his hands.

"She knew…she knew," he repeated.

"Yes," she continued, happy to take revenge. "You don't know your wife. She's smarter than you, than everyone. She puts on this appearance of decency and naivety. She knew everything. Her fiancé confessed it all in a letter and also left her the note I'd written to you. He'd taken it along with a locket that I'd had made for my husband, which he stole from me. With these items, Anna Maria threatened that to reveal everything to Bruno if I didn't end things with you. She was deaf to my tears, my begging. She forced me to bend to her will and let her have you, and all the while she wanted you kept in the dark.

"But now I'm free now. I don't fear her any longer, so I can tell you that the young woman you married, for whom you trampled all over me, had no other aim in becoming your wife than to avenge her dead fiancé."

Mario listened in silence, crushed. Stirring to action, he grabbed Sultana by the wrists.

"Is this true, what you've told me?"

"It's the truth I swear to you. Perhaps I'm a coward to reveal this, but I can't stand seeing your wife lauded by everyone, even by your mother. Whereas I, the victim of her revenge, have to bow down, defeated, before her."

"Why didn't you tell me everything before the wedding?" Mario said, shaken.

"Because you wouldn't have believed me!" Sultana exclaimed vehemently. "Only a while back you said I was lying."

"You're right! I'm sorry," Mario replied, letting Sultana's arms drop to her sides. "And to think I had so much faith in her and her love for me. She really knew how to trick me. Now, I'll have to get my own back."

"Please don't create a scandal," Sultana said, feigning pity. "Just try to get her to confess and retrieve those items that belong to me. We can destroy them together and work out what to do next."

"And will you forgive me, Sultana?" Mario asked in an uncertain voice.

"Perhaps. We'll talk again. Now let me return to my guests to avoid any suspicion. Stay here a little longer so you can collect yourself a bit. You need to."

"Yes, you're right," Mario murmured, obedient like a child. "When will I be able to see you again?"

"I'll be at home every afternoon from two until four," she replied, opening the door to leave.

Mario slumped in an armchair, his palms covering his burning brow. If what Sultana had said was true, he had rejected a woman who loved him for another who had used him to avenge the only man she really loved. This now explained Anna Maria's sudden bouts of melancholy and why she occasionally pulled back when he came to embrace her. He had thought this was due to her shyness. What a hypocrite! what a despicable individual! And to think she was the mother of his child. For the sake of his son, he would suppress any violent feelings and avoid a scandal, but Alceste was now a barrier between him and his wife. She had accepted his revenge mission, playing her role with candor, acting out noble sentiments just to make him fall, naïve and unaware, into her trap.

There was nothing left between them now. Even though he would not seek a legal separation because of his son, they would have to live apart. He would have liked to stay in the chair ruminating, but hasty footsteps outside made him get up quickly. Teresa, Sultana's trusted servant, entered the room.

"My mistress begs you to come to the dining room because they're looking for you. Come this way. You won't bump into anyone."

Mario had regained a modicum of calm, a certain sangfroid.

"I'll follow you," he said. When he appeared, he saw his wife talking with the duke and Sultana with his father. They were laughingly cheerfully. His mother was with Countess Flaminio as before. The other guests had all departed.

"Where have you been hiding out?" Sultana asked so all could hear. "People were looking for you but couldn't find you."

"I'm afraid, signora, that I have to blame your exquisite champagne," replied Mario. "It gave me a bit of a woozy head, and I retired to the darkest corner of your winter garden to sleep it off on one of your wicker chairs behind a palm tree."

This amused those gathered.

"Did you, at the very least, have a nice dream?" Sultana asked.

"Indeed, lovely!" Mario answered.

"What a pity, though, that you missed the pleasure of hearing the countess sing," added the duke enthusiastically. "She was better than the artists at tonight's concert."

Anna Maria blushed.

"I know my wife's voice well, but she's often somewhat coy about it with me."

"That's because at home your son takes up almost all of her time," said Jolanda, "as well as mine. Anyway, that's enough of all that. We should be going. Don't you know it's three in the morning, Mario?"

He forced himself to laugh.

"I've already had a sleep. I'm not tied anymore," he replied. "When we get home, I'll shut myself up in the study and have a read and a smoke."

Anna Maria showed no surprise at this suggestion, persuaded as she was that he had nodded off in the winter garden. She had not noticed that Sultana had gone missing since she had been preoccupied with her music and with talking with Giorgiano. She had spent an enchanting evening and had said as much to Sultana.

"Let's hope it's not the last," she had replied with a peculiar smile.

When everyone had finally left and Sultana was alone, she could not resist a cacophonous laugh, which contorted her face in a hideous expression. As she retired to her bedroom, she vowed that revenge would not escape her this time.

22

Mario got into the car and sat next to his father, while his mother and wife took their places on the seat in front. During the journey, all but Mario spoke of the party's success and of Duke Farelli who they all thought would become Signora Sigrano's husband.

"But he's much younger than she," observed Anna Maria.

"I don't see youth as an obstacle," said Count Giorgio, "because Sultana is as fresh as a woman of twenty-five. Although, I rather fear if the duke learns about Signora Sigrano's past, he might change his mind about marrying her."

"Such information, just like appearances, is always false," said Mario, who, up until that point, had been silent. "It would be better for Farelli to hear the truth from the signora's own mouth. Even if she has faults to be forgiven, she also has a quality frequently lacking in women — sincerity. And it won't be she, for fear of seeing a marriage go awry, who hides her thoughts. Unfortunately, many young women do that to capture the gullible sap who believes their naivety."

Anna Maria was troubled by this comment but had no idea that her husband was planning his escape. His parents did not reply as the car had pulled up outside their home at that very moment.

After kissing them goodnight, Giorgio and Jolanda left the couple and went to their rooms on the first floor. Mario and Anna Maria went upstairs. The servants had been told not to wait up for them. When Anna Maria was at the bedroom door, Mario took her hand in a weary manner.

"Have a good rest. I'm going for a smoke."

She looked at him with a wan expression and surprise in her eyes. She seemed upset by his lack of tiredness.

"Aren't you coming to kiss our son?" she asked.

"I don't want to wake him," Mario replied. "I'll see him in a few hours. It's almost daylight."

Without further ado, he turned away, walked into the adjoining drawing room, and then on to the study. He sank into a low armchair, crossed his arms, and started to think about the night's events. The more he thought of Anna Maria's deception, the more indignant he became, and the quicker his love turned to hate. Had Sultana been telling the truth? Yes, he thought so, especially since she had pushed him to make his wife confess and get back the items Anna Maria had used to plot her revenge.

He had the crazy thought that he should rush to his wife's room and force her to confess at that very moment. However, he was afraid that if he behaved in a violent manner, it would cause a disturbance, and his parents would come to defend her. Yet even his mother and father must be ignorant of the truth, if not how could they have allowed the marriage to go ahead.

Anna Maria had deceived them all, which diminished the image of his wife even further and made Sultana stand out amid the chaos. Unfortunately, she had admitted to taking other lovers, Alceste being one, but had, so to speak, been more upfront in her affection after meeting him. Sultana had truly loved him. It was no momentary lapse that had led to their relationship but love, and he couldn't see his way to condemning it.

She had cried and suffered for him, had lamented their breakup. She had allowed herself to be squashed, trampled, and torn apart, bowing before a girl who had avenged her fiancé, but he had been the main reason for Alceste's death. Mario had taken a handkerchief from his pocket. He bit down on it to avoid screaming out with frustration. Gradually, his troubled state of mind began to ease, much to his relief, as he realized he could dominate his emotions.

He was about to get up and go to his room when he heard the drawing room door open and light footsteps approach. Anna Maria, gaunt and wrapped in a white dressing gown, appeared in the doorway. Mario remained in the armchair.

"Didn't you go to bed?" he asked her calmly.

She stared at him without saying anything, then took a seat next to him.

"I couldn't, my dear," she replied tenderly, leaning towards his chair. "I was restless because of you."

"Really?" Why?"

"I've never seen you like you were tonight," she added softly, "and I thought that perhaps you were upset that I'd played the piano and sung without asking you."

"That's ridiculous, and if you've got nothing else on your conscience...."

He made this comment with such force that it made Anna Maria flinch.

"Mario, you're frightening me!"

"Oh!" he exclaimed, a sardonic smile on his face. "My poor little thing. My poor naïve little creature."

The expression on Anna Maria's face changed. Her eyes narrowed, and she took a deep breath.

"What a way to talk to your son's mother! What's this ironical tone all about?" she asked in a curt voice. "What have I done to deserve this?"

Mario had been a little shocked by his wife's entrance. He wanted to avoid saying anything and to forget about it all but was ashamed of his own weakness. He thought of Sultana and decided to challenge Anna Maria's frowning stare.

"What have you done?" he said. "You've deceived me from the very start."

"Me?" she said, more surprised than indignant.

"Yes, you. It's pointless trying to pose as an outraged wife. Instead, just answer my questions."

"Ok, I will."

"Before you moved to Turin, had you ever heard about me? Had anyone ever mentioned me?"

The color drained from Anna Maria's cheeks.

"No, never!" she replied despite her reaction.

"You're lying, as always."

"Mario!"

"Yes, you're lying. You knew about me. You came to me. You made me fall in love with you, playing out your ingenious but unworthy comedy, laced with tenderness — all for the purpose of stealing me away from your rival and avenging Alceste, the man you loved."

Anna Maria was thunderstruck. Pale as a ghost, she fell to her knees, extending her trembling hands to her husband.

"Mario, listen to me."

"Tell me the truth. Confess it all," he shouted violently. "How much of what I've just said is really true?"

"Yes, but let me tell you everything. Let me explain…."

"It's useless. I wouldn't believe you. How stupid I was to trust your honesty! You must've been laughing at me."

Anna Maria looked at him, her eyes full of tears, her expression humble.

"Mario, listen to me," she said, shaking, "I'm not as guilty as you think. I've told your mother the full story, and she's forgiven me. She, herself, advised me to refrain from telling you. It's true, before I got to know you, I had no affectionate thoughts. I knew you were Signora Sigrano's lover and that, because of you, she had killed the man I was engaged to. Alceste had a premonition that he would die at that woman's hands,… and he wrote to me the day before the tragic events unfolded."

"I want that letter!" Mario interrupted aggressively. "I want it. I have the right to read it."

Anna Maria remained on her knees, still clinging to her husband. Between sobs, she continued: "You will have it," she stammered, "but let me finish. I won't deny it and can't deny that before meeting you in person I had promised to take revenge for Alceste and steal you away from her. But when I got to know your kindness and began to understand that you loved me, I pushed away any thoughts of vengeance. I only thought of loving you, getting you to trust me, forgetting about the past. I couldn't forgive myself for having once wanted to make you suffer thanks to that woman. The better you treated me, the more that memory haunted me. I was often on the point of confessing it all and asking for your forgiveness, but I never had the courage for fear of losing you. Yet I told your mother everything, even handing her Alceste's letter and the other objects, which she returned to me a few days ago. We were going to destroy them together, but thank God, we didn't."

Anna Maria appeared sincere. Nonetheless, Mario who had adored her and had more than enough proof of her decency and honesty, seemed to feel no pity. Instead, he had an almost cruel satisfaction in seeing her so distressed, pleading at his feet. With little effort on his part, he had reached the moment he had hoped for.

"Give me the letter and those objects," he repeated.

Anna Maria got up without answering, wiped her tears from her eyes, and left the room. She returned shortly after, bringing with her a package that, although no longer sealed, still bore Alceste's words: 'To Anna Maria, to be opened in the event of my death or to be returned intact on the day of our wedding.' The young woman handed it over to her husband, then sat down, still clearly distraught.

Mario paid no attention to her. He opened the package and immediately saw the locket with the initials A. B.: "To Bruno," Mario read aloud and added, "this locket was for the lawyer, and Alceste stole it."

"You're wrong," Anna Maria answered in a thin voice, "those are the initials of Alceste Bianco."

Although Mario believed her, he still wanted to contradict his wife: "Well, you could see it either way," he added, "but that's not what matters to me."

He picked up the note Sultana had written to him, his face reddening as he did so.

"And this, surely this was stolen?"

Anna Maria nodded her head without replying. Mario then took Alceste's letter and began to read it. The words revealed all of Sultana's treachery. He winced, although it was not from the shame of having loved such a woman but from jealousy. Alceste, who had received her attentions before him, had been totally besotted. On the other hand though, the words served as a pretext to further criticize Anna Maria, who at that moment was atoning for the guilt of others.

"Here they are, your guilty instructions!" he suddenly shouted. With an unsteady, angry voice, he started to read without a pause for breath.

I am writing to you, not only to tell you of my fears, but to confess my guilt and ask for your forgiveness. If I die, above all, I would like you to exact my revenge and to do the same for yourself. I am giving you the means, use them well.... You, alone, my dear, can repay the harm she has done to us both.

"Your Alceste knew that he wouldn't appeal to you in vain. Yet, I alone was the victim of your revenge. You hurt me in a way that I could never have hurt him in return because I had no idea he was my rival. And would you care to forgive me? Or perhaps I should hate myself?"

Anna Maria was sobbing.

"Yes, it was bad of me," she said, "but I've suffered a great deal."

"And was it me who made you suffer?"

Anna Maria bowed her head, dejected. Owing to her sense of right and wrong and an awareness of his mistakes, she could no longer find an answer. She was unable to hold back more tears. Nevertheless, she wondered who had revealed the secret, a secret only Sultana and Countess Jolanda knew. It could not have been Jolanda, since she would not have waited until then to pierce her son's heart and wound his pride. She had also wanted things dead and buried. Had Sultana been alone with Mario at some point?

His wife's wordless torment started to affect Mario, but he still had no intention of showing it, particularly as he was haunted by the image of Sultana, triumphant, declaring that she had told him the truth and that Anna Maria had only married him to break them up and avenge Alceste.

After a few minutes of terrible silence punctuated by her tears, Mario pocketed the letters and the locket.

"Stop your whining. It's useless, and it's only getting on my nerves. Listen! Does my father know anything about this?"

"Nothing," Anna Maria replied, her voice laden with emotion.

"Well," added Mario, "he must stay in the dark, and you also have to ensure that my mother keeps quiet about it too. I don't want any more of my loved ones to suffer because of me."

Anna Maria was clutching to a foolish hope: "So…will you forgive me?" she stammered.

Mario hesitated for a few seconds. Anna Maria stared at him, causing a fleeting moment of doubt, but it proved brief. Once more, Sultana dominated his thoughts.

"Even if I wanted to, I couldn't," he said slowly. "I don't respect you anymore. When I think that you've deceived me, I just feel anger, hatred. While you were telling me you loved me, you were only remembering him, and you enjoyed tricking me even when I was in love with you. I've got this image of you all wrapped up in your plot for revenge. But I'll say it again, for the sake of my parents and our son, I'll put on a brave face and keep quiet in front of everyone. I'll laugh despite feeling dreadful. And you, Anna Maria, will do the same thing. I insist that you do."

Anna Maria gasped, receiving the news like a blow to the chest.

"I will," she answered in a voice that betrayed her anguish.

"In front of anyone else, all this rancor has to disappear. I'll be the caring husband, the tender father, and you'll carry on playing the part of the loving wife and mother, just as you have up now. But when we're alone, the mask will drop. There'll be no more affection. We'll just spend the night apart."

"You're cruel, Mario! You've got no idea how much I'm suffering," Anna Maria replied in a weak, reedy voice.

"I'm suffering more than you, and I'm the innocent party. I've done nothing but love you from the first moment I saw you. I believed all your lies...."

Anna Maria started to wring her hands desperately: "I loved you too and always will, Mario. I regret having a single thought about hurting you."

"Did I hurt you? Did I? When I met Signora Sigrano, I didn't even know you existed, and from the moment I met you, I've been in love with you. I've been scrupulously faithful, even at the cost of appearing weak and spineless to others."

"Mario, Mario.... If you won't forgive me, if you don't believe me anymore, then it's over. Yes, it's over!"

"You're not going to obey me then?" he said angrily. "Do you want to cause a scandal that will rebound on our son's innocent head? Do you really want me to end up hating you?"

"No!" Anna Maria shouted. "I still hope that my remorse and the fact I still love you will, one day, touch your heart again, and things can be the same as before."

She stood up with difficulty, her face deathly pale.

"I've been wicked, briefly thinking of hurting you, but I've paid for it with these feelings of burning regret. When I thought it was all over, I tried to made amends. Your mother, who understood things better, forgave me because she felt, after I'd told her everything, that I'd not lost my innocence and still felt the same about you. You've got no intention of understanding me. You just want to punish me. I have to bow my head in resignation because, as well as my judge, you're the father of my son. Alright, I'll accept all the conditions you're imposing and won't let anything slip in front of your family. If your mother asks me for the letters and locket, I'll tell her that I destroyed everything so I could forget about the incident.

"Thank you for not wanting a formal break. If and when you've reconsidered and come to me with open arms, I'll remind you how much I loved you and continue to do so, how much I'll deserve your forgiveness."

Anna Maria turned to go. Mario made a gesture as if he wanted to hold her back, but let his hand fall, remaining silent, rooted to the spot. The young woman opened the door and left. On entering her room, she threw herself face down on the bed, her head buried in the pillows to stifle her anxious cries. As she abandoned herself to these feelings of desperation, the dawn began to break.

23

Sultana was in her parlor, reclining in an armchair. She was carefully reading a letter whose envelope, placed on a nearby table, bore a French stamp. The contents were certainly good news. A smile drifted across her face, and her eyes had lit up with malevolent intent. She looked more striking than ever in a light pink dressing gown that gave the illusion of nakedness. She was wondering if her aim would be successful as she put the letter back in the envelope and hid it in the coffee table drawer.

Sultana had given orders not to let anyone pass except Mario Herbert. She was waiting for him, sure that he would come, and happy in the knowledge of the harm she could inflict in revenge for all that had gone before. She no longer loved him. On the contrary, she wondered how she could have loved him so much that she was prepared to kill Alceste merely to fulfil her whims. Perhaps things had been more drawn out because of Mario's resistance and his love for Anna Maria. Now though, Sultana supposed that four years of marriage had dissipated that love to such an extent that he was beginning to find her attractive again. She wanted to take her revenge in a far more effective way than simply shooting a pistol. She smiled at the thought that she had only briefly considered suppressing her desire for vengeance.

As Sultana indulged these fantasies, feeling the voluptuous thrill of their potential impact, Teresa opened the door and announced the arrival of the young count.

"Bring him in," said Sultana, "and ensure that I'm not bothered. Has my mother gone out?"

"Yes, signora, in the car. She has to make four or five visits and won't be back until the evening."

"It's better that way."

A moment later, Mario entered. He looked washed out and had dark bags under his dejected eyes. Sultana stared at him sharply, then held out her hand with a smile.

"As you can see, I'm receiving you in private," she said straightaway, using the informal mode of address, "but I'll always consider you a friend."

"And I am, Sultana," Mario replied, bringing her hand to his lips. "Now more than ever."

"Truly?"

"I swear."

"There's no need for that. Let's just sit down and talk."

Tears came to Mario's eyes.

"I don't deserve your kindness," he said in an anguished voice. "I have cruelly offended you in the past."

Sultana's eyes suddenly widened.

"So now you realize?"

"I really do."

Sultana understood Mario's outburst but hid her reaction.

"Did your wife confess to everything?" she asked eagerly.

"Everything. You were right. She knew it all and had no other purpose in approaching me and getting engaged to me than avenging her dead fiancé and stealing me away from you. Although she hid the truth from me, Anna Maria told my mother. She told her that she was sorry for her thoughts of revenge because she'd fallen in love with me. And it seems my mother believed her."

Sultana continued to stare at him.

"And what about you?"

"I don't anymore. The only reason I'm not going to initiate a public break is to avoid a scandal and stop your name getting dragged into it. Anna Maria means nothing to me anymore, and we'll live like strangers behind closed doors."

"Has she accepted this?"

"Yes, for the sake of her son and because she knows she was guilty."

"One day you'll go back to her. You will forgive her!"

"No!" Mario answered resolutely. "I no longer love her, and I owe you an apology for all that you've suffered because of me. No, no, I can't forget that while Anna Maria was in the process of deceiving me, you loved me, you loved me to such an extent that you did what you did. And now I'm the one who's begging to have you back. I want you. I need you."

"Calm down, my friend!" Sultana said, her lips pursed in a sarcastic smile. "We haven't finished talking. Did Anna Maria show you the objects that she'd used against me?"

"Yes, I've brought them with me."

Sultana's face lit up as Mario removed them from his inside pocket in the packet that he'd received from his wife.

"Here they are," he added. "I'm giving them to you because the letter to me and the locket are your property. I really should've returned Alceste's letter to Anna Maria since it was addressed to her, but I wanted to bring it to you to confirm what you've revealed to me. Besides, I didn't want a document that compromises you to remain in her hands, and I'd be a coward if I kept it myself as a weapon against you."

"Oh, now you're your old self. My wonderful, generous Mario!" exclaimed Sultana, grabbing the package. "As I've already said, we'll destroy the evidence together so nothing remains of this painful past."

The fire was glowing in the fireplace. Sultana unwrapped the package, checking the contents for Alceste's letter, the copy of which she'd already read. Along with her note, plus the picture and hair from the locket, she threw it into the fire. She was silent, absorbed, until the fire had destroyed everything. She then broke the fragile locket with the fire tongs and turned her flushed but joyful face to look at Mario.

"Finally," she said, her voice still convulsed with emotion, "there's nothing left from that horrible period of my life."

"I'll always be here with you, Sultana," Mario said, trying to appeal to her. "I'll be yours, body and soul, from now on."

Sultana reacted with a laugh, which chilled him to the core.

"Why are you laughing?" he stammered, bewildered and humiliated.

"Because you've just made me a promise without knowing whether I'm willing to accept it."

Mario lost his color, and his attitude darkened.

"So, you don't want me anymore?"

"Even if I wanted you, I couldn't do anything about it. I'm with someone else."

He shuddered, livid with anger.

"I see!" he exclaimed, full of scorn. "Those who said your new favorite was Duke Farelli weren't wrong."

"No, my dear Mario," answered Sultana with a hint of irony, shrugging, "they were very wrong. Duke Farelli isn't my type. He might be able to please the likes of Anna Maria, but not a woman like me."

Mario went paler still.

"Why are you telling me this?"

"What! I'm telling you this to convince you that the duke is nothing to me."

"So, who are you with instead?"

Sultana smiled, diffident

"I ought to keep my mouth shut," she said, her tone now serious, "but since I've always considered you a friend, I'll tell you what until now has been a secret. Listen carefully."

She lent back in her chair, deliberately provocative, staring at him with that gaze, sweet and sensual, that both troubled him and bent him to her will.

"I'm listening," he managed to reply.

"You know how much I love you, so it's useless saying it again," added Sultana, her voice like a caress, "but you'll never know what I suffered in the months before your marriage when everyone believed I was grieving my father's death. It wasn't that anguish that made me despair, but not being able to come to you and shout that Anna Maria didn't love you and that by marrying you she was only avenging her fiancé. Her relentless figure was always there before me, appearing to threaten me with the evidence she had and her ability to drag my name through the mud. It was all a horrible torture for me."

Breathing heavily, she went silent for a moment. Her bloodshot eyes were filled with tears. Feeling bewildered, Mario knelt at her feet.

"You've suffered so much because of me. I didn't realize. Forgive me, please!" he said, tripping over his words.

Sultana seemed to collect herself.

"Get up," she said. "Reproach and repentance are useless now. Listen to me again."

Mario obeyed, unsteady, a frown beginning to spread over his face. Sultana continued: "Once your marriage had taken place and realizing that you were lost to me forever, your distance from Turin helped change my pain into resignation. I was already thinking of making amends for my past by dedicating myself entirely to my husband and children and then I became a widow. I'd never been in love with him, but I had a sincere affection for my husband. His death, if not pushing me into poverty, did curtail my lifestyle a lot. It also affected me a great deal. I was reduced to a few thousand lire a year, which was never enough for me. If it had happened when we were together, your love would've been enough of a compensation and I would've been happy to live in a simple bourgeois style, providing you were there."

"My dear Sultana," Mario murmured, moved by her words.

She pretended that she had not heard him and picked up the story.

"But you were already lost to me then, and I had to think about my own situation. I had the idea of looking for a rich and generous lover.…"

Mario shuddered at the thought, turning pale.

Nevertheless, Sultana still paid him no attention.

"Yes, I was determined, but one evening, since my uncle, Count Daniele Sigrano, was dying, he asked to see me. I'd only ever seen him a few times, but I knew he was a millionaire. Therefore, you can understand how quickly I hurried to him. He immediately asked to be alone with me so that we could talk. As I approached his bedside, he looked me straight in the eye and said: 'Yes, you are beautiful, and I can understand his passion for you'. I asked him who he was talking about, thinking he was raving. He then said: 'Have you never met a certain Ezio Marcelliano, who worked at your husband's office for a time?' I smiled and blushed. Ezio was a young man in his twenties, a clerk who was a poet and writer in his spare time. He had fallen madly in love with me and had written me sonnets, madrigals, and some incendiary letters. He was a handsome young man, but I was in love with you at the time and didn't care about him. I sent all his missives back, letting him know that if he didn't stop, I would tell my husband. A week later, Ezio left the office, and I never saw him again, so I was most surprised at my uncle's dying question, but I replied: 'Yes, I saw him sometimes, but he disappeared suddenly, and I heard no more about him.'

"My uncle admitted that he was the one who had suggested he leave. Realizing that his love would never be reciprocated, he'd tried to kill himself, but my uncle had been there to save him and to show him the insanity of his passion for someone else's wife whom he believed to be virtuous and honest. So, it was Daniele who ordered him to travel and forget me. Ezio obeyed and went to France where, under the name of Renier, he didn't take long to distinguish himself in the world of letters. My uncle was sure that he'd soon be famous the world over. Still in contact, despite his frequent travels, Daniele let him know that I was a widow and that he could aspire to my hand.

"More and more amazed, I leaned towards the dying man and asked him why he was so interested in Ezio. He looked at me, his eyes already veiled and said: 'Ezio, or Renier, is my son'. I just repeated what he had said. I was astonished. 'Yes,' he murmured, 'my natural son whom I didn't want to recognize when he was born. His poor mother has urged me to now, on my death bed, and so I've already made a will leaving him all my assets. However, Carli the notary, who is the only one to know the secret, will keep the document in a deposit box and won't enforce it on my death if you promise to marry my son and make him happy.' Daniele, my uncle, looked at me, imploring me, tears in his eyes. I couldn't resist. I told him he could die in peace and that I promised Ezio would be my beloved husband. 'Oh, thank you, Sultana,' he stammered with a great deal of effort. 'Carli will share everything with you and will give you the will to destroy as soon as the marriage has taken place'. He wasn't able to add anything else as all the emotion had hastened his end."

As Sultana was speaking, Mario felt his senses grow colder.

"So will you marry him?" he asked in an uncertain voice.

"Of course!" Sultana replied with surprising frankness. "I'd be stupid if I gave up my uncle's millions. I'll get married before the mayor and the priest, but my new husband must remain in the dark about the whole truth and continue to believe that my uncle was a mere benefactor whose memory will be a blessing."

"But you're going to marry him without loving him?" said Mario.

Sultana straightened up, raising her statuesque head.

"You're wrong!" she exclaimed. "How could I not love him? He tried to kill himself because of me and has longed for nobody else but me. It's thanks to him that I'm rich and can continue to live my life surrounded by love and respect. My poor Ezio, handsome and decent, was made to make others happy. Here read, read the letter in which he says he's going to arrive in a few days."

She opened the table drawer, took out the envelope with the French stamp, and gave it to Mario. He pushed it away, disconcerted.

"I'm not interested in what he writes to you," he said. "I'm only going to ask you this: what about me?"

"What! You!"

"Yes, I still love you, I still want you."

"That's enough!" Sultana interrupted indignantly. "I can forgive the harm you caused me and still consider you a friend, but I'll never be your lover again, never!"

"Sultana...."

"It's pointless. I can't forget."

"Why then," Mario shouted, jumping to his feet, "did you ruin my happiness by revealing Anna Maria's deception if you didn't want me anymore?"

Sultana also rose to her feet, staring at him with arrogance as if at that very moment she wanted to take revenge for all the humiliations she had suffered.

"Because I wanted to retaliate against Anna Maria and get hold of the objects from my odious past so I could destroy them. I didn't want anything to cloud my future."

Mario was shaken. "That's despicable! And that's what you used me for?"

"Didn't you use me in a much more cowardly manner to reach your goal?"

Mario, beside himself, raised his hand in anger as if he was intending to hit Sultana. She just looked at him defiantly with a mocking smile that made him ashamed of his threatening behavior. Nonetheless, he couldn't help letting an insult slip: "Well excuse me, but I seem to have a courtesan in front of me."

"And there I was thinking you had mistaken me for your wife."

Mario would never know how, in that moment, he had refrained from striking such a venomous woman. Perhaps he had been afraid of himself, or maybe he had realized that Sultana had secretly pressed the bell for her servants. Teresa came to the door in response.

"The count wants to leave," said Sultana. "Accompany him out."

Mario staggered from the room without saying a word. His face was so livid and full of dismay that even Teresa noticed.

"Is the count not feeling well?" she asked him. The question was enough to bring him to his senses.

"I'm fine, thank you," he replied, "but the signora's room was so hot I felt as if I couldn't breathe."

"Your right. I really don't know how my mistress puts up with it."

She helped Mario put on his coat, handed him his hat, and opened a window in the anteroom.

"Give my greetings to the countess."

"Thank you. Goodbye."

Mario found himself outside in the street, his mind in complete turmoil.

24

Although Anna Maria, seated at a table with her husband and in-laws at midday, tried to appear as happy as usual, her complexion, wandering gaze, and agitated lips betrayed her internal anxiety. Count Herbert attributed his daughter-in-law's drawn appearance to the night before.

"You see, my girl, that party has worn you out."

"It's true," Anna Maria replied, blushing and smiling at the same time. "I'm not used to spending the night out enjoying myself and dining out."

"It's your fault," said Mario, cheerfully. "I know I said I wasn't tired, but if you'd copied me and gone to bed, you'd be fresh as a daisy and ready for the day. I slept like a log and didn't even bother calling for breakfast."

Countess Jolanda, who had been observing her closely, had noticed something more in her appearance than mere tiredness. "What was that? Didn't you go to bed?

"No, mamma," answered Anna Maria softly. "It was almost daybreak, and Gino had woken up."

"Well, have a nap in the afternoon," added Mario, "while I go and get the music you wanted."

"Yes, that'll be good," replied Anna Maria without glancing at him.

After they had eaten, father and son went to have a smoke. Jolanda and Anna Maria went into the parlor where the governess was looking after the child, who distracted the ladies with his chatter. Eventually, Mario and the count entered.

"I'm going to rest," said the elder Herbert.

"Gino, do you want to kiss your grandfather?" said Anna Maria.

"One for me too," Mario added, "I'm going out."

The child passed from the count's hands to Mario, who kissed him and passed him to Anna Maria.

"Go and put him to bed. Let him have his nice afternoon nap, and get some sleep yourself. See you in a bit."

"Aren't you going to kiss your wife before you leave?" said Countess Jolanda, surprised by his forgetfulness, given he always did.

"Sorry!" Mario replied with a false smile, approaching his wife who had stayed silent. "I was distracted." He bent to kiss her. Jolanda watched them intently, seeing the young woman's complexion change further, but she did not utter a word. Mario turned to face her: "And you, mamma, aren't you joining papa?" he asked.

"I never sleep during the day. You know that," Jolanda answered, "and beside, I'm not tired at all because I didn't rise until eleven o'clock. Go, all of you, go and do whatever you need to do. I'll stay here and read the newspapers."

"See you then, mamma," Anna Maria said gently, leaving with the governess and with her son in her arms. Mario left in turn. His father had already gone downstairs to his bedroom. A maid came into the room to ask Countess Jolanda if she needed anything.

"Yes," she answered. "Make sure my son has left, then go, and call my daughter-in-law. Tell her I need a moment to talk to her. It's a problem trying to catch her without her husband, and I'd like to arrange something secretly while Mario's away so we can surprise him at Christmas. Make sure you're not seen by my son, and if he's anywhere near his wife, just say you're there to ask if she needs anything."

"Yes, countess, I understand."

The maid believed Jolanda because the house was a peaceful united one, and she had not the slightest suspicion about the unfolding drama. The countess had randomly picked up a magazine about embroidery that had been lying on the small table and seemed intent on examining the designs, but she was looking at them without really seeing them, absorbed in her disturbing thoughts.

Suddenly a door opened, and Anna Maria appeared. She seemed calm again, and her color had returned.

"Here I am, mamma," she said.

"Close the door, please, and come here. I need to talk to you."

Anna Maria went over to sit in an armchair facing the countess.

"What do you want to say to me, mamma?" she asked in a calm tone.

"Before explaining, I want to be sure that Mario has really gone out."

"Yes, mamma. I saw hm cross the avenue when I glanced out the window."

"Right then, look me in the eye and answer me: has something happened?"

"No, mamma, no!" the young woman replied, her voice wavering, and face showing her anxiety.

Jolanda shook her head. "You're not telling the truth, and I can see you're hurting. You know you promised to be straight with me about your relationship with my son and his behavior, whatever the story. I noticed something happened last night. Yes…Sultana wasn't in the room when Mario was in the winter garden."

Anna Maria was startled.

"Did Sultana leave the hall?" she said, gripped by shock.

"Yes, you didn't notice because you were playing the piano, but I spotted it all, and when she returned, she seemed quite distracted. Even Mario's demeanor had altered, and I think the tale about sleeping in the garden was a pack of lies. Look, you're beginning to cry.… What is it? You're hiding something from me. Aren't I like a second mother to you?"

Anna Maria could resist no more in the face of Jolanda's care and concern. She dropped to the floor before the countess, buried her face in the woman's lap, and let the tears flow. Jolanda let her vent, gently stroking her head.

"Open up to me completely. Let me know what's hurting you so I can find a remedy," she said when the young woman had calmed slightly.

"You won't be able to anymore, mamma dear," she replied in desperation.

"And why?"

"Because Mario has found out that I knew everything before I married him, and he can't forgive me. He no longer believes in me and thinks I approached him out of revenge."

Jolanda was stunned. "But who could have told him all this?"

"Who?!" Anna Maria shouted, wiping her remaining tears while trying to stem new ones about to fall. "Sultana, herself, who clearly isn't frightened of me anymore."

Still kneeling before the countess, her hands in Jolanda's lap, she told her of the argument with Mario and her agreement to keep quiet, but it was evident she could no longer hold it all in. Jolanda understood her turmoil and the ordeal her son must have endured because of Sultana's brutal revenge.

"And you gave those precious items to your husband?" she asked. "Didn't you realize Sultana had audaciously set a trap to get them back, and Mario had walked straight into it. I bet she's taken them, and now we don't have anything against her anymore."

Anna Maria felt like her world was collapsing.

"My God!" she stuttered, "That woman, that vile woman, and to think we believed she was harmless these days. She's stronger and more dangerous than ever. I reckon she'll make us pay for the humiliation she's had to put up with! And we've got nothing left to fight her with. Mario despises me now. He hates me because of her. It's all thanks to her he'll abandon me and his son."

Anna was heartbroken, succumbing to floods of seemingly endless tears. The countess lifted her into her arms like a child and clasped her tightly, kissing her tenderly.

"Hush now, don't take on so, my daughter," she said, "I'm here to defend you. I won't let such wickedness triumph. You've had ample opportunity to know Mario, and you know that if it's in his nature to be a little weak, even impressionable, he's got a generous heart. He's been too deeply in love with you to refuse to forgive you such a fleeting flirtation with revenge, especially as, over these past four years of life together, he knows your feelings for him and your kind heart. If, at that woman's behest, he didn't believe you, he will believe me, his mother, who's never lied to him in his life."

Anna Maria stared at her, assailed by a tentative hope.

"Oh, mamma!" she said. "If only that were true, what you're saying…. If he would just come back to me. Mamma, if only you knew how much I love him."

"If I weren't sure about that, I wouldn't try and rescue the situation," replied Jolanda, "but I'm convinced that your life, your happiness, depends on your husband's love. Before you'd met my son, you made no attempt to reflect on the feelings that were making you act. You knew nothing but the fact that Mario was that woman's lover and she had killed your fiancé because of him. When you realized my Mario was a victim who had tried to escape her clutches, your heart won out. You didn't grasp that by saving him, you were loving him in a way you'd never loved Alceste. The sincerity of your sentiments made your conscience clean."

"Yes, mamma, that's right!" Anna Maria cried out eagerly. "Only you understand me."

Countess Jolanda kissed her again.

"Take hope," she added, smiling serenely, "and try not to worry anymore. I really suggest you go and rest, you need to regain your strength so that Mario sees you as beautiful and calm as before. I'll wait here for him. Trust me and don't leave your room until I let you know, either that or I'll come and get you myself. Have a good rest, my dear."

Anna Maria hugged her once more.

"Mamma, I haven't lost everything because I know you still love me. May God reward you for this. All I can do is dedicate my life to you."

"Dedicate it to your husband and child. Their happiness will be my reward."

Once Anna Maria had gone, Jolanda was left alone with her thoughts. A black cloud hovered on the horizon. She vowed that Sultana would not have her son and that she would snatch him back from her grasping hands. She knew that any attempt to attract him had nothing to do with love but was an act of retaliation against her and Anna Maria. She was astonished at Sultana's capacity for malevolent deeds.

Mario's poor mother saw an abyss open before her son and was unsure how to pull him back. Was it really possible that he had forgotten the past four years of comfortable domesticity with Anna Maria and the baby. The clock ticked away, and the countess thought of going to the study adjacent to the bedroom, which Mario would be using, given he had severed any intimacy with Anna Maria. The room was in darkness when she arrived. The window shutters and heavy curtains were closed, as was the door to the bedroom. Jolanda was not bothered by the lack of light. She sat down in a chair and waited impatiently for Mario's return.

She had warned the maid that if anyone came to ask for her, she should tell them that she had gone out. Jolanda's thoughts were still focused on her son, wondering what would become of him if he fell back into that woman's hands. Sultana was the very model of the modern sinner who shamefully betrayed the most wholesome of duties, following an immoral path with no remorse, no shame, and a smile on her lips, defying with impunity a society that believed in her good name and bowed before her triumphs as a rich, elegant, and beautiful woman. Her thoughts then passed to Anna Maria, decent, honest, and so wounded that she had to lower her head before such a brazen woman as if she were guilty. No, it was simply not fair.

After several hours, Jolanda suddenly heard her son's voice in the corridor telling the maid that he had no need anything and was not to be disturbed. The countess had just enough time to get up and hide behind the heavy window curtain. Mario came in, switched on the electric light, and locked the door behind him to ensure nobody else could enter. From a small gap in the curtains, Jolanda could see that Mario looked drawn, his face showing signs of stress. He bore no resemblance to a man just returned from a tryst. He went into the bedroom, staying there for a few minutes. Jolanda heard him close another door, the one leading to Anna Maria's room. When he returned, he had removed his hat and coat. Under the glare of the electric light, he had a ghostly appearance. He took the same seat his mother had just been using and, resting his elbows on the nearby desk, buried his head in his hands. What was he thinking? Was he tearful? Jolanda was unsure. It was then she heard him utter these words: "Yes, I have to. How can I go on now?"

It would not have taken much for his poor mother to give herself away, shocked as she was by the words he had said. What did they mean? Her thoughts in turmoil, she was almost afraid to understand. Mario muttered something else that Jolanda was unable to catch, then she saw him drop his arms, revealing his horribly altered face. He hastily opened a drawer and took out a revolver. Terrified, she rushed towards him.

"Son, what are you trying to do?" she shouted, throwing her arms around him amid floods of tears. Mario looked at her, dazed, before putting the revolver back in the drawer and returning her embrace.

"I'm so unhappy,..." he said, his voice faltering.

"Don't say that!" interrupted the countess, kissing his head. "That wretched woman has tried to break your heart by slandering your angel of a wife, but I'll defend Anna Maria against her, against everyone," she added impetuously, straightening herself up.

"Oh, mamma. I know she loves me."

"And you were about to kill yourself? That's shocking! Weren't you thinking about her, about me, your son, your father, who knows nothing about this and thinks you have a happy home life? For that snake who's poisoned our lives, were you really going to offer yours as some kind of sacrifice, regardless of your honor? Were you honestly going to stain the noble name you bear and cast the wife who adores you into mourning?"

"No! It wasn't for Sultana," said Mario, "but for Anna Maria."

Jolanda ran her hand over her forehead. "I don't understand," she said. "Come here, my dear, and don't hide anything from me."

They both sat on the sofa. Mario moved closer to his mother and put his head on her shoulder, weeping even before he could say anything. Jolanda let him vent his feelings, treating him tenderly as she did when he was a child.

"Let it out. It's good for you. You'll feel better," she whispered to him gently.

"Mamma," Mario said after a few moments, "if you hadn't been here, I'd be dead."

"Shush now," she murmured, holding him closer. "It was God's will that I waited for you here. Actually, it wasn't my intention to hide, but your brusque order not to be disturbed made me feel a bit worried, so I dashed behind the curtains to see what you were doing."

"But why were you waiting for me, mamma?"

"Because I'd noticed that your behavior towards your wife had changed lately. Also, Anna Maria's mood had worsened, which made me think that the pair of you had quarreled. When you left, I wanted to confirm my suspicions, so I called Anna Maria, and she's told me everything."

"She must have said that I rejected her," interrupted Mario. "I was horrified and didn't want to believe her justifications for all the lies and deception before our marriage."

"No lies, no deception," Jolanda retorted forcefully. "Anna Maria confessed everything to me. She'd given me Alceste's letter and yours, as well as the locket. The poor girl was struggling with her conscience for fear that she wasn't worthy of you, especially since she'd once thought of revenge when she believed you were in love with Sultana and had persuaded her to kill the poor man."

"Oh my God! Did she truly think that?" Mario said in a choked voice.

"Yes, but only briefly," continued Jolanda. "As she got to know you, she understood that you were also a victim. She was then determined to save you. She loved you like no other, and when you asked her to be your wife, she swore she would dedicate her life to your happiness."

Mario could not help but groan.

"And I've insulted her," he said, agonized by the thought.

"I, myself," said Jolanda, "urged her not to tell you after I'd forgiven her. I didn't want her to disturb your peace of mind. She then gave me the items, fearing that Sultana would try something to ruin your marriage. I also kept it all from your father so that nothing would upset our family harmony."

"And I, with all my selfishness, have ruined everything you and Anna Maria have done," Mario lamented. "I've forgotten the past four years of happiness. Under the influence of that damn woman, who only wanted those compromising things back, I believed her grievances about Anna Maria. I railed against the mother of my child. I was numb to her imploring, her tears, and broke her heart, telling her that she meant nothing to me anymore. I took the objects from her and gave them back to the woman I thought deserved my love, but I was deluded. I told Sultana what I'd done for her and that my life was now linked to hers, yet after she'd destroyed them, she told me, laughing, that she was engaged to someone else."

Jolanda was startled.

"Duke Farelli?" she asked

"Oh, no. On the contrary, she led me to understand that the duke has a weakness for my wife, which may be true."

"Wretched woman!"

"I was tormented by this, along with the anger of appearing ridiculous in Sultana's eyes. She was totally untroubled by the trick she'd played, and laughing, she sent me away. I left feeling utterly at sea. All I could imagine was everything in ruins because I'd rejected my wife and was about to lose my honor and integrity. There seemed no other solution but to end it all."

"That would have been a far greater mistake," said Jolanda. "Not to mention the fact that your death would have been another triumph for Sultana. And do you think that's what you deserved? And what about your wife, who adores you and wants a future with you? And your son? Should they both be so unjustly harmed?"

"Mamma, forgive me, please!"

Jolanda understood how much Mario had suffered despite the disgust, bordering on hatred, she felt for the woman who had led him down this path. She firmly wished that she could see him happy again.

"My dear son," she said, her arms resting gently around his neck, "I'm so sorry you're hurting inside. All this pain because you trusted Sultana, and she's done nothing but create chaos around her, and all this remorse for trampling on the very woman who saved you. You've pushed her away, blaming her for being the guilty party, and she never fought back. You, Mario, must ask for forgiveness, but not from me."

Mario shuddered at the thought.

"Do you think she'll forgive me?"

"Are you in any doubt?" Jolanda said. "Come with me. Let's go and see her."

Mario went along with her suggestion, unable to resist, although he was overtaken by a wave of apprehension, fearing his wife would reject him. The pair of them walked to Anna Maria's room where the young woman was sitting on a sofa, her son on her lap. She had clearly been suffering but was smiling radiantly at the child. She was trying to get him to repeat a prayer intended to encourage his father to be loving and to ensure his grandparents stayed healthy.

Mario and his mother heard the gentle prayer from the adjoining room. Mario's feelings softened.

"Anna Maria, Gino!" he called out in a voice broken with emotion as he entered the room.

The young woman felt faint with delight as she heard his voice, and then he appeared. She understood what had happened the moment she saw Jolanda follow him. She immediately stood up and ran to meet them, carrying the child in her arms."

"Mario, have you come back to me? Do you believe me now? Do you forgive me?" she exclaimed, her face beaming.

Mario hugged his wife and son.

"Yes, I'm back," he answered, "and I won't be leaving again. And it's I who have to ask your forgiveness and beg you to love me once more."

"I never stopped, not for a moment!" Anna Maria added, overcome by the moment. "And I will love you for the rest of my life."

Countess Jolanda was deeply affected. Thinking of Sultana, she knew there was no danger of her coming between them anymore.

Just a few days later, Sultana learned from Count and Countess Herbert themselves, during a visit they paid her, that Mario, somewhat preoccupied about Anna Maria's health, had taken her and their son to the Riviera. Jolanda and her husband were to join them in due course because the winter in Turin was too harsh.

"Yesterday," added the countess, "I had a letter from my son who is overjoyed because Anna Maria's delicate state, which has now eased, was due to her pregnancy. He's very pleased at the thought of having another child and told me he's never been so happy. He'll surround his beloved wife with all the loving care possible until he can enjoy the happiness of fatherhood again."

Sultana managed to control herself, but the sudden change in her features betrayed her inner turmoil. Her attempt at revenge had failed, achieving the opposite of what she had intended: Mario loved his wife more than before. Perhaps, however, the day for vengeance would still come, although Mario and his wife did not deserve to remain the focus of her attention. With this idea in mind, Sultana parted her lips in a wry smile.

"All my best wishes to Mario and Anna Maria," she said. "May happiness follow them wherever they go, and let's hope they're blessed with a big family."

Countess Jolanda who recognized how empty these wishes were, merely thanked her with a slight bow of the head. The count, though, who was still unaware of events, was much more effusive.

"Thank you, thank you…we'll give the family all your best. You're so kind and decent, just like our Anna Maria."

Two months later Sultana married her uncle's son, known by the name of Ezio Renier. The wider world, however, knew nothing of the secret of the young man's birth and therefore the reason for the marriage, namely, to allow Sultana to keep her inheritance. It was said to be a love match. Once the religious and civil ceremonies were completed, the notary handed over the will that would have given everything to her husband, which she hastened to destroy. The millions now belonged to her and could no longer be contested, and furthermore, she had acquired a younger husband who idolized her.

She really had no choice but to enjoy all these advantages. Ezio Renier, who knew nothing of the will, thought he had won the lottery. He was now the husband of the woman he had worshipped from afar and had nothing more to wish for. He thought Sultana had wonderful qualities and considered her a heroine for having the courage to confront Alceste.

A few days after their honeymoon, Ezio returned one afternoon from an errand that he had done for Sultana only to find that she had gone out with a friend who had dropped by to pick her up. He went into his wife's parlor to put the embroidery designs and samples he had bought on the coffee table. Next to the table was an unusual but elegant chest with a small golden key glinting in the lock.

Ezio, assailed by curiosity, sat down in front of the bizarre item, examining it's features closely before opening it. Inside the lid were skeins of silk, sewing knickknacks and trinkets, including a decorated box with a mirror embedded in the lid. Ezio picked it up with a smile and opened it. There were two letters and a folded sheet of paper inside. He was far from having the slightest suspicion about his wife, but nonetheless felt the need to read the contents. His excused his actions by thinking of his intense feelings for Sultana.

He was happy to see that the letters were from his wife's children. They had written about boarding school life and had expressed a desire to see her and meet their new stepfather. Ezio read the words feeling a certain emotion and was about to put them back on top of the sheet of paper with no envelope when, with nothing better to do, he decided to read that too. It was the copy of Alceste's letter written out by Anna Maria. Sultana had decided not to destroy it in case she ever needed to copy the young woman's handwriting for some nefarious purpose.

Ezio started to read the note and was, at first astonished, a sentiment that soon turned to anger and disgust. At the same time, he felt the pain of heartbreak. Sultana arrived just as he had just finished reading.

"Ezio, you're here?" she said. "Well, what's up?"

She had asked the second question after her husband had turned around, his face sunken and eyes frighteningly wide. He handed her the open sheet of paper.

"Are all these horrors true?" he asked in a hollow voice. "Was Alceste your lover? Did you kill him to get him out of the way"

Sultana gasped when faced with the accusations.

"Lies…lies written by the fiancé of the coward who died. She was trying to slander me," Sultana replied, visibly upset. "And you believe her? She's a terrible woman…terrible." She had placed her head on his chest in a display of dismay. "Remember," she continued, collecting herself, "remember that before marrying you, I wanted to tell you everything that had happened in the past. Well, that despicable man, to excuse his behavior and crazy obsession with me, decided to paint me as an abject creature. His fiancée wrote to me repeating the accusations. But I was able to prove my innocence and ended up acting as a second mother to that young woman, helping her find a husband who's made her happy. Back then, you didn't want to know anything…."

Ezio, who was listening intently, bowed his head.

"It's true," he replied, "but why did you want to keep this vile note?"

"I'm not sure what to tell you as I really don't know," Sultana added. "When Alceste's fiancée gave it to me, saying it was a copy of the letter left to her — the original of which I never saw and never knew if it ever truly existed — I was in my parlor at home. I put it in that box so my husband could read it. After my explanations, Anna Maria asked me to forgive her and begged me to destroy it."

Sultana had coiled around him like a serpent, and Ezio had no defense against her sensuous attentions.

"Well, no, I'm not going to believe his accusations," he replied. "I'll destroy the note and forget its contents. I've got no right to delve into your past, especially as I didn't want to know about it before marrying you. But, mind you, Sultana, if I'm wrong about you and one day you betray me, I'll be a harsh judge, and you might not live to tell the tale!"

Sultana smiled sweetly.

"That'll never happen," she said, moving closer still, "because I love you. There is no man in the world who can make me so happy."

She kissed him triumphantly. He narrowed his eyes, enjoying the thrill of her words and attention. The sinner had won again. She would continue her life of deception and corruption until the hour of punishment finally arrived, without which, there would be no justice.

ରେ

This Book Was Completed on 19 April 2023
At Italica Press in Bristol UK.
It Was Typeset in Adobe
Garamond Pro &
Wingdings.
 CℲCℲCℲ
CℲCℲ
CℲ

Printed in Great Britain
by Amazon

27488236R00148